FROM TH

"Relax, Hatch; it's all right," he soothed. "I think it's time you let someone take care of you for a change."

She felt the softening in his tone; it was so strong that she felt she could reach out and touch it. She loosened her grip on his waist, pulling back a little so she could look at him. "Do you really mean that?"

"I really mean it." He pulled her closer with the hand around her waist; his other hand cupped her jaw, simultaneously raising her chin. His mouth closed in on hers hungrily, powerfully. She raised her hands to his shoulders and returned his passion, knowing that a kiss this potent would not be enough to satisfy either of them. And when the thunder rumbled again, as explosively loud as it had been before, she barely heard it.

At last they stopped, if for no other reason than to give their lips a rest.

"Your clothes are wet," Hatch said with a composure that surprised her.

"And so are yours now."

She hesitated only for a moment before voicing her thoughts aloud. "Maybe we should take them off."

FROM THIS DAY FORWARD

Bettye Griffin

ARABESQUE

★BET

BOOKS™

BET Publications LLC

http://www.bet.com

http://www.arabesquebooks.com

In memory of two who left this life too soon:
Gordon E. Griffin (1949–2001).
and
Dianne Gibbs Griffin (1951–2001).
And with thoughts of Alisha and Erica—the precious
gifts they left behind.

ACKNOWLEDGMENTS

Many thanks to: Mrs. Eva Mae Griffin, because she's my mom; Timothy, Katrina, and Aaron Underwood, because they're my kids; Toni Bonita Robinson, Cynthia White, and all the other members of the Prominent Women of Color Book Club; Joyce Long and Gwen Sellers of Touch of Elegance Salon (shameless plug!); Karen and Vicki of the downtown and suburban Jacksonville locations of B. Dalton (shameless plug!); Felecia Wintons of Books for Thoughts in Tampa (shameless plug!); Sharon McDaniel Hollis, Maureen King, Kimberly Rowe-Van Allen, and Anneliese Von Gruenberg, because they've been so supportive; Mrs. Anita Clowers, because she shared all those family papers and legends about my spunky great-grandmother, Hattie Jackson Griffin; Mrs. Cornelia Hatchet Golden, because she lent me her name (I've got it in writing!); Bill, Brian, and Richard of B&B Quality Automotive (shameless plug!), because they keep our vehicles rolling; The Bard Group, including Frank, Jeffrey, Steve, the author of the upcoming *Dummy's Guide to Private Investigation* (shameless plug!); Ellen, Marjorie, Julian, Larry, and Cheryl Ferguson, because their blunt honesty and sometimes downright ruthlessness have helped me become a better writer; Gwyn McGee, because I misspelled her first name the last time around; Beverly Griffin Love, because her dedication got buried on the copyright page last time around; Bernard Underwood, because he's the love of my life; and anyone else I might have forgotten, because my memory is awful.

One

"Okay, we've got a great idea for a story. . . ."

Skye Audsley barely heard the conversation of the production meeting; he was lost in his own thoughts. *How am I going to find someone as good as Ruth Perkins?*

"My brother-in-law got lost trying to follow a shortcut from Indianapolis to Chicago. He ended up in this miserable township called Farmingdale. . . ."

Ruth's been with Grandma for six years. Grandma loves her.

"Their so-called business district consists of a convenience store and a Laundromat. People live in rented shotgun houses and trailers, some without heat or running water. God only knows how they stay warm in the winters. He said he thought he was driving through rural Arkansas or Mississippi. You'd never expect to see these conditions an hour outside of the third largest city in the country."

It's almost too bad Ruth has a family of her own. If she didn't, it'd be ideal for me to move in with Grandma.

"America needs to know about this."

Because she just can't live alone anymore.

"Skye's going to cover this one."

He snapped to attention at the sound of his name. "What?"

Jack Laughlin, the producer who was conducting the meeting, looked him in the eye, holding his gaze for a few seconds before speaking. "I'm sending you to Farmingdale, Illinois, to report on the deplorable living conditions there."

"Where?"

"Am I seeing things, or have you been sitting in this room for the past ten minutes?"

Busted. "I'm sorry, Jack. I guess my mind was wandering."

"It can wander on the plane. I want you out there Thursday. Do some preliminary screening. I'll get a cameraman down from our Chicago affiliate to join you on the weekend."

"Wait a minute. I'm spending a weekend at some dinky little town in the Midwest, a place I'm sure doesn't even have a decent place to stay?"

"We'll get you in a hotel in one of the nearby towns, but if you're very good, I'll give you a break and put you up in Chicago on Saturday night." Jack turned his head, suggesting he was about to speak to the entire group seated around the long rectangular table. "Now, where are we with that piece on the marathon runner who lost a foot?"

Skye slammed his notebook shut and filed out of the conference room with the other staff members, a scowl marring his features. In three days he would be on a plane to Illinois, and the timing couldn't be worse. He had to find a caretaker for his grandmother, someone who could live in, and he needed to do it as soon as possible. Just last week Grandma had slipped during a trip to the bathroom in the middle of the night. She hadn't broken any bones, but she had been unable to get to her feet and had spent the rest of the night on the floor, where she remained until Ruth Perkins found her when she arrived at nine-thirty the next morning.

Ruth had been in his employ since Grandma had her knee replaced when she was eighty-two. Ruth did housework, cooking, took Grandma on all her errands, and most important of all, provided companionship.

Skye knew he should spend more time with his grandmother, but his position as correspondent for the weekly television newsmagazine program *A Day in the Life* required frequent travel. It was the position he'd always wanted, but perhaps he needed to go back to local reporting. He owed his first allegiance to family, and ever since he was nineteen years old Harriet Jackson had been the only family he had.

He parked his Cougar sloppily, not caring that he was not only crooked but a good two feet from the curb, in front of his grandmother's home in Tarrytown, a New York suburb on the Hudson River. He had lived in the small, two-story frame house at the foot of a steep hill from the time of his parents' divorce when he was ten until he left for college.

He let himself in with the same key he'd had since childhood. Immediately the aroma of onion gravy wafted into his nostrils. That aroma was as familiar as the room with its lived-in furniture that Grandma had had as long as Skye could remember. He had offered to redecorate the entire house, but other than worn carpet and mattresses, plus structural improvements to accommodate her advanced age, she had declined. Skye supposed that if he was blessed with his grandmother's longevity—she was eighty-eight—he wouldn't be too concerned about getting new furniture either.

She was sitting in a black club-style chair that was remarkably preserved, considering it was probably as old as he was. The oversize chair dwarfed her small body, the white lace doily pinned to the upper back blending nicely with her wavy gray hair. She was one of those people who would never go completely white, even if she lived to be a hundred. She had never used hair dye, and at eighty-three she announced she had spent her last afternoon in the hairdresser's chair. In the years since, her thick tresses had grown out in their natural texture and were now long enough to be arranged in braids, which she wore pinned across the top of her head.

"Well, hello there!" she greeted.

"Hi, Grandma." He crossed the room to where she sat and bent his six-one frame to kiss her cheek. He glanced at the embroidery in her lap. "What does that one say?"

" 'There's no right way to do the wrong thing.' "

He smiled. "Good advice." Grandma was always embroidering wall hangings, most of which included proverbs, that she would later have framed. Her handiwork was on display all around the house. She had been an excellent seamstress in her younger years, but declining up-close vision had forced her to give it up. He actually preferred to see her relaxing in a chair rather than hunched over her latest project under the scant light of her sewing machine. When she wasn't working on embroidery she was usually crocheting. His apartment was full of throws she had made him. If his heat ever went off in the midst of winter, he'd be fine.

"Are you hungry? Ruth and I made a meat loaf."

"No, thanks."

"Well, in that case, sit down and tell me all about the trip you're going on."

"How did you know?" But even as he posed the question, he knew it had to be Mrs. Williams from next door who'd told her.

"Norma was over earlier. She said you called her."

"I wish she hadn't said anything, but it never occurred to me to ask her to let me tell you."

"You didn't do anything wrong. I know you're just looking out for me."

"It's a delicate situation, Grandma."

"I'm old, Schuyler," she said, using his given name, the way she always did when she was serious. "That's a fact. There's nothing delicate about it. It happens to most of us, except those who are denied the opportunity."

He knew she was thinking of his mother, who had been her only child, and his own heart grew heavy. Over twenty years had passed since her death, but he would never stop missing her.

"Norma and I already have it worked out," Grandma continued. "She's going to call every night at ten to make sure I'm upstairs, plus every morning at seven-thirty. If I don't answer she and Harry will be right over. I've given her a key. I'm also going to go shopping with her on Friday and have dinner with them on Saturday. Their son is coming with his wife and their new baby. I've seen pictures of him, and he's truly beautiful. It'll be nice to hold a baby again."

"Sounds like she's keeping you busy." Secretly he was relieved, so much that he didn't mind the subtle dig about his still being single at thirty-eight.

It was funny how neighbors were either distant or friendly. Until recently, he called a high rise on West End Avenue home, and in six years, his contact with his neighbors were limited to polite nods. His grandparents bought this house over fifty years ago, and while most of the people living here then had either died or moved away, Grandma knew everyone on the block. Norma Williams was always telling him that if she could do anything to help him with Grandma, all he had to do was ask, and with her agreeing so readily to look in on her while he was away, he was convinced that she was the type of person who gave neighbors a good name.

Harriet shrugged. "Maybe just a little more than usual. I'll probably be so tired from running around with her that I won't make it to church."

"I'm really sorry about this trip, Grandma. I was hoping my next assignment would be something I could work on here in New York. I know we have to find you someone who can live in—"

"Don't you worry about me. The doctor at the emergency room said I'm in great shape. He didn't even admit me, remember?"

"That's because it's September and it isn't cold yet." *Thank God,* he added silently. Had it been January, there could have been a much different ending than a twelve-hour hospital stay for observation. But he would have someone here with her well before then.

"He said I'm as fit as a spry young girl of seventy-five. Now, where are you going?"

"A town called Farmingdale, Illinois."

"I never heard of it."

"Neither has anyone else, apparently. The conditions there are supposed to be horrendous."

"Why?"

Skye recounted the information he'd learned about his destination after leaving the production meeting. "It used to be populated by farm workers who had migrated from the South, but for years it's been in a decline."

"And no one cares."

"Isn't that always the way when you're poor? But a profile on *A Day in the Life* might change that. It'll be hard for the local officials to ignore once the show airs."

Skye couldn't believe it. He had known that much of Illinois was farmland, but he imagined simple but dignified homes on large lots of land, not these closely set ramshackle structures, all appearing to need fresh paint, and trailers, some surrounded by debris in the high, patchy grass. He caught sight of a few chickens strutting in crudely fenced-in areas by the trailers. Neither the houses nor the trailers appeared sturdy enough to withstand a strong gust of wind.

That day was devoted to travel. He wasn't expected to do any scouting until the next day, Friday, but decided it wouldn't hurt to take a look around before he drove to his hotel in nearby Bourbonnais. Had this impoverished township once been a thriving community? He couldn't remember the last time he'd seen so many boarded-up businesses. He had passed a small post office and a lone gas station, and the seriously inflated price per gallon made his jaw tense. He hated it when merchants took advantage of poor folks. Across the street there was a mom-and-pop-style convenience store with no name over the door, as well as a Laundromat. That appeared to be the extent of the services available. He didn't even see a school or a public library. Did people have to drive all the way to Kankakee, probably close to a half hour each way, just to get their coats dry cleaned or to cash a check?

He noted several churches of different denominations, all of them simple frame buildings with pointed roofs. A minibus was pulling onto the grassy lot surrounding the Baptist church. It was empty of passengers other than the driver. Skye noted the street name from the corner sign and spoke it into the microphone of the hand-held tape recorder he carried with him when scouting. The small sign's white letters on a navy background clearly predated the larger ones with iridescent white lettering on green in most cities. If it was nighttime he wouldn't be able to read it without stopping to get out of the car. He wanted to remember where it was so he could come by tomorrow and talk with the pastor. There was a possibility that no one would be there on a Friday, but of course there would be on Sunday morning. Better yet, he would attend the service; that would probably make the pastor more willing to share information about the town.

It didn't take long to drive through the small town, and Skye reached for the sheet of paper upon which he'd written his directions so he could head for Kankakee. He remembered tossing it on the passenger seat, but it wasn't there anymore. A steady breeze was blowing, and he did have the windows partially lowered. Perhaps it had blown out of the window without him noticing.

Not a problem, he decided. He was pretty sure he could find the gas station. He pulled to the right, intending to make a U-turn. In the side view mirror he saw a school bus approaching. He sat waiting while it slowly passed, came to a stop, and then flashed its lights and lowered the red-and-white Stop sign as passengers disembarked. As a safety precaution, he planned to wait until the kids had passed by before he turned the car around.

But these passengers weren't small children; they were teens. Most of them went off in the other direction, but two girls were walking toward him. He leaned toward the passenger side and called out to them, "Hi, girls. Can you tell me how to get to Route 2?"

The teens first looked at him, and then at the late-model Chrysler he had rented at Midway Airport. Most of the cars he'd seen in Farmingdale were from the 1980s or earlier. He could see the girls' expressions change from mere curiosity to flashing dollar signs. In the instant before the older one spoke, he had a premonition of what she was going to say. And she didn't disappoint him.

"We'll tell you . . . for twenty dollars."

He decided to see what he could get out of them, or at least out of the older one, who seemed to be the spokesperson. "You're kidding, right?"

"No. I ain't lost, either. Twenty dollars."

Skye remained calm. "And why would you want to charge me such an exorbitant sum?"

"Come on, you know you can afford it. Look at this shiny new car you're driving. I'll bet you're from Chicago. If you wanna get back there, you'd better pay up. It's gonna start getting dark soon."

"You act like there's no one else in town who'll tell me how to get to the highway."

"No, that's not true. But they'll charge you more than we will. We're being nice."

" 'Cuz you got a nice face," her companion said, speaking for the first time.

Skye studied the pair. They had the same brown doelike eyes and tall, slim builds, and they both wore their shoulder-length hair caught in clips at the napes of their necks. They were probably sisters. "I think I'll pass. I'll ask at the gas station," he said.

The talkative one snorted. "That Curtis Crawford is the biggest crook going. Haven't you seen how much he charges for gas?"

He remembered the high price of the gas he had seen posted there. Could she have a point?

He was still considering this when a dull blue-green Impala, easily thirty years old, and with its bottom half generously sprinkled with rust spots, pulled up in front of them. A woman jumped out from behind the wheel and confronted the two girls. "What's going on here?" she demanded in a stern voice.

Skye, too, got out of the car and walked around to the front of it, standing with his right hand resting on the hood. "I was just asking these girls for directions to Route 2. They said they would tell me for a fee of twenty dollars."

"Twenty dollars?" The woman looked at the girls. "You told him that?"

The girls shrugged guiltily, and she said, "You two should know better than that. Now go in the house. Right now. And not another word," she added in a threatening tone when the talkative one opened her mouth to say something.

Skye watched as the girls rushed down the front walk of a blue wood-frame cottage. Then he looked at the woman, whose resemblance to the girls, including the same willowy figure, was emphasized by her similar hairstyle. He put her age at about thirty and decided she must be their mother. Getting pregnant at sixteen certainly wasn't unusual, in the poshest of neighborhoods as well as areas of abject poverty, but a repeat of the same a year or two later might be more common in poorer areas where hope tended to be in shorter supply. He wondered if she had more children at home. It was too bad; she was an attractive woman, or at least she probably would be if she smiled. Who knew what she might have accomplished had she not taken the route of teenage mother in this god-forsaken town.

"I want to apologize for their behavior," she was saying now, her hands stuffed inside the pockets of her jeans, head and chin high in a manner that suggested defiance, despite her humble words. "They're good girls, really. It's just that we don't often see strangers in Farmingdale, and when we do, they're usually lost. I'm afraid it's become customary to try to hustle them."

"No harm done. Can you tell me how to get to the highway?"

"Of course. You go down to the corner, turn left, and keep going until. . . ."

In his hotel room in nearby Bourbonnais, Skye typed his dictated observations on his laptop. His mind kept going back to the woman and the two girls. Their tiny house, like the others on that street, appeared to be a cut above the shacks and trailers he'd seen nearby. Maybe there was a husband who worked. There was a new prison on the outskirts of town, and he imagined many of the men in town worked as guards. Perhaps the woman and her family would agree to be interviewed. He didn't know their names, but he did know where they lived. He could find them easily.

Two

Cornelia Hatchet faced her teenaged sisters, Chantal and Sinclair. "I'm disappointed in you girls," she said quietly. "Daddy always taught you better. *I've* always taught you better. I know the other kids try to get money out of people who are lost, but that's no excuse for you to try it, too."

"I'm sorry, Hatch," Sinclair said.

"It was my fault; I started it," Chantal added.

Hatch was sure she had. She had always been a handful, and now that Chantal was fifteen, Hatch found herself worrying about what the future held for her adventurous sister. On the other hand, Sinclair, two years Chantal's junior, was more like herself, asking questions that hinted at a vivid imagination, and happy to stand by while someone else took the lead.

"All right," she said. "I want you two to do your homework. You can take care of making dinner tonight. Fish sticks, French fries, and salad. Make sure Daddy has his plate by six o'clock. I'm going to get some sleep. I drove to Kankakee to pick up Daddy's medicine, and I'm tired."

Henry Hatchet was in his small bedroom, sitting in the lumpy dark green chair he loved, his left leg and right stump resting on the matching and equally well-worn ottoman. His crutches rested between the chair and the wall. A twelve-inch television perched atop the highboy was tuned to something in black and white. Chantal and Sinclair were always whining about not having HBO and Showtime, but Hatch was grateful that the cable company offered a package that allowed them to receive the classic movie channels and skip the expensive premiums. Between her father's disability check and her earnings from Super Kmart, where she worked as cashier supervisor on the graveyard shift, they barely got by. She suspected she'd go through her entire life hunting down bargains at Big Lots, but still, they were better off than a lot of families here in Farmingdale.

"Hi, Daddy. You all right?"

"I'm fine, Hatch."

"What's that you're watching?"

"*The Postman Always Rings Twice.* I never understood why everybody made such a fuss about Lana Turner. She had a pretty face, but her figure was straight up and down, no curves. She sure didn't do nothin' for me. She didn't even have a waistline."

Hatch crossed in front of him and sat on the edge of his double bed. She was thankful for the classic movie stations. Daddy spent many a happy hour in front of the set, going on and on about Hollywood beauties and their flaws: Audrey Hepburn's big hips, Lena Horne's skinny legs, Grace Kelly's flat chest, and how he didn't see what all the fuss was about Betty Grable's legs—"I can name a dozen gals right here in Farmingdale with nicer ones." If it wasn't that he was scoffing at the absurdity of pairing a young girl in her twenties with a middle-aged man in his fifties. "Now I ask you, would that cute Nia Long look at *me* twice?"

"The girls are home," she said. "They'll be in to see you in a few. I had to give them a lecture, at least a minilecture."

"What'd they do?"

"They were trying to get twenty dollars out of a motorist who was lost in exchange for directions."

"They must have gotten that from Curtis at the filling station. That man doesn't have an honest bone in his body."

"I don't care where they learned it from. It's wrong, and they know it."

"Don't be so hard on yourself, Hatch. Remember they're kids. You were one yourself, and you gave Anna Maria and me a devil of a time when you wanted to."

She sighed. "That may be, but I want them to be better than I was. I want them to *do* better than I did."

"I understand that, Hatch, but they're still kids. Misbehaving every now and then is all part of being young. Lord knows I wanted more for you than what you got, but I never expected you to be a saint. And you weren't."

"I'm fine, Daddy."

"No, you're not. I know how you wanted to go to college, wanted to be an architect and all. I pray to God every day that you'll be able to do it one day."

He was too thoughtful to add that she also wanted to get married and have kids, she noted, lowering her eyes sadly. "It's too late for me, Daddy. But Chantal and Sinclair are both going to college."

"It's not too late. You're only thirty-one."

"I'm thirty-two, Daddy."

"That's right. You just had a birthday. But things are getting better around here now that they've opened the new jail. Next thing you'll know we'll be getting a supermarket and a bank—"

She hastily stood. "Daddy, I've got to check on dinner. I'll be in to see you later, okay?"

Hatch had given that chore to her sisters, of course, and she doubted she had fooled her father, but she felt tears about to spill like water from an overflowing bathtub, and she needed to be alone.

Her bedroom was the smallest in the house, not counting the one in the basement, which was hot in the summer and cold in the winter. Her stepmother, Anna Maria, used to joke that it was really a storage closet. It only contained two pieces of furniture, a double-wide dresser and an ancient three-quarter-size bed that desperately needed a new mattress, not that she thought they even made that size anymore. It would be cheaper to go to Home Depot and buy a board to put between the mattress and box spring. The dresser and bed filled the room—she didn't even have a nightstand. The room Chantal and Sinclair shared was larger, but Daddy and Anna Maria thought she should have her own room since she was so much older than her sisters.

She was glad she had a space, no matter how small, to call her own, where she could close her eyes and imagine her life was different. What if she had been able to go to school and have the career of her dreams? She wouldn't be living in Farmingdale, and neither would her father and sisters, who would be wherever she was. Farmingdale was largely a town of the forgotten. Children grew up and left, made good, and in many cases abandoned their struggling parents. Young mothers grew tired of the never-ending battle to keep a roof overhead and food in the cupboards and took off for the bright lights of Chicago or Indianapolis, leaving their children behind to be cared for mostly by grandparents.

Trevor Burton, her high school boyfriend, had gotten out. He'd earned a degree from Lincoln University in Missouri and now was an administrator at some big hospital in St. Louis. His parents still lived in Farmingdale, but this was no case of an offspring forgetting about the plight of those who raised him. Mrs. Burton was always telling people, and Trevor had told her himself, how he had tried to get them to move to Missouri, but they hadn't wanted to leave their longtime home. Trevor came to visit every once and again, and in recent years he was accompanied by the girl he'd married. The last time they were here, just a few months ago, they were expecting a baby.

Her own mother fell in the latter category of women who found life in Farmingdale unbearable. Hatch hadn't seen Elaine Hatchet since she was seven years old, and she could no longer clearly remember the features of the woman who had birthed her. Her father got a divorce on the grounds of desertion, and for several years it was just the two of them until he married Anna Maria, who filled the void in both their lives. It was Anna Maria who taught her how to cook and clean, and after Chantal and Sinclair were born, how to take care of babies.

She had planned to leave Farmingdale, as well, and to attend college with Trevor, even after her father had to have his leg amputated below the knee due to numerous nonhealing diabetic ulcers. But just months after the surgery, Anna Maria was killed when she lost control of the family car on an icy night and slammed head-on into a streetlight, and Hatch gave up her scholarship. There was no way her father could manage to raise two small children—Sinclair was an infant—with his disability.

Thirteen years later she was still here, and now she knew she would probably always be here. She had no doubts about the wisdom of her decision—her family needed her, and that was that—but to compensate she frequently got lost in her daydreams about the people she saw. The fading town of Farmingdale was all she had known, but working the night shift at the Super Kmart in the town of Bradley gave her contact with people she knew had lives much different from hers. There was the young stay-at-home mother who did her grocery shopping in the wee hours of the morning before her husband and children awakened. Then there was Dave, the white-haired store greeter, who enjoyed getting out of the house for a four-hour shift in the evenings after his wife, who was in poor health, went to sleep for the night.

The people she didn't talk to she merely studied. She knew she could learn a lot about a person by what they purchased. The obese shoppers who loaded up on doughnuts, ice cream, and potato chips probably used food for comfort purposes. Women whose carts were full of clothing, underwear, and socks for men and children, with perhaps a single paperback romance novel for themselves, were obviously chiefly concerned with the needs of their families. Men who purchased drills, hardware, and paint were clearly handy to have around the house.

Most of her contact with strangers was limited

to people she saw at work, but today she had seen a new face right here in town. Who was the handsome mustached stranger driving the new champagne-colored Chrysler? Where was he going?

She knew it didn't matter. He'd gotten on the road and on to his destination. She'd never see him again.

Three

When Hatch's shift ended at seven. Saturday morning, she did the week's grocery shopping, sticking carefully to the list she had made at home. She worked hard at keeping their food budget to a minimum. A boneless pork roast was more economical than individual chops, a small eye round easier on her wallet than steaks. Chicken and ever-reliable ground beef rounded out the meat portion of their dinners. She picked up other staples, skipping over the expensive prepared frozen foods and packaged cookies. Every weekend Chantal and Sinclair baked cookies from scratch or brownies from packaged mixes so there would always be something around to satisfy the craving for something sweet. But Daddy loved strawberry ice cream, and their supply was running low, so just before getting on line she stopped at the frozen-food section and picked up a half gallon.

She cashed her paycheck at the register, then loaded the car with the groceries and headed for home, ignoring the amused stares of the better-heeled patrons who drove newer vehicles as she eased the ancient Chevy out of the parking lot. She had the car maintained religiously, praying that the inevitable would be slow in occurring, for there wasn't much money in her savings account

to buy a replacement. Many residents of Farmingdale didn't own cars, especially the senior citizens,
most of whom cashed their meager Social Security
checks at the convenience store and utilized the
shuttle service offered by local churches, riding
into Kankakee to do their marketing or to see the
doctor.

A crowd had gathered on the sidewalk outside
the Laundromat. Hatch knew Saturday morning
was a popular time to do the wash for those who
preferred machinery to washboards and buckets,
but surely these sixty or seventy people couldn't
all be doing laundry. The Laundromat wasn't large
enough to accommodate them all, for one. She
decided to go home first and unload, then she
would walk over and see what was going on. She
wheeled her father to the store every morning,
and she figured he could appreciate a little excitement as much as she would.

Their house buzzed with the sounds and scents
of housecleaning. Chantal was sweeping the
kitchen floor while a load of sheets and towels agi-
tated in the secondhand washer Hatch had
bought, which was still going strong after four
years. Meanwhile, Sinclair was scrubbing the bathroom tile with a pleasantly perfumed liquid. Hatch
got both of them to temporarily stop their chores
and help her carry the groceries inside.

"There's a lot of people down by the Laundromat," Hatch remarked as she tucked away a roast
inside the nearly empty freezer.

"Oh, really?" Chantal said. "Any idea of what's
happenin'?"

"No, but I think I'll take Daddy and walk back
over. I'm sure it can't be anything *too* exciting."

"Can we go?" Sinclair asked.

Hatch shrugged. "Sure. After you finish your chores." She pretended not to notice her youngest sister make a face before skunking out of the room. "Did Daddy eat?" she asked Chantal.

"He didn't finish his cereal."

"Is he feeling okay?"

"He said he was."

When all the food had been put away, Hatch went to her father's room. She knocked on the closed door. "Daddy, you dressed?"

"Yeah, come on in."

Hatch's father had undergone physical therapy after his amputation and had long since mastered the basic movements necessary to maintain personal hygiene and to get dressed. He was sitting up in bed—the mattress covered only by a quilted cover that was clean but faded and thin in spots—fully dressed in a royal blue sweat suit. The television was turned to something featuring a dashing clean-shaven Clark Gable in a military uniform and ponytail. *Mutiny on the Bounty,* she guessed.

"You must be kidding, asking me if I'm up yet. Chantal was in to strip my bed half an hour ago." He chuckled, then looked at her expectantly. "Looks like a nice day out. Are you about ready to take our walk?"

"Sure, Daddy." She went to a corner and retrieved his folded wheelchair, and in one skilled motion obtained from years of practice, placed it in the upright position with the safety catch in place. She positioned the chair just opposite her father's ottoman. He swung his foot and stump to the right and reached for one of his crutches. Hatch found herself holding her breath. Since his appetite declined, neither his strength nor his balance were what they used to be, but he got to his

feet without incident. Leaning on the crutch, he
hopped toward the chair, carefully turned around,
and lowered himself into the seat.

"You need a jacket, Daddy. It's a bit chilly out."
She took a lightweight tan jacket from his closet
and helped him put it on.

She wheeled him out to the back door in the
kitchen. Years back, she engaged the local handy-
man to build a ramp over the existing step to make
it wheelchair accessible. "See you later," she said
to Chantal, who was now mopping the kitchen
floor. "Make sure you and your sister have all your
work done before you come nosing around."

"You're not going to wait for us?"

"I don't see why. You know where the Laundromat is."

"What's going on at the Laundromat?" Daddy
asked. On their daily regimen he always made two
purchases: a newspaper, and a candy bar to soothe
his strong sweet tooth, both bought at the convenience store.

"Hatch said there's a big crowd over there. Sinclair and I wanted to see what's going on."

"And you will, as soon as Sinclair finishes clean-
ing your bedroom, and as soon as you finish mopping the floor and hanging the wash," Hatch said
with a smile. "See y'all," she added as she opened
the door and tightly gripped the handles of the
chair in preparation for the incline of the ramp.

It was a crisp autumn morning, the type when
the air felt deceivingly fresh. The streets of Farmingdale were littered with rust-colored leaves that
gave the town an almost picturesque look; only
the freshly fallen snow that would come later was
more pleasing to the eye.

"Daddy, Chantal said you didn't finish your cereal."

"I wasn't very hungry."

"But you hardly ate dinner last night."

"I wasn't hungry then, either."

"Why not?"

"What am I, under arrest or somethin'?"

"Of course not. I'm just worried about you."

"Don't worry about me."

"You haven't been eating much, Daddy. I can tell you've lost weight."

"I'm fine, Hatch," he said evenly.

She recognized his tone. She was dangerously close to making him lose his temper, so she let it drop and stayed quiet for the remainder of their walk.

The crowd in front of the Laundromat had gotten even bigger in the time since she'd passed by earlier. It had moved across the street to the filling station.

"Wow. They must be giving something away," Henry said. "Like money." He laughed at his joke.

"Well, something out of the norm is definitely going on." She guided the wheelchair to the outskirts of the crowd. "What's happening?" she asked the tall youth who stood next to her.

"That dude from *A Day in the Life* is here," he said excitedly, speaking surprisingly clearly for someone who had a toothpick protruding from between his lips on the right side of his mouth. "He is gonna be interviewin' people to be on TV."

Hatch looked at her father for explanation. She knew little about *A Day in the Life* or any other nighttime programming; they were all broadcast while she was asleep in the hours before going to work. Most of her television watching was confined to the documentaries of cable channels like Discover and A&E, old movies on TCM or AMC, or more contemporary films on the two Lifetime networks.

"Oh!" Henry said. "That must be that Audsley fella."

"Yeah, that's him. He's in the middle, talkin' to people. It's not fair, him not talkin' to everybody. I wanna be on TV, too."

"Well, this is certainly exciting," Henry said. He leaned to one side of his chair so he could look back at Hatch. "See, Daughter, I told you things are changing around here."

"Oh, wait. I see him coming," the young man next to Hatch exclaimed as he began jumping up and down while waving. "Over here, man!"

Skye was amazed at the number of excited townsfolk around him. He had thought going to the Laundromat early on Saturday morning might be beneficial, but he hadn't expected all this. It seemed as if the whole town were out.

He'd been surrounded from the first moment he'd entered the storefront. Now that the crowd had grown so huge, he was feeling uncomfortable. He'd gotten an earful from the people he'd spoken to. Many Farmingdale residents lived in homes without indoor plumbing. Others lived on such tight budgets they couldn't afford electricity. No wonder Jack Laughlin had been so insistent about publicizing the conditions here.

"Thank you, everybody. I'll see you tomorrow after church," he said loudly as he made his way through the gathering. People called out greetings, and one woman tugged at his sleeve and asked if he knew Bryant Gumbel.

"I've met him, yes," he said. To the crowd he waved and kept repeating, "Thank you."

Then he saw the woman from Thursday.

She was standing behind an old man—no, it was just an *older* man, maybe about sixty—in a wheelchair, a confused look on her face. The gentleman, on the other hand, was impatiently gesturing for people to move from in front of him so he could see.

Skye changed direction and walked toward them. "Hello," he said to the woman.

"You know him?" asked a tall youth standing near the woman. Skye didn't like his tone; it sounded like an accusation.

"This lady was nice enough to give me directions when I got lost driving through town the other day," he told the boy. Then he fixed his attention on the gentleman in the wheelchair. Only his left foot protruded from the bottom of his sweatpants. The bottom of the right pants leg blew in the breeze. An amputee. "How are you, sir?" he said, holding out his hand, careful not to bend. He didn't want the man to think he was patronizing him.

"Fine, fine," he said as they shook hands. "Hatch, why didn't you tell me you met Skye Audsley?"

The woman shook her head. "I didn't know who he was." She met Skye's gaze. "I work nights. I don't get to watch much television unless it's in the daytime."

"Well, let me introduce myself. My name is Schuyler Audsley, and I'm a correspondent on a

newsmagazine show called *A Day in the Life.* We're
on every Wednesday night, and what we do is visit
specific people or communities all over the United
States and air profiles about them."

"And you came to *Farmingdale?*"

"People need to know places like Farmingdale
exist, especially in times of prosperity. And your
name is . . . ?"

"Oh, I'm sorry. I'm Cornelia Hatchet. This is
my father, Henry."

"Pleased to meet you both. Mr. Hatchet, I'll bet
you could tell me a lot about the history of the
town. I'd like to include miniprofiles of several
residents of different age groups. Would you care
to participate?"

"And be on TV? Sure!"

"It might be a good idea to speak to your entire
family." Once more he looked at the woman.
"Cornelia, is it?"

"Everybody calls me Hatch."

"Hatch, then. Where are your daughters today?"

"My . . . daughters?"

Her bewilderment combined with Mr. Hatchet's
booming laughter told Skye he'd said something
off target.

"Chantal and Sinclair are *my* daughters," Mr.
Hatchet said between gasps. "They're a lot
younger than Hatch, and she helped raise them
when my wife died, but they're her sisters. Technically, half sisters."

"Oh. I'm sorry. I just assumed . . ." Skye wished
he could take the words back. Hatch looked so
stricken, as if she'd never thought of herself as old
enough to be the girls' mother. He felt awful for
having hurt her feelings. "Please forgive me."

"Sure," she mumbled in an unsteady voice.

"Why don't I take the four of you to lunch?" Skye suggested. "You can tell me about your experiences in Farmingdale." A voice inside his head screamed, *What are you doing?* But he had started it; he couldn't drop it now. "Uh, do the four of you make up your entire household?"

"Yes," Henry answered. "But there's no restaurant here in Farmingdale."

"I'm staying in Bourbonnais. I'd be happy to drive over and pick you up."

"No, that won't be necessary," Hatch said. He noticed she was speaking naturally for the first time since his gaffe. "It's too far for you to drive back and forth. We have a car; we can drive and meet you there."

Her spine seemed to straighten as she spoke. He supposed she had a right to feel a little proud after clearing up the blunder he'd made regarding her sisters. "Are you familiar with Bourbonnais?" he asked.

"Yes. I work nearby, in Bradley."

"Well, there's a Ruby Tuesday, which should work nicely, since it's casual dress and has something on the menu for everybody. It's in the mall."

"Yes, I know."

"Say about noon?"

"Do you think you could make it at one? I worked last night. I usually sleep a few hours in the morning."

"Sure, that's fine. I'll see all of you then."

"You headin' back to Bourbonnais now?" Henry asked.

"Yes, sir. I'm going to have a busy day tomorrow. I lined up a number of people to interview."

* * *

As he drove off in the rented Chrysler, Skye wondered what had possessed him to invite the
Hatchet family to lunch. His plan of going to the
minimal town center of Farmingdale, or whatever
it could be called, and photographing the extent
of it with the video camera the program furnished
him had worked beautifully. All it took was one
woman asking him what he was doing for the word
to spread like the flu. He'd spoken to a number
of people he wished to interview: the sixtyish
woman who told him she was raising three of her
school-age grandchildren, the offspring of a
daughter whom she believed was somewhere in
Chicago but whom she hadn't heard from in years;
the arthritic seventy-four-year-old woman whose
bathroom was a hole in the ground; the woman
who was doing laundry here because her kitchen
had no sink and her bathtub was filled with stag-
nant water. He planned to go back to his hotel,
sort them all out, and make a neat graph of the
addresses he'd hurriedly scribbled, along with the
times he'd agreed to call on the interviewees.

From there he'd planned to drive to Chicago,
as there certainly wasn't much happening in Bourbonnais. He would only have to carry what he
needed if he decided to stay overnight; his room
at an efficient Holiday Inn Express had been paid
for by the program through Monday.

He easily could have made an appointment to
meet with the Hatchets on Sunday, as well, but he
felt he had to do something to make amends for
his initial thoughts about Hatch. Her shocked expression was something he wouldn't soon forget.
Besides, the reporter in him was curious about
their situation, and he felt it would take more time
than what he'd allotted for his Sunday appoint-

ments. How did Hatch manage, caring for her invalid father and being a mother figure for her much-younger sisters, *plus* working full-time, nights no less? That was a heavy load. He wondered if she ever felt trapped.

He was certainly devoted to Grandma, and it was fortunate that she was in good health while he attended Syracuse University. Her independence allowed him to build the broadcast journalism career he'd always wanted, and in turn his success allowed him to care for all her needs as she aged. But what if her health had begun to fail after his mother died? His mother had been Grandma's only child, and her death had been a crushing blow. What if she couldn't be left alone? While he could have taken college classes locally, he never could have taken that first job at a station in far-off Des Moines, Iowa, and that meant there would be no offer from a New York affiliate, and no subsequent offer from the newsmagazine. He could live decently on the salary of a white-collar professional, but he wouldn't be able to afford a live-in companion for Grandma, which would make her care his personal responsibility. But would he feel even the tiniest bit of resentment at having sacrificed the career he dreamed of and his life?

It was a certainly a sobering thought, for he enjoyed the material comforts his work brought him. He had everything . . . except someone to share it with. He'd had plenty of fun as a single man, but now he wanted something different. In two years he'd be forty, and he was still alone.

He tapped his fingers on the steering wheel in time to the music on the radio. It shouldn't be too bad. The fact that the Hatchets were driving

into Bourbonnais to meet him would make the
afternoon a lot less tiresome. Two round trips to
Farmingdale from his hotel would add up to nearly
a hundred miles. But he'd made the commitment,
and of course he would honor it either way.

Afterward he could still drive up to Chicago.

Four

"Oh, shucks. They're all gone?" Chantal repeated, her voice sullen with disappointment. She and Sinclair, on their way to the Laundromat, ran into Hatch and Henry a block from their home.

"And I don't get it. What's *A Day in the Life?*" Sinclair asked.

"It's a news show. I think they call it a newsmagazine," Henry replied. "It's something you'd know about if you watched something other than those music videos."

Hatch hid a smile. She couldn't agree more, but she supposed that when she'd been their age, she hadn't been much interested in anything other than the latest dance music and steps herself. "He's doing a piece about Farmingdale," she said as they all fell into step, with her behind her father's wheelchair.

"What about it?" Chantal said, clearly unimpressed.

"I think it's something that people will find very interesting," Daddy said.

Chantal and Sinclair looked at each other and giggled.

"I think so, too," Hatch added. "I think a lot of people will be shocked."

"Shocked? At what?" Sinclair asked.

"This might come as news to both of you girls, but the great majority of Americans don't live like we do," Henry said.

"What? They live worse?" This from Chantal. "I know some people in Farmingdale do, but people in other places, too?"

"No, they live better," Hatch said.

"Oh, you mean like the people on TV, like the *Brady Bunch,* where they've got all those kids and they still get to go to neat places like Hawaii and the Grand Canyon. That's not real."

"Maybe for some people it is real, Chantal," Hatch said. "Flying six kids to Hawaii is probably out of most families' financial reach, even if they do live in California and aren't all that far away. But the majority of people do live better than we do. The services that we have to drive to Kankakee for are right nearby, like hospitals, doctor's offices, banks, movies, and restaurants; and people live in nice homes."

Chantal made a *hmph* sound. "Yeah, white people and *Cosby.*"

"And *The Fresh Prince of Bel Air,*" Sinclair added. The girls dissolved into giggles.

"No, that's not true."

"What do you know about it, Hatch?" Sinclair asked. "You haven't been outside Kankakee County, just like we haven't."

"Your sister's right," Henry said. "There used to be a time, when I was coming up, where being black automatically meant you were poor. That's why my family left the South to come here. We're still poor, but I do believe that leaving Round Pond, Arkansas—where change happens slowly, if at all—was the right choice. But it's not that way anymore. Lots of black folks are gettin' real comfortable or downright rich these days."

"I just wish we hadn't missed all the excitement," Sinclair said with a sigh.

"Well, maybe you haven't," Hatch replied. She tapped her father's shoulder. "You tell them, Daddy."

Chantal and Sinclair stopped walking, faced their father and clamored simultaneously, "What? What?"

Henry chuckled. "Well, it seems that the gentleman remembered you girls from the other day. Something about directions . . ."

The girls' expressions fell like a soufflé, and they looked at each other guiltily.

"Anyway," he continued, "he wants to interview us. We're what they call a multigenerational family. I remember Farmingdale in the old days, when there was plenty of work and the House of Blue Lights used to jump every Friday and Saturday night, and you girls can give the point of view of the younger generation."

"You mean we're gonna be on TV?"

Hatch marveled at her sisters' swift change in demeanor, from that "aw-shucks-we're-busted" look to "omigosh" excitement.

"It looks that way," Henry said. He reached up and touched his fingertips to Hatch's forearm, and she knew he wanted her to tell them the rest.

"And that's not all," she said. "Mr. Audsley is taking us to lunch."

"Where're we going? Someplace real fancy?"

"Don't be ridiculous, Chantal. We're going to Ruby Tuesday, over in Bourbonnais, because Mr. Audsley is staying near there."

"When?"

"This afternoon. We're supposed to meet him there at one o'clock."

Chantal and Sinclair hugged each other and jumped up and down. "I've got to find something to wear," Chantal said.

"Me, too."

The girls ran toward the house.

"I think I'd like to sit out front while I read my paper," Henry said when he and Hatch reached their home a minute later.

"Sure, Daddy. I'm going to go in and get some sleep, but I'll have the girls check on you."

"Tell them to come get me in twenty minutes. That should be enough time for them to do their primping." His wheelchair, a lightweight model that folded for storage, was not equipped with turnstiles that would allow him to move about independently; he had to be pushed.

It wasn't until Hatch closed her bedroom door behind her that she allowed herself to break out into a wide grin. She'd been acting awfully nonchalant about the whole thing. Anyone would think she went out to lunch every day, when the truth was she couldn't remember ever having eaten out at lunchtime. Of course, lunchtime for her was the middle of the night, when most places were closed. She probably could count on one hand the times she'd gone to dinner, a special occasion here and there after her father and Anna Maria were married, and certainly none at all since she'd died.

Because of her schedule, her few forays into restaurants were generally for breakfast. There had been a few fellows who lived nearby who had expressed interest in getting to know her better, but working Friday and Saturday nights made dating difficult. The men she knew from work all lived in the Kankakee area and considered Farmingdale too far to drive to pick her up, and consequently when she was invited out it was to the local diner for breakfast immediately after their shift ended.

She had walked past the Ruby Tuesday restaurant during her rare trips to the mall in Bourbonnais, but her pocketbook ran more toward a quick snack at the food court. Skye Audsley must have known this; he'd all but come out and announced that there was no dress code. She couldn't be upset at him for that. All he had to do was take one look at their family car and the small house they rented for it to be clear that meals out were something in which her family did not indulge.

She set her alarm for eleven A.M. That didn't give her much time, but at least she would get a little bit of rest. She needed her reflexes to be sharp for the drive to Bourbonnais, and she certainly didn't want to look tired.

As she fell into the unconscious state of sleep she thought about Skye thinking she was her sisters' mother. Teenage pregnancy wasn't unusual in Farmingdale, but she'd managed to avoid it. *This* was the age when she should be having her children.

Like Trevor was.

"Okay, let's hit the road," Hatch said as she slid behind the wheel. It was a quarter past noon, and she had just placed Henry's wheelchair in the trunk.

"I'm really hungry," Sinclair said from the back seat, where she sat with Chantal.

"Me, too," Chantal added. "I could eat everything they've got."

Hatch and Henry exchanged glances.

"Girls," he began, "I know this is exciting and different, but I don't want y'all to embarrass me, hear. It's not like you don't get enough to eat at home. We might not eat steak or lobster, but Hatch makes sure we eat good. You each order one meal, and if you finish it, you can order dessert. You can probably even share a dessert if you don't think you can eat a whole one by yourself. Remember, you didn't make the best first impression on Mr. Audsley. I told you I know all about that directions business. I won't have you taking advantage of his kindness."

"And be sure to put your napkin in your lap as soon as you sit at the table," Hatch added.

"Next you're going to tell us which fork to use," Chantal said.

"You mean there'll be more than one fork?" Sinclair asked, sounding incredulous.

"Don't worry, Sinclair. It's just like they said to Leonardo in *Titanic.* You start from the outside and work your way in." Chantal spoke with all the wisdom of a fifteen-year-old whose impressions of life were based on what she'd seen at the movies.

"I don't think they'll have more than one fork," Hatch said. She hoped she was right. She was only going from her experience of eating at the diner, where the place setting included a knife and single fork inside a rolled paper napkin.

They were immediately shown to the table where Skye waited. Hatch was sure the hostess was alerted by his description of three black females accompanying a disabled black male. The hostess took them around the long way, bypassing the stairs. Henry generally only used his crutches when moving about at home; he preferred his wheelchair when walking any distance was involved.

Skye rose when he saw them approaching. The table was round, with an empty space where the fifth chair normally would be. Hatch wheeled her father to this space while Skye pulled out chairs and seated Chantal and Sinclair. He then pulled out the remaining chair, which was the one next to his, with Sinclair on his other side.

"Thank you," Hatch said, feeling a tad self-conscious; it wasn't every day that she was on the receiving end of courtesy by such a handsome, successful man.

The waitress took their beverage orders. Chantal and Sinclair were busy looking at their menus. Their slightly open mouths attested to their amazement at the extensive choices, and Hatch suddenly wished she'd been able to afford to take them to a restaurant at some earlier point in their life. Their experience was limited to fast food and the pizza or Chinese food she occasionally brought home. She had hoped Skye would be unable to tell this was their first restaurant meal, but their lack of familiarity was painfully obvious.

"Mmm, beef fajitas sound good," Sinclair said.

"I think I want the barbecue ribs," Chantal said, sounding breathless, like she had just run around the block.

"I think I'll have the roast beef sandwich with that dipping sauce," Henry said.

"I can't decide," Hatch said.

"Neither can I," Skye said. "Maybe I should just close my eyes and point to something."

Their waitress appeared with their drinking glasses. "I'll make up my mind in just a minute, I promise," Hatch said.

"It's all right. Mr. Hatchet, why don't you and the girls tell the waitress what you want? I'm sure Hatch and I will be ready by the time it's our turn."

In the end Hatch ordered a salad featuring boneless fried chicken pieces, and Skye chose one of the specialty burgers.

Their conversation was centered around everyone's impressions of living in Farmingdale, from Daddy's recollections about his days as a young man over forty years ago up to Chantal's and Sinclair's answers to Skye's questions, most of which were given in five words or less, with a description from Hatch of what a typical day was like.

While the others talked, Hatch found her imagination running overtime. How nice it would be if Skye wasn't simply showing them kindness, but if he was her date, or even—she could hardly bear the thought—her boyfriend, taking all of them out to lunch. He was so handsome, like a movie star. What was his life like? she wondered. Where did he live? He wore no wedding band, but did he have a girlfriend back in New York? She wished she could ask, but he was there to interview them, not the other way around.

"I guess our little boring town must be quite a change of pace for you, Skye," Henry commented.

"It's certainly different, Mr. Hatchet. I'm planning to drive up to Chicago this afternoon and spend some time with friends."

Hatch liked the deft way he handled a sticky situation, not coming right out and agreeing that Farmingdale was a nothing town, but saying it was merely "different." She was curious about who his friends were. Probably cut from the same high-quality cloth, she decided. Wealthy, successful, college-educated types who felt perfectly at home, whether in corporate boardrooms, arguing cases before judges, or asking nurses to hand them scalpels.

When their plates were cleared—Hatch noted with disappointment that Daddy only ate a little more than half of his sandwich—and the waitress asked if anyone cared for dessert, Chantal immediately said that she and Sinclair would share the brownie sundae. Skye surprised Hatch by asking if she'd like to share a dessert with him. She agreed, and the waitress brought a white-covered concoction that looked like a miniature snow-covered mountain. The hard surface was white chocolate, as was the vanilla-appearing ice cream it covered that was inside on a bed of crushed Oreo cookies. "This is delicious," she said at her first taste.

"It's my favorite. I'm glad you like it."

"So when do you talk to us for TV, Mr. Skye?" Sinclair asked.

Skye brushed a drop of ice cream from his moustache. "I'd like to interview you on-camera tomorrow afternoon. I've made appointments with a number of residents already, so I hope you don't mind being last." He turned to Hatch. "How's four P.M.?"

She loved the sound of his voice. It was so smooth, with perfect diction. Her ear should have told her right away that he was in radio or TV. "That's fine." She quickly took a bite of dessert, for an idea was already beginning to form in her mind, and it made her want to smile.

* * *

She put the chicken in the oven at three P.M., knowing the scent of it roasting would fill the house by the time Skye arrived. She would serve flavored yellow rice, green beans, and her special homemade biscuits. It had all the makings of a typical Sunday dinner for them, but if Skye accepted her invitation to join them, it would be different from all the others.

She fixed her hair in a single French braid down from crown to nape, tucking the end in neatly. When she was satisfied the braid was straight, she applied her makeup. She had never been much for cosmetics. Usually she just wore lipstick, but since she was going to be on television she felt she needed a little more, so she dabbed on blusher to color her cheeks.

She looked at her reflection. Her skin was unblemished, but something wasn't right. It was her eyebrows, she realized. They were straggly. Funny how she'd never noticed that before.

There wasn't time to tweeze out all the unruly hairs, so she made feathery little strokes with an eyebrow pencil to thicken them. The effect was quite attractive, but she hoped Skye wouldn't notice how her eyebrows had seemed to grow since yesterday.

She never considered her looks any more than just average. She didn't have prominent cheekbones, luminous eyes, or any other standout feature. Actually, her nose was a tad too large for her face, but the additional makeup did make a difference. She looked . . . well, kind of pretty. Better than that, she *felt* pretty.

The knock on the door came at four-twenty. Hatch took one last look at the living room, making sure nothing was out of place.

"Hello," she said when she opened the door.

"Hi, Hatch," Skye said. "We're a few minutes late. I'm sorry about that. We got a little behind schedule."

"That's fine. I'm sure it's difficult to keep up when you've got so many people to see."

He introduced her to the cameraman, John Kirby, a short, muscular black man casually dressed in khakis and a plaid shirt.

She invited them inside, more conscious than ever of the small living room with its outdated sixties furniture. "Excuse me a moment. I want to get my father."

She called out to Chantal and Sinclair while unfolding her father's wheelchair. "Mr. Audsley is here."

When they were all in the living room, John looked through the viewfinder of his camera. "Do you mind if I adjust your shades?" he asked Hatch.

"No, go ahead."

It only took a few moments to set the proper lighting. Skye began by asking Henry a series of questions as John stood nearby and filmed his responses. Hatch watched her father visibly relax. He must have forgotten all about the camera.

The interview went pretty quickly. Many of Skye's questions were repeats of the ones he had asked yesterday at lunch. Chantal and Sinclair were interviewed together, and then it was her turn.

Skye looked at John. "I think that about does it."

"I think you've got more than enough film." John sniffed. "We should probably leave so the Hatchets can sit down to their dinner. It smells delicious."

It was the opening Hatch had been hoping for. "Would the two of you care to join us? We have plenty."

"It's tempting, but I've got a long drive home, and my wife is holding dinner for me," John said.

"It's been a while since I've had a home-cooked meal," Skye began. "If you're sure it won't be an imposition . . ."

"Not at all. We'd love to have you join us."

"When are we going to be on TV, Mr. Skye?" Chantal asked when they were all at the table.

"I'm not sure of the airdate. It'll probably be two or three weeks out. I'm flying back to New York tomorrow. When I get there I'll be sitting down with a film editor and will determine which parts of what John shot will be used and which parts won't be. Most of the film is going to be tossed, I'm afraid. It all has to fit inside a window of about twenty minutes, not including introductions and stand-ups at the beginning, the end, and before and after commercial breaks."

Chantal frowned. "What's a stand-up?"

"It's what the reporter says after the feature has run, sort of a summary. The final one runs twenty or thirty seconds. One before a commercial will be a little shorter."

"Your work must be fascinating," Henry commented.

"I enjoy it."

"Do you know where'll you be sent next?" Hatch asked tonelessly. She'd known all along that Skye would be moving on after completing his assignment, but it was an unpleasant thought, just another reminder that everyone but her got to leave Farmingdale.

"I won't know until I turn the edited tape in to the producer. But first I've got a few days off coming."

Most of the meal was filled by Skye telling them amusing anecdotes about his work experiences. Hatch kept hoping he would say something about his personal life, but he didn't. And she couldn't think of a gracious way to bring it up without sounding as if she were prying.

"Something I've been meaning to ask you, Hatch," Skye said as he discreetly wiped his mouth with a napkin. "Why does everyone call you that?"

She laughed. "Because it's better than being called Cornelia."

"Now that's a perfectly nice name," Henry said. "It was my mother's name."

She made a face. "It's so old-fashioned. My mother gave me that nickname, Skye. I don't think she much cared for the name, either."

Skye nodded. She thought he looked a bit uncomfortable. He knew from lunch about the story of their family, how her mother had run off years before. Perhaps he was embarrassed that he'd brought it up, but the truth was that talking about her mother didn't upset her or Daddy. They had long since stopped asking themselves why she left. Elaine Hatchet's abandonment had become a mere footnote on a page of their lives; it was Anna Maria Hatchet whose memory was cherished.

"This is delicious, Hatch. You're a wonderful cook."

Hatch wasn't sure if he really meant it or if he was merely trying to cover his discomfort. Still, she mentally thanked Anna Maria for teaching her what to do in the kitchen. "Thank you. I wish I could say *everybody* felt the same," she said with a pointed look at her father.

All eyes turned to him as he pushed his food around on his plate, and he looked up almost guiltily. "I've always enjoyed your cooking, Hatch. I'm just not very hungry this afternoon."

"You weren't very hungry this morning, either."

He shrugged. "Must be all the excitement. It's not every day a man gets interviewed for television. But don't take it personal, son," he added, addressing Skye.

"I won't. And I hope once I'm gone your appetite will improve, Mr. Hatchet," Skye said.

"I'll bring my plate with me while I'm watching my movie tonight."

"What's it going to be tonight, Daddy?" Hatch asked.

"He loves old movies," Sinclair explained to Skye.

"I can't remember the name of it, but that Dee girl is in it. She's one of my favorites. I'll bet in real life she's got as much love in her as all those sweet young characters she played."

Skye's forehead wrinkled in confusion. "Sandra Dee?"

"No. *Ruby* Dee."

Hatch's spirits were leaden as her family walked Skye to the door. It was time for him to leave.

"I've certainly enjoyed spending time with all of you," Skye said. "I'll sleep good tonight after such a wonderful and filling meal."

"I'll think about you being fast asleep while I'm at work," Hatch said.

"You're working this evening?"

"My days off are Tuesday and Wednesday. I requested those days so I can drive my father to his doctor appointments. On nights I work I usually sleep in shifts, five hours in the morning and three hours in the evening. The girls will clean the kitchen."

"Yeah, 'the girls' will do it," Chantal said sullenly.

Everyone laughed, and Skye held out his hand to Henry. "Thank you, sir. Your family's hospitality has meant a lot to me."

"We were glad to have you, Skye."

Hatch watched as Skye shook Chantal's and Sinclair's hands, and then it was her turn. She was glad she'd used lotion after dinner.

"I really enjoyed dinner, Hatch. I hope you like the segment. And I truly hope improvements get made. There's a lot of good people living here in Farmingdale."

"I think so, too. Thank you."

The familiar weight continued to hold her mood down as she lay in the dark of her bedroom. This weekend had been remarkable, but now the excitement was over, save for when the show actually aired. Now it was back to the same routine, day after day, with little variance, the only change being the increasing strands of gray in her hair, reminding her that she was rapidly approaching entry into middle age.

At least she had the show to look forward to, seeing herself and her family and neighbors on television. But the events of the weekend had been so much fun she wished there could be more.

Skye Audsley would never know how much
brightness he had brought into her bleak existence.

Five

Hatch hesitated in the doorway to her father's room. "I made some baloney and cheese crackers. Would you like some?"

"No, I'm not really hungry."

She placed the plate on top of his dresser. "Oh, Daddy. You told me the nurse said you lost another twelve pounds. You're down nearly thirty pounds in the last six months. If you keep this up, if you turn sideways we won't see you."

"I guess I can't help it if I don't feel like eating."

"It's nothing but some crackers and a little baloney and cheese. Nibble food, Daddy. Won't take hardly any effort at all for you to eat."

"Hatch. C'mere." He gestured with a curling index finger.

She sat on the edge of his bed and waited for him to speak.

"Wait a minute; I want to see something."

He was watching *The Price Is Right*. Spokesmodels were presenting prizes, accenting the goodies with raised arms and that twirling wrist motion Hatch was sure would eventually lead to carpal tunnel syndrome.

"Can you believe it? That woman there passed on a week's vacation at a resort in the Arizona desert, plus a week's vacation in Monte Carlo *and* a beautiful boat, and I'll bet anything it was because she was looking for a car. People can be so foolish sometimes. Most working people can manage to buy themselves some kind of transportation, but how many chances do they get to take eight-day, seven-night vacations? And in such nice places?"

"So did she get a car?" Hatch asked, even though she didn't care.

"Ha! All they offered her was some new living room furniture, carpeting, and a pool table. And I hope Miss Greedy Gut loses."

She blinked repeatedly, trying to hold back tears. Daddy was diminishing before her very eyes. What's more, he didn't seem to care. He took more interest in game show contestants than he did in his own health.

He reached forward and patted her hand. "I didn't want to tell you this, Daughter. I knew you would get upset."

It never occurred to her that perhaps there was a reason for him being so calm in the face of his steady weight loss, but he only called her "Daughter" when he was serious about something. She leaned forward in concern. "Daddy? What is it? Something's wrong, isn't it?"

He removed his hand and sat back in his chair. "I'm not saying another word unless you promise not to say anything to your sisters."

"But if something's wrong, don't you think they have a right to know?"

He simply gave her a stern look, and she knew he meant what he said.

"All right, Daddy. Tell me."

"Well, last spring Dr. Sheffield told me my kidneys are starting to go. It was after I had some lab tests drawn."

"So there's dialysis when it gets to be real bad. You'd probably qualify to have someone come to the house because of your disability. I know it isn't a pleasant thought, but it really shouldn't be particularly inconvenient for you."

"That wasn't all he noticed."

"What else?"

"I had something called a PSA that was very high. They did a biopsy, and they told me I've got prostate cancer. Apparently it's a very aggressive type."

"Daddy, why didn't you tell me?"

"Because I knew you wouldn't understand."

"What's not to understand?" She held out her hands in front of her, palms up.

"I told him I didn't want any treatment."

"Daddy! How could you? If you tell him that, you won't get any better. The cancer will just keep growing—" She broke off abruptly, suddenly realizing she didn't have to tell him what the outcome would be.

"Now you know why I don't eat much anymore."

This time she couldn't hold her tears. She put her face in her palms and sobbed. Daddy had been there for her all her life; after her mother left it was just the two of them until he met and married Anna Maria years later. He was only fifty-nine years old. She expected to have him around for years and years yet, but he was telling her he was dying.

"I know you feel bad, Daughter, but believe me, it's best this way. I'm sorry not to stick around and see Chantal and Sinclair grow up to be women, but I'm just so tired of fighting. I stuck it out as long as I could."

She stopped crying. "Daddy, don't say that."

"And as much as I hate to admit it, I think y'all will have a better chance without me."

"That's not true, Daddy."

He put a hand on his chest, and it was several seconds before he spoke again. "I kept up my insurance policies. It's not a whole lot, but there should be something left over after my expenses are taken care of. Don't even think about putting me away in one of those expensive mahogany caskets. I want you to take the girls and leave Farmingdale. Just leave. Give the landlord notice, rent a truck, and hit the road. Move closer to your job. You should have enough money to at least get you started. You'll have to do the rest. It won't be easy. You might even have to use some of that money the girls get every month. . . ."

Hatch knew he meant the Social Security benefits Chantal and Sinclair received because of his disability.

". . . that we were putting away for their college, but they'll get there. It's not too late for you, Hatch. I know how you see Trevor and that girl he married when they come to visit and wish that could be you. Don't think for a minute that you haven't done anything of importance, because you have. You've raised two children, and that's the most important job there is. You've done a fine job with Chantal and Sinclair, and I know you'll continue. Don't worry about me. I'll be with Anna Maria. She and I were meant for each other. Your mama and I, well, that just wasn't meant to last. I may have found Anna Maria late, but it was perfect. I'm sure you'll find your true love, and when you do he'll understand your responsibility for your sisters. They'll be grown anyway in another couple of years. I'm real proud of you, Hatch. I know you gave up a hell of a lot to take care of us, and I don't know what we would have done without you."

She made no sound, but inside her a dam had burst, and tears came spilling out, turning her cheeks into waterfalls. She knew she wouldn't be able to stop them, and she didn't try.

"My body is giving out, Hatch. Sometimes acceptance is the best route to take. Don't be sad. Besides, it's not like I'm going anywhere next week." He placed a comforting hand on her knee. "Come on, perk up. I'm finished talking. *Waterloo Bridge* is about to come on, and I want to see it. That Vivien Leigh was a real beauty, even if she had the biggest hands I've ever seen on a woman."

Once Hatch stopped crying, she put on a good face for her father. She hugged him and told him to enjoy the movie. She was all cried out, and now she felt like a failure. She should have been able to do something to make his life more comfortable, more meaningful.

His words kept playing over and over inside her head when she prepared to take her afternoon nap, and all she could do was remind herself that he wasn't going to die right away.

"Wow, he's really good-looking," Sinclair commented.

The whole family was watching *A Day in the Life*. Skye Audsley did look especially handsome in a brown suit, multicolored geometric print tie, and a shirt the color of deli mustard as he introduced the segment on Farmingdale. Hatch could hardly believe this gorgeous man had taken them all to lunch. The woman in his life was certainly lucky.

She was lying crosswise on Daddy's bed, along with Chantal and Sinclair, and they all oohed and aahed each time the scene changed, as they recognized every setting and every face. When their own living room flashed on the screen, the females screamed. Even Daddy was beaming. "I don't look half bad," he remarked.

It was true. He was thinner than he had ever been, but on television he appeared heavier. Hatch gripped the quilt in a reflex reaction; she knew that this time next year he wouldn't be with them.

Her mood didn't brighten when the segment focused on the poorest of Farmingdale's citizens. Close-up shots were taken of holes in floors and shacks equipped only with outhouses. "Something has to be done about this," she said.

Even Chantal and Sinclair were sobered. "I didn't know there were people in town living like that," Sinclair said.

"You girls are among the fortunate," Daddy said. "And to think you complain about not having HBO."

"I guess that means we're spoiled, doesn't it?" Chantal said softly.

"There really isn't anything wrong with wanting more than what you've got, or striving to better your circumstances. Just keep in mind that no matter how bad things are, there's always someone who's worse off."

* * *

The program aired on Tuesday. Friday morning when Hatch came home she ate a light breakfast, then knocked on the door of her father's bedroom as she usually did when it was time to take their walk. When he didn't answer, she opened the door a few inches and peered inside. "Daddy?"

He was lying in bed on his side, his mouth open. As she approached she noticed his lids were only partly shut. She gasped and quickly moved to him. When her palm connected to his shoulder she felt the coldness of his skin. With shaking hands, she reached for the phone to call 911 . . . but she knew it was too late.

Henry Hatchet's sudden death from a heart attack came as a shock to the residents of Farmingdale. Chantal and Sinclair were inconsolable. Hatch allowed herself one session to cry her heart out, but at the funeral she was stoic, comforted by her father's acceptance of his fate and his wishes for her not to let her grief stop her from reaching her goals. She truly believed he was with Anna Maria, who had been the love of his life.

Six

Skye didn't know what made him want to go back to Farmingdale, even as he drove south on I-57. His position with the network included reporting on breaking news, and he was on assignment in Chicago to report on a major story. He'd been on the first plane out of LaGuardia at dawn, and now by midafternoon, the edited tape was ready for airing on the evening news. He'd spoken with Grandma on his cell phone and assured her he would be back by nine P.M.

He'd had no choice but to move in with her himself, even though he kept his Greenwich Village apartment, and he would stay in Tarrytown until he found someone who could care for her. The few possible candidates who had passed the initial screening had been rejected by Grandma as "phony," "too nervous," or "Good heavens, she'd talk me to death," when they met for a joint interview.

His return flight wasn't until eight P.M., and he had several hours to kill. Everyone he knew in Chicago was at work, so he decided to use the time to make the long drive to Farmingdale. The program had aired two weeks before, and he was curious to know what the residents thought of it, especially the Hatchets.

He saw Violet Pettiford, the woman who was raising her grandchildren, shepherding the youngsters into her trailer. He pulled the rental car to the curb and got out. "Hello, Mrs. Pettiford."

She squinted as he got closer. "My, my, is that you from the television program?"

"Yes, it's me. Skye Audsley." He knew she couldn't remember his name.

"Well, hello. What brings you back here?"

He explained about the story he was covering. "I do segments for the evening network news, too."

"Well, I think you ought to tell that fellow who sits at the anchor desk that it's time to retire and let some young blood take over."

He chuckled. "How did you like the program?"

"Oh, I loved it. So did my grandchildren. I never thought I'd get to be on TV."

"Are there any changes being discussed? New housing or shopping?"

"No, not really. There's some rumblings about building some decent housing, but I'll believe it when I see it. I think things are about to get better for us, though. We're going to take over the lease on the Hatchet house when they leave."

"The Hatchets? They're moving?"

"The girls are. Henry died week before last. It was a heart attack, but from what I understand he was very ill and wasn't long for this world anyway."

"That's awful. I had no idea."

"I guess you couldn't have. You'd have to have known Henry before he started losing all that weight. He was a good man, Henry Hatchet. He loved his family. For years he took care of his oldest all by himself."

"How did his daughters cope with it?"

"The younger girls took it pretty hard. Hatch, bless her, is a strong girl, and family means everything to her. Not anything like that mother of hers." Mrs. Pettiford rolled her eyes to demonstrate how little she thought of Henry Hatchet's first wife. "She'll keep them together. But she told me they're gonna leave. She said Henry didn't want them to live out their lives here in Farmingdale. This really is no place for young people, unless they get on at the prison. And even thought it pays decent, it ain't much of a career."

"I think I'll go see them. They were very nice to me while I was reporting my story."

"You remember where the house is, don't you? I've got to see after the kids and get dinner started. Oscar'll be home soon."

"Sure, ma'am. Thank you."

Skye got in his rented vehicle and drove the few blocks to the Hatchet home. At first he wondered if anyone was home. It was too early for the middle and high school buses from the neighboring town to be in, and Hatch might be asleep. No, wait, she'd said she was off Tuesday and Wednesday nights, and today was Wednesday.

He parked in front of the house and knocked on the front door. Hatch opened it. Only the screen door separated them, and from the way she blinked and stared at him through widened eyes, he knew she was shocked to see him.

"Skye?" she said, her tone barely louder than a whisper.

Her face looked thinner than he remembered. "Yes, it's me. I was doing some work in Chicago, and I had a couple of hours before my flight back. I decided to drive down and see how everyone was doing. Mrs. Pettiford told me about your father.

My sincerest condolences to you and your sisters. He was a fine man."

"Thank you. He was." She pushed the screen door open. "Come in."

They sat on opposite ends of the sofa. He quickly shifted position to avoid a hard patch in the sofa cushion. "How are you and your sisters managing?"

"It came as a big shock to them, and to me, too. He did tell me about some other health problems he was having, but still, I didn't expect his heart would give out. I thought he'd be with us for a couple more months at least." She paused, and he was afraid she was going to cry, but when she spoke again her voice was steady and quiet. "You know, he died just a few days after the segment with us in it aired. He liked your work very much. I think I can say that he died contented, if not truly happy. That helps a lot."

"Mrs. Pettiford mentioned you and the girls are leaving town. What are your plans?"

"I'm not really sure. There's really no need for us to stay here. Daddy had a bit of insurance, but the funeral costs were more than I expected. Less than half is left. I was thinking about moving to Chicago, or at least the Chicago area."

"It's expensive there, Hatch. It'll be hard for you to find a place to live that you can afford. Even though the cost of living is higher, there probably won't be much difference in your salary."

"I can't stay here, Skye. I feel like this town has got me by the neck and is squeezing the life out of me. I was going to go to college, you know. I gave up my scholarship when my stepmother got killed. I've been here all my life, and if I don't get out of here now, while I have the chance, I'm going to grow old and die right here." She touched gentle fingertips to the still-smooth skin of her throat.

"I'm just asking that you give it a lot of thought before you jump in. It's a big step, and I'd hate to see you make the move and then find that what you can make as a head cashier won't be enough to support you and your sisters."

Her forehead wrinkled and her eyes closed tightly, and this time he was sure she was going to break down. The frustration she so clearly felt broke his heart, and at that precise moment the idea hit him.

"I've got a suggestion for you."

"What's that?"

"My grandmother will be turning eighty-nine in a few weeks. She has a caretaker during weekdays, but now she really needs someone to live in. I've been looking, and I can't seem to find the right person. I think you'd be perfect."

"*Me?*"

"Don't look so shocked, Hatch. You may have worked outside the house, too, but your main function all these years has been taking care of your father and running the household."

"But it wouldn't be just me. Where I go, my sisters go. I'm their guardian now."

"There's enough room for you, Chantal, and Sinclair in the house."

"She doesn't want to live with your parents?"

She sounded incredulous, he thought, like she couldn't imagine a daughter or son wanting to hire a stranger to take care of their own mother. But of course that's how she would look at it. She was too devoted to her family to even consider such an idea. "My parents are both dead."

"Oh. I'm sorry. I didn't know."

"And I'm always traveling. So tell me, are you interested?"

"Yes. What happens now?"

"The first step would be to do a background check on you, so I hope you don't have any objections to that."

She shrugged. "No objections. Nothing to hide, either."

"Good. Room and board are included. I'd give you a household allowance to buy food with, plus a small salary."

"What about Chantal and Sinclair? Would the allowance include them?"

"Of course. They're part of the household. I don't see why it can't work much the same way it works now"—he broke off, realizing his error—"the way it worked with your father, where all of you pitched in. You can spend the days with Grandma, and when the girls come home from school they can keep an eye on her and you'll have time to yourself. Technically, they'll be earning their portion. Maybe you can work part-time or use the insurance money to take college courses in the evening." He could tell from the way her mouth opened, then closed, that the word *college* brought her hope. "I think it'll be good for Grandma to have young people in the house," he continued. "Most of her friends have died, and that can be very depressing for an old person. And if you take the job you'll get to live near New York, the most exciting city in the world, even more exciting than Chicago." He watched her chew on her lower lip and gave her time to think.

"It sounds like a wonderful opportunity. . . ."

He didn't want to give her a chance to express any doubt. "I'll tell you what. Let's arrange for you to meet my grandmother. She's vetoed the few people I thought might be good for the job. She's got this wonderful sixth sense about people, but I think she'll like the three of you." He felt no one could dislike Hatch. He was sure Chantal and Sinclair could be a handful, but heaven help them if they tried to pull any fast ones on Grandma. She might weigh less than a hundred pounds, but she was sharp as a Ginsu knife.

"Is she going to come out here?"

He laughed. "No, I think it would be better to fly you and the girls in to New York."

She brightened right away. "Us? Go to New York? On a plane?"

"Yes. You're not afraid to fly, are you?"

"Well, I never have, but I think it'd be more exciting than frightening."

"Good. I'm sure I can get you all on a flight this weekend, say on Thursday? We can make it in the evening so Chantal and Sinclair won't have to miss school that day, but they'd have to miss Friday. I'd have you back on Sunday."

"One day of missed school won't hurt. Skye, do you really mean it?"

He smiled; her enthusiasm was infectious. He was certain his grandmother would approve of the Hatchet sisters, and he was suddenly very glad he'd decided to drive to Farmingdale. "I really mean it."

Seven

Hatch hooked her arm through Chantal's on one side and Sinclair's on the other as they rode the escalator to the baggage claim area. "So, did y'all enjoy your first plane ride?"

"It was a little on the bumpy side," Sinclair said. "But New York looks like it does in all the pictures and movies I've seen."

"Didn't this trip cost Mr. Skye a lot of money?" Chantal asked.

"I'm sure it wasn't cheap, but he can probably write it off on his tax return or something. Oh, I see him!" Hatch waved, and Skye waved back, as did the tiny woman standing next to him. She looked sweet. Hatch prayed she would like them, for this was an opportunity she didn't want to miss.

It only took a few seconds to reach them. "Hello, Skye," Hatch said, holding out her hand.

"Welcome to New York, Hatch. How was your flight?"

"Wonderful. It's incredible how fast you can get from one place to another."

Hatch was taken off guard when Sinclair gave Skye a hug and Chantal followed suit. She stood opposite his grandmother and extended her hand. "Hello, ma'am. It's so nice to meet you. I'm Cornelia Hatchet, but everybody calls me Hatch."

"Harriet Jackson. I've heard quite a bit about you, dear."

Hatch shook the woman's hand gingerly, but was surprised by her strength. This was no little old lady with a macaroni grip. "Mrs. Jackson, these are my sisters, Chantal and Sinclair. Girls, this is Mr. Skye's grandmother, Mrs. Jackson."

"Oh, that sounds too formal," Mrs. Jackson said. "Call me Miss Hattie, like all the young people do."

"All right. Miss Hattie it is."

"Let's go get your luggage," Skye suggested. He seated Miss Hattie in her wheelchair and they all began walking toward the terminal. "Grandma actually walks quite well, but not long distances," he explained to Hatch as they waited for the elevator.

Hatch had packed all their clothes for the weekend in one large suitcase. She had worried that it was a little shabby looking, but she saw plenty of bags that looked worse. She'd seen how the handlers carelessly threw passengers' luggage into the plane and decided it would be silly for someone of her modest means to purchase expensive bags just to have them tossed around like Frisbees.

When they stood at the carousel marked with their flight number, Skye asked for their claim checks.

"We only checked one bag," Hatch said, handing him the ticket.

He reached for the bag she pointed out and checked the identification tag. He carried it to the exit, where he showed the claim check to the official. Hatch, having taken over pushing Miss Hattie's wheelchair, followed, with Chantal and Sinclair bringing up the rear.

It was a crisp autumn evening. Hatch was surprised at the freshness of the air. She thought her nostrils would recoil at breathing air filled with soot and other unpleasant scents of the big city.

Skye instructed them to wait while he brought the car around. After he was gone, Hatch moved in front of the wheelchair so Miss Hattie could see her as she spoke. "I can't believe we're in New York," she said. "It's so exciting. I never thought I'd get to see it."

"You'll love it. Skye has told me so much about you, Hatch. He said you took wonderful care of your father, and that you lost him recently. I'm sorry." Miss Hattie reached out and patted Hatch's hand. "All of you are so young to be without parents. My Skye was young, too."

"Oh, I didn't know."

"I guess I can't say I'm surprised he didn't mention it. Skye and his mother—my daughter, Barbara—came to live with my husband and me after Barbara left Skye's father." She shook her head. "I get feelings about people, and I always felt that Arthur Audsley would bring my daughter nothing but heartache. But you can't tell kids anything. She was in love. Anyway, Arthur died not too long after she left him, and she went to glory a couple of years later."

"That must have been hard for you," Chantal said.

"Oh, it was. Children are supposed to bury their parents, not the other way around. But you have to go on." She smiled at the teenagers. "Now, tell me how old you are and what grades you're in."

As Chantal and Sinclair complied with her request, Hatch hoped Miss Hattie had a good feeling about them. She'd easily passed the background check Skye ran on her, but his grandmother's opinion was the final hurdle. But Miss Hattie was certainly making them feel comfortable.

The four of them were chatting easily by the time Skye pulled up. He popped the trunk from inside the car and quickly lifted the bag inside. He then helped Miss Hattie to her feet and folded the wheelchair—Hatch could tell it was a light-weight model similar to the one Daddy had used—and inserted it in the trunk, as well. Hatch was horrified to see Miss Hattie heading for the back seat of the four-door Grand Marquis. "Miss Hattie, you sit up front. My sisters and I will ride in the back."

Skye laughed. "Grandma always rides in the back. She's afraid of the air bag."

"It's only because I'm little," Miss Hattie said in protest. "I've heard about how those air bags come flying out like they were just shot out of a cannon and crush people my size."

"So people who see us think I'm her chauffeur," Skye joked. "It's okay, Hatch. You go ahead and get in front."

She felt a little self-conscious riding in the front seat alongside Skye, so close she could reach out and touch him. His right arm was resting on the arm rest between their seats, with his elbow just inches from her left arm. This was an unexpected plus and an almost foreign feeling for her. She knew Daddy mainly meant her love life when he said he knew how much she'd given up for their family. Her eyes filled with tears; she missed him terribly.

She looked out of her window and blinked furiously to dry her eyes. Miss Hattie, Chantal, and Sinclair were having quite a conversation in the back seat. Miss Hattie was telling them about the village of Tarrytown, where she lived.

"The schools for junior and senior high are both called Sleepy Hollow."

"Sleepy Hollow? The town with the headless horseman?" Chantal asked.

"Ichabod Crane and the headless horseman weren't real, they were made up by Washington Irving—he's buried in the Sleepy Hollow Cemetery, by the way—but Sleepy Hollow is a real town. It's right next to Tarrytown, and for years they called it North Tarrytown. They didn't change the name back until just a couple of years ago."

"Oh, look, there's the skyline again!" Hatch said. They were crossing a bridge, and the famed Manhattan skyline they had seen aerially from the plane glistened in the night. "Look at the Empire State Building."

"I've never seen so many lights in my life," Sinclair said.

"How far away from the city is Tarrytown, Miss Hattie?" Chantal asked.

"Oh, about forty minutes or so."

Skye leaned closer to Hatch and spoke in a low voice. "She likes you guys. I can tell."

"I hope so. She looks like a real sweetheart."

"She is. She raised me after my mother died. I'm like Chantal and Sinclair; I was orphaned at a young age."

She shuddered. "I hate that word *orphan*. There's something creepy about it."

"I guess the phrase 'orphaned at a young age' is redundant, since I'm pretty sure the word itself refers only to young people." He moved his hand so that his palm rested atop the back of her hand

and applied a gentle pressure. "But don't worry. It looks like you're in."

Hatch drew in her breath. Skye's hand rested on hers for just a few seconds, but it was the first time he'd ever touched her other than to shake her hand, and while she knew he was only trying to reassure her, she nonetheless found his touch exciting. She felt flushed as she told herself it was simply her imagination working overtime. She'd had many crushes over the years when she came into contact with good-looking men, imagining how it would be to have a courtship going on. It was almost natural for her to have a special feeling for Skye, for unlike other men she'd admired from a distance, she'd actually spent a little time with him, and if everything worked out he would be the one to rescue her from a life of despair in Farmingdale.

"This is the car you'll be driving," Skye said. "I'm sure you won't have any problem, since you're used to driving a large car."

"Oh. I had no idea I'd be driving something so nice. I thought this was your car."

He laughed, then spoke loudly enough to be heard in the back seat. "Grandma likes a heavier car. She says it makes her feel safer. I have a little two-seater, which she hates. It really sits too low for her anyway."

Hatch had a visual picture of herself sitting beside Skye in a red sports car, zooming down the highway with the top down, her hair blowing in the breeze. She blinked. She was really getting carried away. Skye's car probably wasn't even a convertible, and besides, it was highly unlikely that she would accompany him anywhere in it.

She heard Miss Hattie talking with Chantal and

Sinclair in the back; once more they had broken off into their own conversation. "I don't know my way around. Will your grandmother be able to direct me?"

"No problem there. Grandma's sharp. She'll probably give you a tour of the town and of the historic sites in the area tomorrow. On Saturday she'll bring you to the supermarket. I've already told her you're a fabulous cook."

"Thank you. I'm sure she can cook circles around me, though; she's been doing it a lot longer."

"I don't know about that. That chicken you made that day was the juiciest I've ever tasted."

Hatch smiled. She realized early on, when she would stand alongside Anna Maria in their tiny kitchen in Farmingdale, that she had a knack for preparing food. But unlike her stepmother, Hatch wasn't content to merely make the same meals week after week. She frequently experimented with new recipes and had discovered new ways to fix ground beef and chicken that had become staples in their household. It boosted her morale to know that she could cook better than just about anyone she knew, and hearing that Skye thought she had a special talent made her feel especially good.

"On Sunday," Skye continued, "Grandma usually goes to church with her neighbors from next door. You and the girls will have plenty time to explore on your own."

"Do you live near here?"

"I've been staying up here while I've tried to find someone to live in, but I have an apartment in the city, down in Greenwich Village."

"Oh, I've heard of that."

"Living in the city is convenient to the studio and the network's offices. But I'll be up on Saturday."

"Is there anything special you wanted me to do this weekend, Skye?"

"No, not really. Grandma will let you know. Just relax, and you and the girls get to know her. We'll go from there."

Hatch looked out of the window at the passing scenery. They were on a rather picturesque two-lane highway, surrounded by grass and trees. When they left the highway they drove down a street of retail shops and restaurants, and then Skye steered the Mercury down a steep hill. Farmingdale was flat, and this incline made Hatch feel as if she were sliding down the side of a mountain. "Whatever do you do here when it snows?" she asked.

"We pretty much have to stay in until the road is cleared, but the town gets that done as soon as the snow stops, so it isn't too bad."

The wood frame house Skye parked in front of, although it had a second story, didn't appear to be much larger than their house in Farmingdale. When Skye opened the trunk and removed their single suitcase, she reached for Miss Hattie's wheelchair.

"You don't have to take the chair," Skye said. "Grandma can walk into the house all right."

The house sat close to the street, and they quickly covered the short cement walkway leading to the front door, Miss Hattie with her arm slipped through Chantal's for support. Skye unlocked the door.

Hatch looked in at a flight of stairs against the wall and a living room with large, dark furniture.

The room was saved from looking somber by the nubby tan carpet and beige curtains. "You have a lovely home, Miss Hattie. It looks very comfortable."

"It is. I've lived here fifty-three years. Come with me, girls." Miss Hattie gestured for them to follow her, which they did. "This is the dining room."

"You've got nice furniture," Sinclair said, stroking the brown cherrywood table with the back of her fingers. A matching china cabinet was centered against the wall.

"Thank you. I've had it a long, long time, even before my husband and I lived here. This is the kitchen."

They followed her into a kitchen that had obviously been updated. Its modern wood-toned countertops, wall oven, side-by-side refrigerator, and small island with cooktop were a stark contrast to the old-fashioned furniture of the living and dining rooms.

Miss Hattie opened a door under the stairs. "Skye put that bathroom in here so I wouldn't have to go upstairs every time I needed to go. He even had them put in a shower in case the stairs get to be too much for me, but it's so small I don't think I can turn around in there. Now this," she added, moving into a room at the end of the kitchen, "used to be a porch, but my husband and I had it enclosed when Barbara and Skye came to live with us, so Skye could have his own room. I thought you might like to sleep here, Hatch, since I'm still able to make it up the stairs."

In what had once been Skye's bed, maybe even with Skye's pillow? I'd love to! "Sure," Hatch said in a carefully controlled voice.

"Chantal and Sinclair, you two will share a room upstairs. I'll bet you share a room now, don't you?"

"Yes," they replied simultaneously, smiling at each other.

"I'm going up myself, but I know you two can take the stairs two at a time, so go ahead. It's the room on the right."

Hatch lagged behind as the others went upstairs. She looked at the room that would be hers. It was small and narrow, perhaps six feet wide and ten feet long at the most, but it was larger than her square-shaped room at home in Farmingdale. It was simply furnished with a twin bed, nightstand, pole lamp with three bulbs, and dresser with three drawers. Best of all, she would be the only one downstairs. While everyone was asleep she could sit in the living room and pretend she had her own place. . . .

She left to join Miss Hattie and her sisters upstairs, knowing they would soon be calling for her. Skye was sitting in the living room with the television on, perusing the newspaper. "You're having a late night tonight, aren't you?"

"Oh, I'll be all right. I'm expecting it to be an easy day tomorrow. I just wanted to make sure everyone is settled before I drive home. Go on up."

She wanted to sit with him, talk with him, ask him about himself, get to know the man behind the handsome face, but she knew it wasn't her place. She was here to do a job, not get into his business. Still, she couldn't help thinking that in spite of his success and the comforts it brought, there seemed to be an emptiness in his heart.

She followed his suggestion and climbed the stairs. She heard the laughter when she reached the landing, and when she saw the room Chantal and Sinclair would be sharing she understood what was so funny. There was but one bed, a double. The girls had never shared the same bed before and were giggling about kicking each other in the night. Miss Hattie sat on the bed, obviously enjoying their banter.

"You two remind me of how my sister and I used to tease each other. We were very close."

"What happened to her?" Sinclair asked.

"Oh, she died a long time ago. She had kidney disease. Now they have dialysis and all that, but in those days there wasn't much they could do for you if your kidneys failed. This was back in the 1930s. She was only twenty-four years old."

"That's sad," Chantal said.

"Yes, it is, but my memories of her are all good ones. So, what do you girls think?"

"I think it's lovely," Hatch said, as Chantal and Sinclair echoed her words.

"I'm so glad to have you here. I think we're going to get on fine." Miss Hattie yawned and stood. "I'm getting a little sleepy. I put three sets of towels and facecloths in the bathroom. Hatch, you might want to move yours downstairs. I wasn't sure how you'd feel about that shower being so small. I'm going to bed now. It's been an exciting day for me. Tomorrow I'll show you my little town."

"Good night, Miss Hattie," Chantal said.

The others repeated this, and Miss Hattie walked out to the landing. "Skye, I'm going to bed."

Hatch heard a thumping on the steps, then soft voices on the landing. She turned to her sisters. "Do you like the house?" she asked quickly, not wanting Skye and Miss Hattie to think they were eavesdropping.

"It's cute," Sinclair said.

"Did you see the bathroom, Hatch? It's neat. It's got a real big shower. Miss Hattie said she can roll her wheelchair in there if she needs to," Chantal said.

"Actually, no, I haven't seen it yet."

"The other room is Miss Hattie's," Chantal concluded.

"It's a nice house. Not too big. Keeping it clean will be a snap." Hatch looked over at the doorway when she saw a movement out of the corner of her eye. Skye stood in the doorway, a broad grin on his face, like he'd just heard good news.

"Grandma's gone to bed, and I'm getting ready to go. Did you want me to bring the bag up here before I leave?"

"No, I think it'll work better if I take my things out first, since I'm staying downstairs. I can bring it up after, but thanks for offering." Hatch looked at him curiously. "Why are you smiling like that?"

Instantly his expression returned to normal. "Was I smiling? I wasn't aware of it."

"Your grandmother is really nice, Mr. Skye," Sinclair told him.

"Well, she just told me she thinks all of you are really nice, too."

Hatch felt disoriented when she opened her eyes, not recognizing the small room where she slept. When she remembered, she spread her arms and stretched luxuriously, then lounged with clasped palms cradling her head, remembering what Skye said before he left. Miss Hattie liked them. He seemed as pleased by Miss Hattie's approval as she was.

Funny, but for all the differences in their life experiences and education, when it came to making sure family was taken care of, she and Skye were essentially the same.

Eight

"I guess Skye decided not to come over today," Hatch commented as she added water to the frying pan for the gravy.

"He called and said he'd be here for dinner," Miss Hattie said.

"Oh. That's surprising. I thought he'd have plans on a Saturday evening."

"I can't tell you how long I've been waiting for great-grandchildren. The thrill of being a grand-mother wore off years ago. He's pushing forty, and there haven't been any prospects in nearly two years."

Hatch kept her eyes on the pan, choosing her words carefully. "I'm sure it's not because of a lack of female attention."

"No. I'm afraid he's become a bit of a cynic lately about their motives. He's quite a catch, my grandson—wealthy and handsome. But I do have to laugh about him being worried about losing his hair."

"Is he going bald?"

"His forehead's gotten higher the last couple of years, but I don't think he'll lose much more. His daddy didn't have a receding hairline at all, so I think he's going to be like my husband, whose hairline moved back a little but then stopped, and he didn't lose another inch right up to the day he died."

Hatch tasted her gravy, then frowned. It was missing something. Now that she knew Skye was coming for dinner, it had to be just perfect. She reached for the spicy no-salt blend of seasonings, hoping a dash or two would spice up the flavor.

She and her sisters were thoroughly enjoying their visit to New York. Miss Hattie took them on a tour of the area on Friday. Many of the towns and villages along the Hudson River were settled prior to the Revolution. Madame C.J. Walker's magnificent estate in Irvington reminded Hatch of pictures she'd seen of grand homes in Italy.

Miss Hattie had shown them the main streets of the village, one of which appropriately was called Main Street, with its quaint blend of shopping, services, and restaurants. Tarrytown had not been invaded by large chain retailers like Home Depot, Wal-Mart, Blockbuster, or Walgreens. Miss Hattie surprised Hatch by stating she didn't believe there was a Wal-Mart anywhere in Westchester County, although Kmart had a location in nearby White Plains.

Tarrytown's shopping district consisted of a post office and independently owned businesses specializing in hardware, pharmacy products, video rental, wine and spirits, travel and real estate, and numerous antique dealers. Hatch, Chantal, and Sinclair got a kick out of a boutique called New To You, which Miss Hattie said sold good quality used clothing. The one concession to name recognition was a McDonald's restaurant. Hatch and her sisters, accustomed to the strip malls found in Kankakee and other communities near Farmingdale, found the suburban setting charming.

Since Hatch had no idea where she was going, Miss Hattie directed her. Hatch marveled at the older woman's sharp mind. Miss Hattie explained how she had not driven a car since her right knee was replaced several years back. "But that doesn't mean I don't know where I'm going." They got on a highway, and Miss Hattie told her where to get off and where to turn. She took them to lunch, and after stuffing themselves with oversize hamburgers they went to the Grand Union supermarket to buy groceries for the week.

That night Hatch made honey-dipped chicken wings, which Miss Hattie adored. "Wait 'til Skye tries these," she said.

Hatch remembered Miss Hattie's words, along with Skye's comments about her roast chicken, and she decided to earn a place in his affections with her cooking. She was certain he'd enjoy her smothered pork chops. When the gravy tasted just right she spooned it over the browned chops, covered the baking dish with foil and placed it in the oven. "That's done," she said. "How about some green beans and some mashed potatoes? There'll be plenty of gravy. And of course I'll make biscuits."

"Hatch, you're going to have me too heavy to get into my clothes," Miss Hattie said with a laugh.

"I don't think a few pounds would hurt you." Miss Hattie was a small woman, a shade over five feet and no larger than a size six, but the framed photographs from years past on display in the living room suggested advancing years had diminished her weight. "Of course, I equate being a little chubby with good health. My daddy lost a lot of weight in the months before he died."

"You're certainly slim. So are Chantal and Sinclair."

"It's in the genes, I guess."

"Nothing wrong with that. Men usually like it."

All she could do was shrug. She noticed Miss Hattie looking at her curiously and knew what she was thinking.

"Have you ever had a serious boyfriend, Hatch?"

"Yes, but it was a long time ago. High school."

"Oh, so he was a local boy."

"Then, yes. He lives in St. Louis now with his wife."

"What went wrong between you, if I'm not being nosy?"

"It's all right. Like I said, it was ages ago. We were planning to go to the same college, but my daddy had to have his foot amputated, and then my stepmother was killed in a car accident. I had to take care of Chantal and Sinclair. Sinclair was only a baby at the time. Trevor went on to college, and we just kind of grew apart. He didn't come back to Farmingdale after he graduated . . . not that I can blame him." It didn't hurt her to talk about it; it felt almost cathartic to say it aloud. Perhaps being in Miss Hattie's modern kitchen in Tarrytown made all the difference. It had been many years since Hatch had a mother figure to talk to, and in just two days she felt as though she'd known Harriet Jackson all her life.

Skye called out from the living room. Hatch heard him greeting Chantal and Sinclair, who were watching television. Moments later he joined them in the kitchen, his tall body dwarfing his grandmother as he scooped her up in a bear hug.

"Mmm, something smells good in Hatch's kitchen," he said.

She liked him calling it her kitchen, even if he was being a little premature. Tomorrow she and her sisters were flying back to Farmingdale, and she didn't know if they would be coming back.

While she was heating water and margarine for the mashed potatoes she noticed Skye gesturing to Miss Hattie. "Did you tell Hatch what you told me?" he asked.

"I thought I'd wait for you."

It was impossible to pretend she didn't hear them in the kitchen, which wasn't overly large, but she said nothing. If they had something to say to her, let them say it.

Skye spoke to her. "Well, Hatch, how quickly can you close up your business in Farmingdale and make a permanent move here?"

The spoon she was using to stir the mixture clattered onto the cooktop as her palms clapped just beneath her chin, like his words were an answer to a prayer. "You mean it?"

"I think it'll work out just fine with you and the girls," Miss Hattie said.

"Oh, Miss Hattie, thank you." She bent to hug the older woman. Pools of tears formed in her eyes, a few drops spilling out here and there.

Miss Hattie rubbed her back. "We're going to have a lot of fun together, the four of us."

Hatch straightened up and stepped back. When she turned to the cooktop she saw a rapidly boiling liquid in the pan. She watched helplessly as Skye removed the pan from the heat, poured in the premeasured potato flakes and began whipping them with a fork.

"Potato mashing is one of my many skills," he said, smiling.

"I'm sorry, Skye. I just got so emotional I forgot it was about to start boiling. You don't know how much I've been hoping you guys would want us to come back."

"Not a problem." He removed the pan from the heat and gave her an impromptu hug. "Welcome to the household."

He held her only for a moment, but when it was over she knew it was a memory she would savor for a long time to come. "Thank you, Skye. You don't know how much you've done for me."

Their eyes met and held. "I think I can imagine," he said gently.

The beeping of the timer she'd set for the biscuits went off at that moment, jarring her to take action. Then she thought of Chantal and Sinclair, and she called them in and passed on the good news. Sinclair, still young enough to wear her emotions openly, burst into happy tears and kissed both Miss Hattie and Skye. The more composed Chantal clasped her hands tightly in front of her and thanked them profusely. It was clear both girls preferred Tarrytown over Farmingdale.

When they sat down to eat in the dining room, Skye sat at the head of the table. Hatch expected Miss Hattie to sit at the other head, but she took a chair on the side. Chantal and Sinclair sat in the two chairs on the other side, one of which had been moved from its place flanking the china cabinet, leaving the opposite head the only place for her to sit.

Skye blessed the table, and as she bowed her head she had to rub her arms to keep from trembling. In her imagination they were all sitting together as a family, she and Skye facing each other at each end like any husband and wife. It was a thought more delicious than any meal could be.

"Amen," Skye concluded.

"Amen," the rest of them echoed. Hatch added a private postscript. She knew it was wrong to daydream about being Skye's wife when she should have been thanking the Lord for the bounty before them.

But she had a hunch that God wouldn't mind her one indiscretion.

Nine

As word got out that the Hatchet sisters were leaving Farmingdale, their friends and neighbors began stopping by their home to say good-bye. Hatch informed the landlord they would be gone by the end of the month. There wasn't much to pack—they were bringing their clothing and the television from Henry's room, but little else. The furniture, linens, and housewares were either being sold or discarded. The items Hatch didn't want to part with filled a medium-size box, which, along with the television and excess clothing, would be shipped to their new address in Tarrytown.

"My goodness, you're selling all these lovely things?" Rose Shannon exclaimed.

"There really won't be anyplace to keep them. It's not as if we're going to have our own place, Mrs. Shannon; we're going to be staying with someone." Hatch refrained from pointing out how old their belongings were—she suspected Mrs. Shannon was baiting her to say precisely that so she in turn could bargain for a lower price.

"Oh. Well, how much are you asking for this chair?"

It pained Hatch to sell her father's chair and ottoman, but they were too worn to be of much use, and reupholstery was out of her budget. "Thirty-five dollars."

"That's an awful lot."

"The chair only would be twenty-five. The ottoman is ten."

"Let me think about it. We need a new bedroom set more than we need a chair."

The furniture sold quickly, as did the car, which Hatch sold to the Pettifords, who would also be moving into the house the middle of November. Mrs. Pettiford was thrilled; having a second car would give her transportation to hold down a part-time job while the grandchildren were in school. "It looks like things are really looking up for us," she said happily.

Her remark saddened Hatch. A statement appropriate for a twenty-five-year-old was heartbreaking coming from a woman close to sixty. At twenty-five, achieving all one's dreams was still a possibility. By sixty all of them should have come true . . . if they were ever going to.

Her imagination clicked into motion. *Where do I want to be when I'm sixty?* Hopefully she would be married, maybe celebrating a silver anniversary or at least approaching it. Her children—a boy and a girl, she hoped—would be grown, but it would still be a little early for grandchildren. Chantal and Sinclair would be in their early forties and would probably have children in the adolescent stage, and she would be involved with them, as well. Her main concern would be that she and her husband were in good health as they headed for their golden years. Her husband might be retired, but she expected to still be working, at least part-time; after all, her career began late. They would have an impressive net worth, comprised of a home they owned outright and investments that had done well by them.

She had no idea who that husband would be. Skye Audsley was only a fantasy, of course; but surely the man who would be her lifetime partner was waiting for her in New York. She would meet him after moving to her new home.

If she was ever going to.

Skye informed Hatch they would be traveling to New York by train, apologetically adding that Amtrak was much more receptive to one-way fares than the airlines were. She assured him that she, Chantal, and Sinclair welcomed the new experience, although secretly she felt that twenty hours on a train was too long.

Their train left at seven P.M. on the last Friday of October, and Hatch signed Chantal and Sinclair out of school early so they could catch the bus for the long ride to Chicago's Union Station.

"Will we ever come back, Hatch?" Sinclair asked in a halting voice.

Hatch knew her youngest sister was sentimental as well as emotional. "I don't think so. Not to live, anyway, but if we're ever in Chicago we can come visit."

"Visit who?" Chantal said, in a tone suggesting she never wanted to see Farmingdale again.

"Mama and Daddy, for one," Sinclair said.

Hatch picked up on the sadness in Sinclair's voice, and even Chantal looked sobered. She squeezed their hands. "Remember, there's nothing there but remains. Their spirits are together in heaven. They'll forgive us if we don't visit their graves."

Her words sounded brave, but even she felt a little choked up. In her head she kept hearing the theme from *Picnic* and seeing the bus that carried Kim Novak from the town she'd lived in all her life to the big city to an uncertain future with William Holden. She was now taking a similar bold step, not only for herself but for her sisters, having packed all their clothing and sold just about everything they owned to head for a future that was by no means stable. She was going to be the caregiver for a woman who was eighty-nine years old. She hated to think of anything happening to Miss Hattie, but expecting this job to last for years was simply unrealistic. Anything could happen at any time, and before she had her degree.

She suddenly remembering an old news story about an unfortunate man in France who arranged to take over the lease of a choice Paris apartment from a ninety-year-old woman, with the terms that he would pay her rent for the rest of her life and take up residence after she died. The woman ended up living another thirty years and at one point was the world's oldest living person, having a glass of wine with her dinner and even an occasional cigarette. In an especially ironic twist, she outlived the man who sponsored her all those years, and after he died, his children became responsible for her rent. Maybe Miss Hattie would also be blessed with such longevity. As Fats Waller ungrammatically said in *Stormy Weather*, "One never knows, do one?" Besides, she just couldn't believe that Skye would literally throw them out into the street if their services weren't needed anymore. She began to feel better.

Chantal and Sinclair brightened when they arrived at the station. They checked in and got some sub sandwiches, then went to the newsstand and bought books and magazines for the long trip.

The train had barely crossed over the Indiana state line when Chantal and Sinclair asked permission to go to the lounge car. Hatch, engrossed in the latest issue of *Biography* magazine, nodded with a smile; she'd known they wouldn't be able to sit still for long.

They were gone so long that after two hours she went over to check on them. The first thing she noticed about the car was the haziness from cigarette smoke; it was the only public place where smoking was allowed.

She found her sisters at a table with some other young people, playing Uno. She slipped Chantal a five-dollar bill so they could get something to drink and purchased a bottled water to bring back to her seat. She'd packed some of those prepackaged cheese and cracker snacks to munch on, and crackers always made her thirsty.

The girls returned about thirty minutes later. "Hatch," Chantal said excitedly, "did you know some people on the train will actually sleep in beds? They have their own private rooms to ride in, and then the maid—"

"The porter."

"Okay, the porter. He converts the chairs to a bed and pulls another bed from out of the wall, like a bunk. Sara and Paul showed us theirs. They're going to New York with their parents because somebody in their family died, an old uncle, I think. They're going to be staying someplace called Scarsdale."

"They said that some people even have their own bathrooms in their room," Sinclair added.

"But Sara and Paul have to go down the hall to take a shower or use the toilet."

How awful for them, Hatch thought dryly. "I'll bet it's real expensive to travel like that."

"I wish Mr. Skye had gotten us a room," Chantal said.

"I believe it's called a compartment, Chantal. And Mr. Skye has been very generous. He paid for us to fly round trip to New York just a couple of weeks ago, or have you forgotten?"

"I didn't forget. But he's rich, Hatch. He can afford it."

She sighed. "I guess it's safe to say he's rich. But he doesn't have to lift a finger to do anything to help us."

"But he's not helping us just out of the kindness of his heart," Sinclair said.

"That's true. He saw an opportunity to get good home care for his grandmother. But he also knew there wasn't much of a future for us in Farmingdale. You two tried to take advantage of him the first time you saw him, but I don't ever want that to happen again. I'm going to be working for him, and to a lesser extent the two of you, too. He's going to be paying our living expenses, and because of him, we won't have to worry about finding a decent place to live on what little I can make at this point in my life."

"Hatch, do you think Mr. Skye will get us HBO and Showtime if we ask? A lot of the kids at school talk about how good that *Soul Food* show is."

"Chantal, did you not hear what I just said? Mr. Skye has done quite a bit for us already, and we're not going to ask him to do any more. If we want premium cable channels, we'll have to pay for them ourselves, and right now I don't think there'll be money for that. I plan to start college in January, and I doubt a school loan will cover my entire tuition. In the meantime I won't have you treating Mr. Skye like some kind of a cash cow."

"Well," Chantal said, "I guess you'll just have to marry him, then."

Hatch tossed her empty snack pack at her sister, hitting her on the right shoulder. "Good night, Chantal."

"Good ni-ight," Chantal replied in a singsong, don't-have-a-care-in-the-world voice.

Chantal's remark troubled Hatch. The teenager had a serious attitude adjustment to make. Marrying Skye was her own private, if unobtainable, dream, but the thought of Chantal wanting to marry her off to him merely so she could travel in a private compartment was outrageous, straight out of *Mildred Pierce* or one of those other movies with ingrate children plots.

When they awoke in the morning they looked out on Pennsylvania. The seats were roomy and reasonably comfortable—much wider than those on the airplane—but as Hatch brushed her teeth over the sink in the rest room at the end of the car, she couldn't help wondering how it would feel to have the luxury of a private compartment and to stretch out in this traveling hotel, just like the honeymoon scenes she'd seen in so many films from the thirties and forties.

When the three of them had freshened up, they went to the dining car and ate a hearty breakfast at a table with a view of the passing countryside. Hatch resolved to get a journal when they arrived.

She believed this train ride was just one of many
new experiences awaiting her, and she didn't want
to forget any of them.

"Oh, look, there's Sarah and Paul!" Sinclair
waved.

Hatch looked in that direction and saw the two
teens Chantal and Sinclair had been sitting with
in the lounge car last night, this time accompanied
by a forty-something couple, the man with thin-
ning dark hair and the woman whose blond-high-
lighted brown hair suggested that she was making
a gradual transition to a lighter color. The family
didn't look particularly prosperous, but from what
Hatch had heard about Scarsdale she doubted any
poor folks lived there. She pictured them at the
reading of the deceased's will, rejoicing at the stag-
gering sum he left them.

Must be nice, she thought, even though she
hadn't the slightest idea whether any of what she
had just conjured up in her imagination was ac-
curate. For all she knew, the departed had been
somebody's butler and didn't have a dime, but she
couldn't help feeling a little envious of families
who could travel halfway across the country on a
moment's notice, while she had spent her entire
adult life budgeting every penny and doing without things she would have liked to have but
couldn't afford. Enrolling in college was a start,
but her immediate future held more of the same
penny pinching she'd always known—lots more.

Their excitement increased as the train moved
closer to New York. They had another dining car
meal for lunch, after which Chantal and Sinclair
returned to the lounge car, where they had spent

most of the morning. Hatch decided a change of scenery would be good for herself as well and went with them.

The occupants of the car were mostly adults, including the parents of Chantal and Sinclair's friends, who seemed only too happy to relinquish their seats at one of the tables so all the children could sit together. "Hi. You must be Chantal and Sinclair's sister," the man said, holding out his hand. "I'm Alan Britton, and this is my wife, Pam."

"Cornelia Hatchet, but please call me Hatch." She shook both their hands, and they took seats in the opposite corner. "Are you from New York?" she asked, making small talk, even though she already knew they made their home in the Chicago area.

"I am, originally," Pam said. "My uncle died—actually my great-uncle—and we're going East for the services."

"Oh, I'm sorry."

"Thank you. He and my grandfather were brothers, but my grandfather died before I was born. Uncle Bill was more like a grandfather to my brothers and me. But he lived to a ripe old age, ninety-four. We'll all miss him, but no one can say it's tragic."

"I wish everyone could live that long," Hatch said, seeing her father's and stepmother's faces as she spoke.

"It would certainly be nice to have a guarantee," Alan agreed. "Sara tells me you and your sisters are relocating to Westchester County."

"Yes, from a town near Kankakee."

"Do you have a place to live, or is your job putting you up at a hotel or in a corporate apartment?" Alan asked.

"No, we're all set. We've got a house all ready to move into."

"Who do you work for, Hatch?" Pam asked.

She didn't hesitate. "I'm with Kmart. I'll be working in the regional office." She was surprised at the ease with which the lie rolled off her lips. For all she knew there was no regional office in New York, but no way was she going to tell these people she was merely a cashier supervisor, and would probably have to start at an even lower rank in the White Plains store.

Hatch looked out the window expectantly, although there had been nothing to look at but darkness since the Lake Shore Limited descended into a tunnel. They were just minutes from their expected arrival time at New York's Pennsylvania Station. She had instructed Chantal and Sinclair to use the rest room and had done the same herself, so they wouldn't be delayed. She knew Skye would meet them, but she wondered if Miss Hattie would come along. Probably, she decided. Skye's sports car couldn't accommodate all of them plus their luggage, and if he had to drive to Tarrytown to pick up the Grand Marquis, Miss Hattie might as well ride to the city with him. But regardless of whether Miss Hattie came or not, Hatch would get to share the front seat with Skye, a prospect she found most appealing.

When the dark walls of the tunnel were replaced by the bright lights of the station, the final destination, she had to fight the urge to push disembarking passengers aside and scream, "Hey, I'm about to start a whole new life; that should give my sisters and me priority!" Of course, she didn't do that. Instead she patiently awaited her turn.

"Tell me if you see Skye," she said to Chantal and Sinclair as she scanned the hordes of people who had come to meet the train. "I can't find him."

"I don't see him, either," Chantal said.

Sinclair poked Hatch's arm with her elbow. "Look, Hatch! That man in the black suit is holding up a sign with our name on it."

She stared at the young blond man. In addition to the black suit, he wore a cap that reminded her of the one Jackie Gleason wore for his famous role as Brooklyn bus driver Ralph Kramden. He had to be a chauffeur. But where was Skye?

"Girls, I don't want you to get too excited, but I think we might be riding in a limousine."

"A limousine? With Skye?"

"I don't think Skye is here."

"I thought he was coming to pick us up. It's Saturday."

"Maybe he's working. I can't think of why else that man would be here, holding a sign that says 'Hatchet, party of three,' can you?"

"No."

"Wait here for them to unload our bags. I'll go find out."

She smiled as she approached the driver. "Hi. I'm Cornelia Hatchet."

He instantly lowered the sign. "Hello, ma'am. I'm Jeremy." He named the service he worked for. "I have instructions from Skye Audsley to bring you and your party to Tarrytown." He stated Miss Hattie's street address.

"Yes, my two sisters are over there waiting for the luggage to be unloaded." She gestured toward where Chantal and Sinclair stood. "It looks like they've got them. Uh . . . do you know—" She broke off, deciding it would be futile to ask Jeremy where Skye was. People who ordered limousines to meet arriving trains or flights didn't give explanations.

"All right. Well, why don't I get the bags and bring them out?" Jeremy suggested.

"Sure." They walked over to where the girls were with the bags, and when they were within hearing distance she said, "Girls, this is Jeremy. He's going to drive us up to Miss Hattie's."

"But where's Skye?" Sinclair asked, her face contorted with disappointment.

"I don't know, Sinclair. Perhaps he's away on assignment. He was out in Farmingdale on a weekend, remember?" As Hatch put a comforting arm around the shoulder of her youngest sister, she caught sight of the Britton family watching them, and suddenly she was very glad she had purchased the new luggage when it went on sale at the store. The black canvas bags with tan leather borders were all on casters, three of them small-dimensioned but deep-surfaced, plus one suitcase that was larger. The rest of their clothing had been boxed and sent ahead. She was glad, too, that she'd excused herself so quickly after fibbing about what she did at Kmart. Surely the Brittons recognized that Jeremy was a chauffeur. They were no doubt thinking she must hold quite an important position to rate limousine service.

"Chantal, Sinclair. There are your friends. You should wave good-bye to them." She waved, as well, then signaled to Jeremy that they were ready to leave.

Outside, on busy Seventh Avenue, they stood

with the bags at the curb, waiting for Jeremy to bring the car around. They saw the Brittons once more; Alan Britton was helping a taxi driver put their bags in the trunk. Once more he waved to Hatch. "We're taking a cab to Grand Central so we can get the train to Scarsdale. I guess we're not as important as you are," he called out with a sheepish smile.

Hatch laughed. It was a delicious feeling, knowing Alan and Pam Britton would like to change places with her.

"What did he mean, Hatch?" Sinclair asked.

"He was making a joke. When we were talking in the club car, I kind of gave him the impression that I was a big shot with Kmart. I told him I was with the regional office. I just didn't say what I did." Then she had a disturbing thought. "You two didn't have to mention to their kids what type of job I took in New York, did you?"

"No," Chantal said. "It really isn't any of their business. We just said we were moving because you'd taken a new job."

"I get it," Sinclair said. "They think Kmart sent this man to carry your suitcases and bring the car around, while they have to carry their own bags and get a cab."

"That's right. Now, girls, don't get me wrong. I'm not ashamed of what I do. I make an honest living. It's just that I got the impression that the Brittons are pretty well-to-do, and I didn't want them to think we're poor. So I don't want you guys fibbing to your new friends at school about what I do."

"Are they going to be rich kids?" Sinclair asked.

"No, not necessarily. Some of them might be, and then there will probably be kids just like you."

Hatch had a feeling that most of the other students came from comfortable homes, but she didn't want her sisters to be nervous.

Jeremy pulled up in a shiny black limousine. He alighted, walked around the side, and opened the door for them. Hatch, Chantal, and Sinclair slid onto the black leather seats one at a time while Jeremy stood next to the open door.

Soft music played through the speakers. "Look, there's a TV!" Chantal exclaimed.

"Help yourself to beverages," Jeremy said when he was back behind the wheel. "Just relax, and I'll have you in Tarrytown within forty-five minutes." The partition separating the front seat from the rear then slid closed.

"Hatch, this wasn't anything like the car we had when Daddy died. They've got drinks, they've got television, and it just seems a whole lot bigger."

"I guess limousines come in all different sizes and models, too, just like cars and trucks. I guess they stock refreshments and have televisions when they bring people to or from catching trains or planes so they can be comfortable, especially if traffic is bad and the ride takes a long time."

She looked out at the passing traffic; and noticed drivers and passengers' glances lingered on the limousine, like they were hoping for a glance at the passengers, impossible through the tinted windows. Her fingers toyed with a depressed black leather button on the upholstery. She might only be Cornelia Hatchet from Farmingdale, but right now she felt like Angela Bassett in Hollywood.

Forty minutes later Jeremy parked the limousine in front of Hattie's house. He opened the rear door and helped them out. "I'll get the bags," he said when they had all alighted.

Hatch turned to her sisters. "Go ring the bell." She was sure Miss Hattie was home; otherwise they would literally be left out in the cold. While the girls ran down the front walk, she reached into her purse for her wallet. She knew little about limousine protocol. The only time she ever rode in them was when someone died, but this was a different type of situation. The driver should probably receive a tip, but how much was appropriate?

She looked over at the front door when she heard squeals. Chantal and Sinclair were joyously hugging Miss Hattie, who appeared just as happy to see them as they were to see her. Hatch rushed to join them. They were sharing a group hug when Jeremy approached with the bags, wheeling two and carrying the other two by their handles. He deposited them just inside the front door. "Here you are," Hatch said hastily, handing him a five-dollar bill. "Thank you."

"Thank *you*, ma'am." Jeremy tipped his hat. "It's been my pleasure to have been of service. Good afternoon."

When he was gone, Hatch once more turned to Miss Hattie, who looked well. It was hard to believe she was eighty-nine; she could easily take fifteen years off her age. "Oh, I'm so happy to see you again."

"I'm glad you're here. And just think, this time it's to stay. Skye was so sorry he wasn't able to meet your train. He's on assignment somewhere in Wyoming, of all places."

"Wyoming? It must be exciting, getting to travel all over the country like that."

"He does rather enjoy it, and even more now that he knows he won't have to worry about me."

She beamed. "The girls tell me you had a lovely train ride."

"It was an exciting new experience. The food was good, too. I didn't expect they would have choices of either beef, poultry, or fish. Even vegetarian meals." She smiled at Chantal and Sinclair. "Of course, these two spent most of their time socializing in the club car."

She longed to ask when Skye would be returning, but she didn't want to appear too anxious.

Sinclair came to her rescue. "When is Mr. Skye coming back?"

"Early next week, I believe on Tuesday. He did ask me to call him when you arrived. I hope seeing the driver he sent wasn't too much of a shock."

"It was neat," Chantal said. "I never thought I'd get to ride in a car like that unless someone died, and this one was really fancy."

Hattie laughed. "Skye seemed to think you'd get a kick out of it. I'm glad you did." Her gaze settled on their new luggage. "I like your bags."

"Thank you. I wanted each of us to have one of our own, plus the big one. And them being on wheels makes it so easy to manage."

"This new style of suitcase is probably putting the redcaps out of business."

"What's a redcap, Miss Hattie?" Chantal asked. Hatch had been wondering the same thing, but was embarrassed to ask. She thought it best to conceal her lack of knowledge. She certainly didn't want Miss Hattie to think she was stupid.

"Those are the men who carry the passengers' bags to and from the train. They call them that because they wear red caps, or at least they used to."

"I think I saw a few," Sinclair said. "Some people had a whole lot of suitcases."

"Well, that's good. I hate to see progress eliminate jobs. Oh! Your packages came yesterday."

"They did?"

"Yes. I asked Harry Williams next door to put them in your room, Hatch. It's quite a stack, so you might want to unpack them today. Or else you'll barely have room to turn around in there."

"Okay, girls, let's get busy."

"And the people from the cable company were here last week. They added connections in both your rooms."

"Oh, Miss Hattie, thank you!" Sinclair said.

"You didn't have to do that," Hatch protested. "I could have taken care of it once we got here. I insist on paying the bill for the installation."

"Oh, no. It was nothing, really. Consider it a welcoming gift."

"You are just too sweet, Miss Hattie."

Chantal and Sinclair were getting their respective suitcases from the foyer. "Miss Hattie, you've got money lying on the table here," Sinclair said. "Five dollars."

"You should put it away, or else anyone who comes to your door might reach in and grab it when you're not looking," Chantal said.

"Oh, yes. I put that there so I could tip the driver . . . er—in case you didn't have a five on you, Hatch," Hattie said, walking toward the table. She picked up the bill and stuffed it into the breast pocket of her blouse.

Hatch knew that Miss Hattie's hasty explanation was to cover the fact that she hadn't expected her to know enough to tip the driver at all. She wished she knew more about this type of thing, but knowing she hadn't needed Miss Hattie's intervention made her feel a little better. She grasped the handle of the largest suitcase. "Okay, girls, upstairs. Let's get our things put away," she said, adding, "We're home."

Ten

The following weeks had them settling comfortably in their new routine. Chantal and Sinclair had actually looked forward to beginning classes at Sleepy Hollow Middle and High Schools, respectively. Hatch, wanting to be sure they dressed as well as their classmates, purchased new clothes for them after the trial weekend in New York, so they had new blouses, sweaters, jeans, dress slacks, and skirts, as well as new winter jackets. The girls were about the same size, at least on top, and they could easily interchange blouses and sweaters, which in effect doubled the size of their wardrobes. They made new friends easily, and the phone began to ring almost immediately.

Hatch was hired by the White Plains Kmart to work in the cash office. She worked from five-thirty until closing time five nights a week. Because she had no seniority at this location, she wasn't guaranteed certain days off; they varied each week according to need. The store was gearing itself for the busy Christmas shopping season, and she would continue on after she started school. She had chosen an established technical college with an accelerated program—four-hour classes every weekday evening. Her supervisor assured her she

could work Saturdays and Sundays after classes
started in January.

She continued shopping the same way she did
when she lived in Farmingdale, making a list and
avoiding frozen and other preprepared foods with
high salt content that aggravated Miss Hattie's hy-
pertension. She wanted to impress Skye with her
ability to run a household efficiently.

Being able to sleep at night was a welcome
change. She enjoyed spending time with Miss Hattie during the day. In the morning she did housework—Miss Hattie, declaring she was still capable
of helping out, usually dusted—and after lunch
they went on errands, such as to the library, where
Miss Hattie would check out large-print books; the
bank; or even to the mall in White Plains, where
they would walk around and have ice cream or
pretzels. Hatch was relieved to learn that trips to
the doctor's office for checkups were few, generally
once every three months. She had been to more
doctor's offices in her lifetime than most people
did who lived to be a hundred.

Other days they merely took brief walks around
the neighborhood and watched television together. Miss Hattie enjoyed old films, as well.
"Movies today are too graphic," she complained.
"In the old days they never showed blood, even if
a character was shot."

While her contact with Miss Hattie was constant,
Hatch had seen little of Skye. They all spoke to
him the night they arrived, when Miss Hattie di-
aled his cell phone. He asked all the expected
questions: How was the trip? Were they happy to
be in New York at last? Had she been able to settle
all family business in Farmingdale? And the like.
In turn, she asked him about Wyoming, and he

told her about the remote town he was covering. He apologized for not being there when they arrived.

He returned to New York on Tuesday, but didn't get up to Tarrytown until Saturday. Chantal and Sinclair pleaded for him to take them for a ride in his maroon Cougar, which he did, first one, then the other, since the sports car only held two passengers. Hatch was more than a little envious, but decided it would be silly for her to ask for a ride. She'd never ridden in a sports car, but she wasn't a giddy teenager anxious to feel the wind in her face and hair.

Skye stayed most of the afternoon, and she felt a stabbing disappointment when he left at five-thirty. He was actually whistling as he walked toward his car. His demeanor and the spring in his step told her he was a man with a date . . . and not just any date, but one he was looking forward to.

The next week he stopped by briefly in the evening on Thursday, but she missed him because she was at work. He didn't come by at all that weekend. She casually asked Miss Hattie if he was coming, but she said no. "He mentioned when he was here the other night that he had plans."

Plans. She wondered if it was with the same woman he'd gone out with last weekend.

Skye didn't get to Tarrytown until the following Sunday, when he took them to a brunch buffet. "I was planning on doing the shopping for Thanksgiving dinner on Monday, Skye, if that's all right," Hatch told him when everyone was seated with their plates.

"You don't have to. We're going to be guests."

"Guests?" Hattie repeated. "Where?"

"Out at the Ballards' in Westhampton. We'll get a hotel room overnight. I want to look at some houses on Friday before we come back." To Hatch, Chantal, and Sinclair, he explained, "A couple of months ago I moved into a building owned by the family of one of the cameramen at work. The rest of their family lives out on Long Island, near the beach. I've rented a place out that way for the past couple of years, but now I'd like to buy one. My buddy invited all of us to join them for Thanksgiving dinner so we can look at some houses on the market while we're there."

"Sounds good to me," Hatch said. "I've never been to Long Island."

"Ask him to find out what we can bring," Hattie said. "And don't let him tell you something insignificant, like macaroni and cheese. We should make a real contribution, at least two dishes. It wouldn't be proper for five people to show up with nothing but their appetites."

That night Hatch wrote in her newly purchased journal. She described eating at a buffet—never before had she seen so much food: scrambled eggs, bacon, sausage, ham, potatoes, rice, pancakes, waffles, biscuits, fruit, cereal, and more, just waiting to be moved to patrons' plates for consumption—as well as their plans to go to Westhampton for the holiday. She'd read about the series of villages collectively called the Hamptons on the eastern part of Long Island, where movie people and wealthy folks from the city had summer homes. She'd even seen pictures of some of them in the *People* and *In Style* magazines her father's doctors kept in their waiting rooms, but those were

estates, homes with fifteen or more rooms, horse
stables, and other possessions of the financially fortunate.

She hesitated, her pen still poised above the paper. This was her personal diary, where she was
supposed to reveal her deepest thoughts, yet she
was reluctant to write what she felt.

Deciding it was foolish to hold back, she re-
sumed writing. "I've always had daydreams about
this man or that man. They helped me more than
I can say when it seemed like I couldn't stand my
life another minute . . . but I confess that where
Skye is concerned, it's more than my imagination.
More than anything, I really, truly would like to
be the special woman in his life."

She put the pen down and read what she'd written. She felt relieved at having expressed her feelings, but at the same time she felt sad, for there
was no way she could ever be anything more to
Skye Audsley than the woman he'd plunked out
of obscurity, just two jumps ahead of poverty, and
brought to New York to care for his grandmother.
Chantal and Sinclair would have the chance to
marry successful men, for they would go to college
and become successful themselves; but too much
of her life had been spent living hand-to-mouth
for her to ever be comfortable in the world of the
well-to-do.

Her feelings for Skye would forever be locked
in her heart.

Eleven

"Here comes Santa Claus," Sinclair sang as the TV camera zoomed in on the float carrying a man clad in the trademark red-and-white suit.

"That means the parade's over," Miss Hattie said. "Good job at Macy's."

"We should get ready to leave, then," Skye said, rising. "It'll take about two hours to get there. I'll put the bags in the trunk. If traffic is good, we should be there a little after two."

Hatch stood up, as well, and slipped into her jacket. "All right. I just need a minute to get the food together."

In the kitchen she removed the oblong dish of candied sweet potatoes from the refrigerator. She'd cooked them only partially so they wouldn't be overcooked and dry when they went into the oven for heating at their destination. She slid the dish lengthwise into a brown paper bag and tossed a bag of miniature marshmallows on top. She would arrange the marshmallows on top and let them brown in the oven after the potatoes were fully cooked.

In addition, their hostess sent word that apple and pumpkin pies would nicely supplement the pound cake and sweet-potato pie they planned to serve. Hatch and Miss Hattie baked the pies the

night before. Now she removed the foil-covered
pie dishes from the refrigerator and stacked them
inside a plastic supermarket bag.

"Okay, I'm ready," she said, emerging from the
kitchen, cradling the bag with the sweet potatoes
with one arm while gripping the handles of the
plastic bag in the other.

"Chantal, carry one of those bags for your sister," Miss Hattie commanded.

Chantal, sulking because she hadn't been able
to attend the Thanksgiving-morning football game
at the high school, sullenly took the bag with the
pies.

"Where is it we're going again?" Sinclair asked
when they were on the highway—Miss Hattie informed them they were actually called parkways,
which was appropriate because they were so scenic.

"Long Island. It's an island that starts as part of
New York City. The borough of Queens is on Long
Island, but we're going to be driving about sixty
miles past that."

"Whoop de doo," Chantal said.

"Stop pouting, Chantal; it's beginning to get on
my nerves," Hatch said. "It's only a football game.
You'd think you were head cheerleader or something." Her eyes met Skye's, and he smiled with
understanding.

"I thought everything was closed tomorrow,"
Chantal said. She spoke with just a hint of grumpi-
ness, as if she knew she was on the verge of trouble.

Skye chuckled. "I could probably get someone
to show me a house this afternoon if I wanted to.
Real estate people are surprisingly flexible when
there's a sale at stake."

"Long Island must really be a long island, if
we're going sixty miles out," Sinclair said. Every-

one laughed except Chantal, who merely rolled her eyes.

Traffic was moderate on the busy Long Island Expressway, but Hatch noticed the farther away they got from the city, the fewer cars she saw. At last Skye turned down a street of a mix of houses. Some were tinier than those in Farmingdale, though in much better condition, while others were larger, some with two stories. All the homes were on good-size lots that reminded Hatch of the houses back home; she almost expected to see chickens and ducks waddling about.

Skye steered the Grand Marquis into the driveway of a dark brown shingled ranch house with white shutters. "Here we are."

"Good," Miss Hattie said. "I feel like I've been riding forever."

The front door was opened by a tall, overweight man about forty, wearing a cable-stitched pullover sweater over black slacks, and a Knicks cap on his head. "Hi, folks. Glad you made it." He approached Miss Hattie and bent to kiss her cheek. "Good to see you, Miss Hattie."

"Nice to see you, too, Marshall. I want you to meet my caregiver." She held out a hand toward Hatch, who took it and stepped forward. "Cornelia Hatchet, this is Marshall Ballard, Skye's landlord. We call her Hatch, Marshall."

Marshall and Hatch exchanged hellos, after which Skye, Chantal, and Sinclair came from around the trunk, Chantal and Sinclair holding their group's contribution to dinner. Skye rushed ahead to shake Marshall's hand, and Marshall suggested that everyone come in. "It's cold out here."

Hatch was surprised to see no one in the comfortably furnished living room. Instead they fol-

lowed Marshall down to a roomy furnished basement, Skye assisting Miss Hattie. A washer, dryer,
and freezer stood in one of the far corners, and
Hatch glimpsed a partially open door to a powder
room. Two middle-aged couples and a man about
Skye's age were seated, while two preadolescent
boys shot a game of pool. Introductions were made
all around.

She soon learned that both couples were named
Ballard. They were in the home of Marshall's parents, Eldred and Pauline; and Fred and Dorothy
Ballard, Eldred's brother and sister-in-law, lived in
the house next door. Fred and Dorothy's son, Lucien, was present also, and the two boys were Marshall's sons. Neither Lucien, thin, bespectacled
and quiet, nor his outgoing cousin Marshall appeared to be accompanied by a female.

Hatch watched as Miss Hattie, a full generation
older than all the senior Ballards, was shown to a
comfortable swivel chair and offered a drink. She
accepted a glass of ice water and smiled content-
edly, obviously pleased to be fussed over.

Pauline Ballard picked up an empty ice bucket
and headed for the stairs as her husband fixed
refreshments. Hatch quickly caught up with her.
"Mrs. Ballard, we brought some food for dinner.
I believe my sisters gave the packages to Marshall."

"Why don't you come with me then, and we'll
make sure everything's put away? If I know my son
he put it down someplace and forgot it."

As Hatch followed her hostess, she heard Marshall say to Skye, "Hey, you didn't tell me your
grandmother's caretaker was a fox!" She smiled.
It was always nice to be appreciated by the opposite
sex, but she wished it was Skye making such a comment. She desperately wanted her dream to come

true, like it had for that young Scandinavian maid on one of the Rockefeller estates who ended up marrying one of the sons. She'd seen newsreel footage about the wedding on American Movie Classics. Of course, it all happened before she was born, and she didn't know if it lasted four years or forty, but it was such a lovely idea.

The basement door was just opposite the kitchen, so they merely crossed the hall. "There they are," Hatch said, spotting the familiar bags on the table.

"What'd I tell you?" Mrs. Ballard said with a laugh. She unfolded the brown paper bag and pulled out the foil-covered rectangular baking dish.

"Those are the yams. I only cooked them a little bit. I didn't want them to dry out when I heated them."

"Smart thinking. I see you brought marshmallows, too. I bought some, too, as well as whipped cream for the pies. It's easy to forget toppings when you're carrying food to a destination."

"It was so nice of you to invite us for dinner. There are so many of us. We're almost a mob."

"We're happy to have you here. We've heard so much about Skye and his lovely grandmother from Marshall, and of course we watch his program every week. And five people is nothing. We're accustomed to having a houseful for dinner." She spoke in a confidential tone. "My son and his wife are separated, and she's spending the holiday in Brooklyn with her folks. They usually all come out here."

"I'm sorry to hear that. But it's nice that the boys are here."

"We think so, too. Shari—that's our daughter-in-law—was nice enough to let him bring them out here for the weekend. With them living in the city they see their other grandparents all the time."

"Well, I hope they work it out."

"I hope so. Shari's a fine girl and a good mother. I like to think they will. It's only been two weeks."

Hatch offered to fill the ice bucket while Mrs. Ballard put the food in the refrigerator and basted the turkey. Then they returned downstairs.

"Hatch, can Sinclair and me take a walk around the block or something?" Chantal asked before Hatch could sit down.

"Well, I don't know. . . ." She looked at Mrs. Ballard uncertainly.

"Oh, it's all right. I hadn't planned to serve dinner until four."

"Which means it'll be four-thirty before we eat," her husband interrupted as he helped one of his grandsons aim his cue stick.

"Oh, go on and shoot the eight ball in the corner pocket already," Pauline said to him playfully. "It's fine, Hatch. They've got plenty of time."

"All right." Hatch turned to her sisters. "Just don't get lost, and keep an eye on the time. I want you back here no later than four."

The girls got their coats from a bench at the back of the room and disappeared up the stairs.

"It's hard for kids to go places with their families when there's no one their age around," Dorothy Ballard remarked. She pointed her chin toward the boys. "Of course, if this fellow and his brother were a little older, there'd be no problem."

"Hatch, are you from New York?" Marshall asked.

"No, I'm from northeastern Illinois, about an hour south of Chicago. I'd never even been to

New York until Skye hired me. But this part of New York really reminds me of home."

"That's good," Skye said. "You'll feel right at home when we get a summer place. Last year I brought Grandma out on the weekends because I had to be in the city all week, but now that you and Chantal and Sinclair are with her, you can stay here the entire summer."

Hatch drew in her breath. This was the first she'd heard of this plan. Spending the summer out here meant she would have to miss an entire semester of school. The accelerated program meant she had no long vacation breaks like other college students, just two weeks in the summer and at Christmas. At her age, time was not on her side, and she hated the idea of a delay.

She didn't want her disappointment to show. "Will we be staying right on the beach?" Everyone laughed, and Hatch wondered what she said that was so funny.

"I'm sorry, dear," Miss Hattie said. "We didn't mean to laugh. It's just that beachfront property is very expensive in this area, in the millions. Skye has something a lot more basic in mind, something like the house in Tarrytown. We'll have to drive to the beach."

"Oh, that's fine." She shrugged. "I didn't realize."

"We'll ride past that area tomorrow so you can see what Grandma's talking about," Skye said.

"You might want to take her now," Lucien said. "We're not really doing anything except waiting to eat. I think the girls might want to go, too. And it's a cinch there won't be much traffic."

"Good idea," Skye said. "Are you game, Hatch?"

"I'd love to."

Skye turned to Miss Hattie. "Grandma, did you want to take a ride?"

"No, you young folks go ahead. I'm very comfortable right here."

"I'll drive," Lucien said.

"Can we go?" Marshall's son, Eldred Jr., asked.

"We're not going to see anything you haven't seen a hundred times before, sport," Marshall replied. "Besides, I don't think there's enough room in the van. It only seats seven."

Hatch and Skye, Marshall, and Lucien retrieved their coats and prepared to leave. Lucien got behind the wheel of the minivan parked in the driveway, and Marshall took the passenger seat. Skye climbed in the second row, then turned and held out his gloved hand to help Hatch up. While the van sat higher than a standard car, getting into it wasn't particularly awkward, but Hatch enjoyed his gallantry nonetheless.

They quickly spotted Chantal and Sinclair strolling, and Lucien stopped the van alongside them. Skye lowered his window. "We're going to take a ride along the beach. You two want to come?"

The girls quickly climbed in the back row of seats. "The town looks pretty desolate this time of year," Lucien said. "Lots of businesses cut back on their hours during the winter, while others are only open between May and September."

They passed normal services one would expect to see in a small town: a hardware store, supermarket, real estate office, bank. After that they drove by mansions barely visible behind high, well-trimmed hedges lining the sidewalk. Hatch couldn't be impressed by what she couldn't see, but when they reached Dune Road all she could say was "Wow." While some homes were mere cottages built on stilts with parking underneath, others were brick mansions with four-car garages on the ground floor and elegant curved staircases leading to entrances on the second floor, tennis courts close to the road and swimming pools visible beyond, with the high dunes at the rear indicating the ocean was mere steps away . . . and offering protection from the same when the weather turned fierce. The buildings represented an eclectic mix of old and new. Some of the homes, as well as beach clubs like the Swordfish and Dune Deck, had clearly been around for years, while low-rise condos and the more spectacular homes appeared much newer.

"Wow. I wish I could live in one of those," Chantal said.

"There's an inlet behind the right side of the street, and in the summer you can see all the boats docked," Marshall said.

"Are you going to buy a house like this, Mr. Skye?" Sinclair asked.

"No, not I. But a couple of high-ranking folks at the network do have homes here. Westhampton might be considered nouveau riche by the old-money folks in Southampton, and it's less trendy than East Hampton, and there are fewer celebrities than you'd see in Sagaponack or Amagansett, but it's the closest to the city, which makes it more convenient. That traffic on Sunday nights can be murder."

"Of course, *some* of us occasionally hire limousines for that drive back to the city," Marshall said with a pointed look Skye's way.

"The program will hire a car for me if I have a Monday morning flight. You make it sound like I charter a helicopter or something," Skye said, a defensive edge in his voice.

Hatch nodded. "So that's why you didn't want to buy the house you'd been renting, Skye? It was too far from the city?"

"No, that's more because Grandma didn't particularly care for some of our neighbors in Sag Harbor. The shorter drive home is more of a fringe benefit."

Hatch immediately started wondering what was wrong with the neighbors, but she knew it wouldn't be proper to ask. They were probably busybodies, or perhaps they made too much noise. She decided to change the subject. "There doesn't seem to be much industry out here. What do you do, Lucien?"

"I'm a manager at LILCO in Riverhead, the electric company."

Back at the Ballard home, Hatch assisted both Mrs. Ballards in getting the food on the dining room table. She always enjoyed Thanksgiving, and it was a refreshing change to have so many people to sit down with.

"I think it's wonderful that you live right next door to each other," Hatch said when they were all seated at the dining room table, with Chantal, Sinclair, and the boys sitting at a card table a few feet away.

"It wouldn't make much sense for us not to," Eldred Ballard replied. "Our homes are on land that's been in our family's hands for over a hundred years."

"Really?"

"We have our great-grandmother to thank for

that," Fred Ballard added. "You see, after emancipation, a number of our ancestors went to New York and worked in the households of wealthy families there."

"A lot of people left the South at that time, didn't they?" Skye asked.

"We weren't in the south. We were right here on Long Island."

Hatch was incredulous. "They had slavery in New York?"

"It was legal here up until 1827," Pauline said.

"I didn't know that," Hatch said.

"I thought the northern colonies all abolished slavery in the late 1700s, around the time they stopped burying people in that African cemetery in lower Manhattan," Skye said. "Did you know about that, Grandma?"

"No. Just because I'm old doesn't mean I know *everything*, Skye. My people were slaves in North Carolina. I didn't realize it was going on in New York, too, but even I don't go quite that far back," Miss Hattie said with a smile.

"Slavery was outlawed in the north long before the Civil War broke out," Fred continued, "but racism was rampant. Our great-grandmother was working for a family on Washington Square when she was thrown off a Madison Avenue streetcar because she was black. I think that was in 1883. Anyway, she found a civil rights attorney to take her case and filed suit. She was awarded seven hundred and fifty dollars, a lot of money in those days. Part of that was a down payment on the house Marshall lives in now, and the rest paid for twenty acres out here. The people who built the houses between mine and Montauk Highway had to buy their land from us."

"Except me, of course," Lucien said. "I've got an in with the owners."

"Wow, that's an interesting story," Skye said.

"You're welcome to do a feature about us on your show," Fred said with a smile, and they all laughed.

After dinner, Hatch insisted that the two Mrs. Ballards relax while she, Chantal, and Sinclair loaded the dishwasher. Marshall's sons returned to their pool game, but everyone else relaxed in the living room, where they enjoyed dessert and coffee. At eight o'clock Miss Hattie announced she was tired, so they left for their hotel in nearby Quogue.

The next morning they had breakfast at a local café, after which they went to view the homes the Realtor had lined up for Skye to see. They saw three, but the choice was made when they saw the finished basement in the third one.

"Did you make an offer on the house, Skye?" Miss Hattie asked when they were in the car for the long ride home.

"No. I don't want the Realtor to think I'm too anxious. He doesn't have to know it's perfect for us. I'll call him Monday."

"What about furniture?" Miss Hattie asked.

"I'll let you ladies take care of that."

"You mean we get to pick out our furniture ourselves?" Chantal asked excitedly.

"Anything within reason," Skye answered. "Grandma will determine whether or not it's within reason. Incidentally, I hope everyone enjoyed dinner yesterday."

"Very much. The Ballards are nice people, and Lucien especially is charming," Miss Hattie replied.

Hatch pretended to look out the window, but she thought she'd heard a hint in Miss Hattie's voice. Was she trying to steer her toward Lucien Ballard?

"I wonder why a handsome fellow like that isn't married," Miss Hattie mused.

"A lot of people who happen to be nice looking aren't married, Grandma," Skye said. "I might not be the best-looking man around . . ."

Hatch smiled. He was modest, too. She liked that.

". . . but it's not like women look at me and run away screaming."

"Well, there's nothing like having a family. Sometimes I think I'll have to live to be a hundred just to see you settled down, Skye."

"All right, Grandma."

"You took that broken engagement too hard, dear. You know you did the right thing. When you do make it to the altar it'll be with the real Miss Right."

Skye had been engaged once? Hatch cast a curious eye on him. Even with his moustache, she could tell his mouth was set in a firm line, and he appeared to be gripping the steering wheel with more strength than was necessary.

"Can we talk about something else, please?" he requested.

"All right. Well, now that we know where we'll be living next summer, and that we all agree on how nice the Ballards are, I have a request." Miss Hattie's soft voice hinted that refusal was not an option.

"What's that, Grandma?"

"The church is having their Christmas dance

the week after next. I want my entire family to attend with me, and that means all of you."

Hatch turned around in her seat and saw that Chantal and Sinclair were wearing the same broad smiles she knew was on her own face. How sweet of Miss Hattie to think of them as family.

"It's been so long since anyone saw me with anyone they probably think I'm all alone in the world," Miss Hattie continued.

"Didn't you go last year?" Sinclair asked.

"I went, but Skye wasn't able to make it."

"The network had their Christmas party that same night," he explained. "It's a great time to mix with the top brass in a social setting, so Grandma encouraged me to go. She's determined for me to be the first black person to anchor the network evening news."

"How do you know the same thing won't happen this year?" Hatch asked.

"They've already announced the date. It's going to be the same weekend, but on a Saturday."

"But Miss Hattie didn't say if her party was being held on a Friday or Saturday," Hatch said.

Skye laughed. "Church parties are always held on Fridays. They don't want to keep people out too late the night before church."

"So where's your job's party being held this year, Skye?" Miss Hattie asked.

"The Rainbow Room. We'll all be dancing under the stars."

Hatch wondered whom he would be dancing with.

"Well, the church party is having dancing too, after dinner. It's semiformal, Skye, so you won't have to wear a tux. And girls, there are always young people there. It's really very nice. . . ."

Miss Hattie was still talking, but Hatch was too lost in her own thoughts to hear what she was saying. Suddenly it didn't matter that Skye would be dancing under the stars at the Rainbow Room with the date he would undoubtedly bring to his job's holiday celebration. He was coming to the church affair, and there he would dance with *her,* hold her in his arms as they spun around the room. She didn't know where the money was coming from, but she was going to look like a princess. This would be the night when he would finally see her through different eyes. . . .

Twelve

Skye threw his black nylon gym bag in the small trunk of his Cougar. It was only three-thirty, but he'd had a long day and wanted to go home and stretch out. He had plenty of time; Diana was spending the weekend in Virginia with her family.

He'd met her at B. Smith's, where he'd gone with Marshall for drinks one night after work. She was a surgeon, intelligent, well-read, and witty, about his own age and never married.

He had never been married either, but he had once been engaged to a woman named Monique Oliver. Monique was also intelligent, well-read, and witty, but it became increasingly clear to him that she was more concerned about the lifestyle being married to him would afford her more than anything else. He could tell she enjoyed it when people approached him and asked if he was Skye Audsley from *A Day in the Life* by the way her left hand always moved a little higher on his arm, so the person asking could see her ring. She told him it was rude to decline to shake hands with people who stopped by their table while they were dining, but he thought it inappropriate to thrust out a hand while he was eating.

Those habits along with other things, like her repeated urgings that he get an apartment with more character than the large, bland, prewar building on West End Avenue he called home at that time, as well as a larger summer house, made him wonder if Monique was really the woman with whom he wanted to spend the rest of his life. Their engagement came to an abrupt end when she made an unforgivable suggestion in response to his expressing concern about Grandma.

Afterward he went for months without dating at all, and he found himself carefully studying each woman he met, as if he might be able to see a physical mark of insincerity on her. When he learned Diana Butler was a surgeon, he figured she would be too busy with her own summer home than to nag him about his. He considered that a plus, but her specialization of emergency treatment was not without inconvenience. More than once he had to cancel dinner reservations or return theater tickets because she was called in to remove someone's appendix or spleen. It wouldn't be truthful for him to say it didn't bother him. In a few months he would be thirty-nine, and he didn't want to be alone, but he was realist enough to know Grandma wouldn't live forever.

As anxious as Grandma was for him to find a life partner and have children, she couldn't possibly know how much he wanted that, too. And he wanted her to be around to actually *see* her great-grandchildren, to hold them, for them to know her as she knew them.

At least he didn't worry about her being alone anymore. There was an aura about her that simply hadn't been there before. She'd lived alone since his grandfather died almost twenty years ago, and perhaps even she hadn't realized how much she missed having someone there when she woke up and went to bed. Being with her was good for Hatch, Chantal, and Sinclair, too. They were too young to be alone in the world, without parents or grandparents. Grandma was easily filling that role, having dusted off her sewing machine to help Sinclair with a project for her home economics class, and she was also teaching Chantal how to cook as they prepared dinner together after Hatch left for work.

Funny, he thought as he drifted into the unconsciousness of sleep, Hatch put her family first, like he did. He couldn't imagine her ever suggesting that he put Grandma in a nursing home, like Monique had. . . .

Hatch looked in the window of New To You, the used clothing shop. There were no mannequins, but the outfits—most of them dressy for the current holiday party season—were displayed attractively on padded hangers. She thought the sequined dresses too gaudy for her taste, but she spotted a pretty wine-colored velvet dress with crocheted shawl that would probably work nicely.

She wanted to show up looking regal for the church's dinner dance, but she didn't know if it would be possible. Both Chantal and Sinclair would need new dresses, as well, and she'd forgotten about the cost of tickets. Her mouth dropped open in shocked surprise when Miss Hattie informed her the tickets were thirty-five dollars apiece, and she accepted gratefully when Miss Hattie offered to pay for both Chantal's and Sinclair's tickets.

She went inside. "Can you tell me the size of

that velvet dress in the window?" she asked the salesclerk who approached her.

"Sure. Just a moment." The woman carefully climbed into the window display and peeled back the back of the dress so she could read the label. "It's an eight," she said.

Hatch sighed. She thought it looked a little small, but if it was a ten she would have tried it. "I'm afraid that's too small for me."

"We have plenty of cocktail dresses. They're our biggest sellers. Right over here."

Hatch followed the woman to the middle of the store, where there were three racks of dresses in all sizes. She quickly found a sedately sparkling black dress in her size. When she tried it, it molded to her figure perfectly. The dress actually looked more gray than black because of the way the light hit the sparkles, which were much smaller than most sequined dresses she saw. The skirt was full, falling nearly to her ankles. The fitted bodice tapered to a narrow halter neckline. She had never noticed she had such attractive shoulders.

The dress cost more than she planned on spending—she still had to get shoes, a purse, plus dresses for Chantal and Sinclair—but it was so perfect for her that she didn't hesitate.

She proudly showed it to Miss Hattie when she got home.

"It's beautiful, Hatch!" Miss Hattie exclaimed. "I'll bet it looks great on you. But you have to accessorize."

"I can get a dress and shoes at the store."

"I'm afraid you'll need more than that."

"More? What else do I need?"

"Jewelry, for one. That dress will put your arms on display. You'll need bracelets, silver ones. You'll

also need silver earrings. Because the neckline is
so high you can get by without a necklace. Then
you'll need a shawl. It's usually cold at these func-
tions."

Hatch tensed. "All of that?"

"I'm afraid so. There's more to going out than
merely putting on a pretty dress. I'd loan you my
jewelry, but mine is all gold. I've never been much
for silver. Incidentally, have you realized that you
can't wear your jacket?"

She hadn't thought of that, but of course Miss
Hattie was right. Her hip-length tan wool jacket
would look horrible over her pretty sparkled dress.
Chantal and Sinclair would have similar problems
with their outerwear. The thought of purchasing
new coats for the three of them was out of the
question; she couldn't afford it. Even with Miss
Hattie purchasing Chantal's and Sinclair's tickets,
if she wasn't careful, the expense of her own ticket
and of dressing them for this one evening could
easily eat up the rest of the proceeds from the sale
of their belongings. She was hoping that at least
Chantal and Sinclair could get by with their Sunday shoes. Her own were black skimmers with a
low wedge heel, much too ordinary for such an
alluring dress.

"You know, a dress I saw at the shop might fit
Chantal. It was velvet, kind of plain with short
sleeves and a square neck. The more I think about
it the more it would probably work for her. It's
dressy, but not too sophisticated for her age. I can't
stand seeing fifteen-year-olds who look thirty."

"Sounds perfect."

"I think I'll call the store and ask them to put
it on hold. Or maybe I'll just go to the school and
pick them up, and we can go straight from there.

I hope you can come with us. I'd really like your opinion."

"I'd love to."

Chantal liked the dress when she saw it, and it fit her slim body like a dream. Sinclair found a dress of her own, a beige silk jacquard shirtwaist with a bow in front that Miss Hattie said was entirely appropriate for a thirteen-year-old. Hatch was relieved, for both girls' brown dress shoes would go well with their dresses. Being so young, they could get by without purses, and Chantal's sleeveless dress came with a shawl, not that the crocheted nylon would do much to keep her warm.

Hatch stared at her reflection. Was that really her? The woman she was looking at could have come from the pages of one of those celebrity magazines she rarely had time to look at anymore. She had found high-heeled pumps with crisscross straps in a black shiny fabric—the admiring woman on line behind her said they were made of *peau de soie*—a matching purse, and a heavy black knit shawl at the store, as well as silver jewelry. She was glad she'd taken Miss Hattie's advice and purchased a supersheer pair of seamed off-black hose.

Chantal had touched up her hair, and she'd worked to style it in a replica of the way Ingrid Bergman wore hers in the party scene from the movie *Notorious*. It took several tries before the upturned sides were in perfect symmetry, and the back was caught at the nape with a sparkling silver bow barrette and curled under. Hatch had suffered the discomfort of plucking her eyebrows and was pleased at the difference it made; her entire face seemed to open up. Her upper and lower lids were outlined with a smoky charcoal pencil, her lips with a red pencil that matched her lipstick. Carefully applied blusher completed her cosmetic enhancement.

She draped the shawl over one shoulder before taking her purse out to the living room. "Is everyone ready?"

"Wow, Hatch, you're beautiful!" Sinclair exclaimed.

"You look real pretty," Chantal echoed.

Miss Hattie merely beamed. "I'm so proud of my girls."

"You all look marvelous. And Miss Hattie, I love your hair!"

"Thanks," she said, placing arthritic fingers to her elegant French roll. "Chantal did it for me. I think she's got a real knack for hairstyling."

"So what time is Skye due?" Hatch couldn't wait for him to see her. She felt like a whole new woman, and sitting beside him in the car was going to be heavenly.

"He said he would meet us there, so we might as well leave now, since we're all ready and it's going on seven," Miss Hattie answered.

Hatch hid her disappointment by turning her head as she pulled her shawl across both shoulders. "All right, then. Chantal, Sinclair, I want you two to wear your jackets, but when we get there leave them in the car. I'll drop you by the front door and you can slip inside."

"Here's your coat, Miss Hattie," Chantal said, reaching for the familiar navy wool.

"Oh, I'm going to wear my fur tonight."

"Your fur?"

"Yes. Check the back of the closet. It's in there. I can't believe I'm still around to wear it another season."

"And you'll be around next season, too, and the one after that," Sinclair said with the confidence of a thirteen-year-old.

"Here's one with a fur collar." Chantal ran a hand over the unusual textured pattern of the tan coat. "This is pretty."

"It's Persian lamb. It was a gift from Skye for my eightieth birthday. I was afraid it was too much of an investment for a woman my age, but here it is nine years later and I'm still wearing it, so maybe not." She laughed.

The party was being held in a banquet room at one of the White Plains hotels. It was seven-twenty when Hatch pulled up in front of the main entrance. Sinclair, who had insisted over Chantal's loud objections that it was her turn to sit up front, jumped out and opened the door for Miss Hattie, who looked quite elegant in a cream-colored sweater and long full skirt in a crinkly material the same color. Chantal, whose short-sleeved dress and thin lace shawl were no match for the cold December night, waited until Sinclair and Miss Hattie were at the door before saying a rushed "See you in a few," to Hatch and making a dash to join them.

Hatch parked nearby and made her own scramble for the warmth of the lobby, walking as fast as she could without running, which she felt would look undignified in her elegant ensemble.

Her first stop was the ladies' room, where she made sure none of her luster had been lost. Then she looked for the room where the dinner dance was being held. There wasn't an empty banquet room in the hotel, and from the signs posted at each door she could tell that most of them were corporate holiday parties. Bartenders worked behind makeshift setups in the hall.

The church function was being held in a room at the end of the hall. Hatch slowed her rapid steps, not wanting to appear overly anxious.

She smiled at the finely dressed women who sat at a table just inside the door. "I forgot to get my ticket, but I'm with Mrs. Harriet Jackson."

"Oh, yes. She told us you were coming. Just sign here please, and go right in."

It took Hatch's eyes a moment to adjust to the lighting, which was dimmer than in the hall. Then she noticed Sinclair waving a shimmery white-sleeved arm and walked over to where she sat at the table for eight with only Chantal and Miss Hattie. She had hoped Skye would have already arrived so he could see her entrance.

"You all look so lonely at this big table," she commented when she sat down.

"Miss Hattie said Mr. Skye's bringing some people with him, and then we'll be full," Sinclair said.

Her face hardened in shock. Was Skye bringing a *date*?

"Look, there he is!" Sinclair said in a loud voice.

Hatch had deliberately taken a seat with its back toward the door so that Skye wouldn't see her until he reached the table, but now she turned. Even as she did so, she knew she would see a woman on Skye's arm.

What she didn't expect was that the woman

would be wearing fur from her neck to her ankles. It had come from an unfortunate creature who had had a dark, luxurious coat—she couldn't tell if it was black or a very dark brown—and it looked terribly expensive.

Skye was talking to the women at the front table. He nodded his head and then escorted his date out the door. When they returned, their overcoats were gone. His date wore a boat-necked satin tunic of gold and black horizontal stripes over a pencil-slim black skirt. Her hair was pinned in a bun atop her head, with bangs softening the look. Even from a distance Hatch could tell she had gorgeous skin.

"Hi, everybody," Skye said. He bent to kiss Miss Hattie. "You look wonderful, Grandma. You too, Sinclair. Chantal, you look so grown-up."

Chantal and Sinclair beamed.

Hatch held her breath, hoping to see a reaction when he saw her.

He didn't disappoint her. His expression was one of pleasant surprise. "Hatch! I almost didn't recognize you. You look . . . Wow."

She smiled in delight . . . but then she remembered his companion. Her smile instantly disintegrated when he brought the woman forward and possessively rested his hands on both her shoulders. "Grandma, this is Dr. Diana Butler. Diana, my grandmother, Harriet Jackson."

Hatch watched unhappily as Miss Hattie greeted Diana. Skye's date was lovely, with wide-set eyes, a pert nose, and skin every bit as radiant close up as it had looked from a distance. Even her ears, with their modest diamond studs, looked dainty. And if all that wasn't enough, she was a doctor.

In addition to Diana, Skye's party included Marshall Ballard and Marshall's wife, Shari. Hatch wondered if they had reconciled.

Hatch forced herself to look pleasant during dinner. Shari Ballard sat beside her, and Hatch liked her immediately. Shari had a natural friendliness that belied the image of the coldhearted New Yorker.

"Skye tells me you're going to be spending the summer in Westhampton," Shari said chattily. "We'll see lots of each other. I'm a school librarian, so I have the summer off. The boys and I stay with Marshall's parents, and he comes out on the weekends."

"It'll be fun," Hatch agreed.

As dessert and coffee were being served, the minister made his way around the tables and greeted everyone. "Well, Miss Hattie, I don't believe I recognize any of these fine young people at your table," he said.

Hatch suppressed a smile. She knew the minister was trying to shame the nonchurchgoers into attending services. She nodded politely as Miss Hattie explained that she and her sisters attended a church of a different affiliation.

"Well, we'll just have to kidnap you," he said before greeting Skye.

After he'd circulated, the minister made a brief speech. A drawing was held, followed by the introduction of the band. Hatch was surprised when a young man asked her to dance; she hadn't noticed the admiring looks she'd received upon her entry to the banquet room. Chantal was also asked to dance, and Hatch realized that her sister was blooming. She would be sixteen years old in April, and her dress showed off her youthful figure.

Young boys were attracted to her like to a basketball court.

Hatch wasn't without her own magnetism, and
she did her fair share of dancing. She danced with
both Marshall and Skye. Even Miss Hattie took to
the floor with surprising agility, lifting her skirt to
reveal thin legs encased in cream-colored hose.

When the band slowed the tempo, Hatch, dancing with an admirer, was happy to see Skye leading
Miss Hattie about while Diana sat with Marshall
and Shari.

But what she dreaded did happen eventually;
Skye danced with Diana. By then Hatch had returned to the table and had no other recourse but
to sit and watch them move in tempo to the slow,
dreamy song. Marshall and Shari were also dancing. Miss Hattie had moved to the next table to
talk to the people there, and Chantal and Sinclair
were busy chattering about the teenagers in attendance, one of whom Sinclair apparently knew from
school. She tried to concentrate on the well-
dressed people in the room, but her gaze kept
going back to Skye and Diana . . . and her smile
began to feel like it was pasted on.

"I had a lot of fun, Hatch," Chantal said. She
sounded out of breath, which was understandable,
for she had just been dancing with Skye. Now the
band was playing what they said would be the last
number of the evening, and once more Skye was
dancing with Diana. Hatch was glad for the distraction.

"You've really been Miss Popularity tonight. And
don't look now, but I think another admirer is
coming."

Chantal happily took the hand that was extended to her, and Hatch was also asked for a repeat dance. She found the young man's interest in her amusing; he couldn't be more than twenty-three. Still, he was tall and handsome, and it was nice to have her efforts to look beautiful appreciated, even if he was much younger than she. Besides, in fifteen or twenty years she'd probably be thrilled to have a man a decade her junior ask her to dance.

When the music faded after a deafening last chord, the minister took the microphone, thanked everyone for coming, and said he looked forward to seeing them all in church on Sunday.

"Maybe we should just wait a few minutes," Skye suggested. "There's going to be a mad dash for the coat check room."

"I don't think it'll be too bad," Marshall said. "They're sure to have two people working."

The others agreed they were ready to leave, so they joined the others heading toward the coat check down the hall.

"Good night, Miss Hatchet."

She turned to see André Taylor, who had danced with Chantal several times. "Good night, André."

"Miss Hatchet . . . may I have permission to invite Chantal to a movie?"

She was impressed by the young man's good manners. "Yes, you may." She watched as André rushed off to catch Chantal, possibly to extend an invitation right here and now.

Diana Butler fell into step beside her. "Hatch, I didn't get much of a chance to talk with you, but I wanted to tell you how much I admire your dress."

She hadn't expected this compliment, but why shouldn't Diana be friendly? Diana didn't perceive her as a competitor for Skye's affections . . . because of course she wasn't one. "Thank you, Diana. You look very pretty yourself."

"Thank you. This outfit is actually several years old, but there's usually so many parties to go to during the holidays. I did buy something new for the party Skye's job is giving tomorrow."

"I'm sure it's lovely." She could have guessed Skye was bringing Diana to the network party. Her airway constricted as she wondered if they were serious about each other.

"Marshall and I will get all the coats; just give us your tickets," Skye suggested.

Miss Hattie removed hers from her purse, and as she handed it to him Hatch said, "We left our coats in the car."

"In the car? Why? You must have frozen getting in here."

"It was warm in the car." She shrugged, knowing it sounded feeble. *If I had a full-length mink or whatever that is that Diana was wearing, I wouldn't have to be cold.* "I didn't park very far away."

Skye helped Hattie into her Persian lamb, then Diana with her fur. "If you'll tell me where you parked, Hatch, I'll bring the car around for you so you and the girls don't catch cold."

She told him, and he and Marshall, wearing their overcoats, went out into the cold night. The women waited by the door, and Hatch watched as Diana linked her arm in Miss Hattie's and said, "I'm so glad to have met you at last, Mrs. Jackson. Skye has told me so much about you."

"I'm glad to meet you. Have you and Skye been seeing each other long?"

"Just a few months."

"He's notoriously close-mouthed about telling me who he's seeing," Hattie explained. "He knows how anxious I am to see him settle down. I keep telling him I'm not going to live forever."

Everyone chuckled, and Shari Ballard turned to Hatch. "I'm looking forward to seeing you this summer, if I don't see you before that."

"I hope we see each other before that, too."

"Here they are," Sinclair said. Skye pulled up in the Mercury, with Marshall following in a cream-colored SUV. Both men got out from behind the wheel, leaving the engines running. Hugs and good-nights were exchanged all around, and Marshall escorted Shari and Diana to the SUV while Skye seated Miss Hattie in the back seat of the Grand Marquis. Hatch, Chantal, and Sinclair had dashed to their own seats, but instead of getting into Marshall's vehicle, Skye walked around to the driver's side of the Mercury. Hatch lowered the window.

"All right. Drive carefully. And watch Grandma. She had two glasses of sherry." His broad smile told her he was teasing.

"I'll sleep good tonight," Miss Hattie said enthusiastically from the back seat.

Skye patted Hatch's shoulder. "Keep warm. Good night."

"Good night."

"Hatch, roll up the window; it's cold," Chantal complained.

Hatch pressed the button that controlled her window. She took a moment to adjust the seat, which Skye had pushed back to accommodate his long legs, then put the car in gear and pulled off, leaving the bright reflection of Marshall's head-lights behind her, but very much thinking of the man who sat in the back seat of that vehicle, next to his date.

Thirteen

"Skye, I'm worried about Hatch," Hattie said.

"Worried about her? Why, Grandma? I thought she was doing so well in school and all."

"She is, but she has no social life."

"Social life? She has a full-time job, is guardian for two teenagers, goes to night school, works at Kmart on the weekends. She's already very busy, and a good education means a lot more than a good time to her. She's waited nearly fifteen years to go to college."

"I know, but I don't want her to decide she doesn't want to stay."

"Trust me, Grandma, she's not going to go back to Farmingdale. You saw the segment I did on it for the show. It's a very depressing place."

"I was hoping she'd meet people at school, but she said most of her classmates are either much younger or much older than she is."

"She seemed to be making a friend at the Christmas party."

"Oh, that fella she was dancing with was an adult but still quite young, although I certainly was hoping she would meet someone there. I guess all the men in her age group who were there were either married or involved."

Skye looked at her closely, and she knew he was

hoping she wasn't going to say how much she wanted him to settle down. It wasn't really her disposition to nag; she actually expressed her wishes quite rarely.

"Chantal is the one who has the avid social life," she said. "She's been out several times with the Taylor boy since the party. Sinclair is too young to date, of course, but she's made a lot of friends and is always going to the mall or the movies or the bowling alley with her girlfriends. Hatch is the one who never has contact with people her own age, male or female."

Well, I wish I could help you, Grandma, but I don't see how I can. It's not like *I'm* her age."

"You're not much older."

"Come on. She's what, thirty, thirty-one?"

"Thirty-two. She's only six years younger than you are. Why don't you take her to dinner one night, in appreciation of how happy she and the girls have made me? Consider it an investment in my happiness, because I want her to stay."

"All right, Grandma. I'll do it."

"Good. But don't plan it ahead of time. Do it spontaneously. One time you're sure to catch her at home when both Chantal and Sinclair are out, or else they'll want to go, too."

Hattie was pleased. She'd seen the stricken look on Hatch's face when Skye entered the Christmas dance with Diana. She'd never considered the possibility of Hatch having a crush on Skye, and actually over Thanksgiving she found herself hoping that Hatch and Lucien Ballard would hit it off, for her impression of Lucien was that he was a quiet, thoroughly decent man who would make some woman a fine husband. But after thinking about it, she realized that Hatch and Skye shared similar values, determination and devotion to family among them. That was more than enough on which to build a life together, she felt. Skye was still recovering from being hurt after choosing the wrong girl, but she believed with Hatch he wouldn't go wrong. Perhaps this little nudge from her would help them find their way.

If not, she'd have to stop nudging and start pushing.

Skye sang along with the catchy song on the car radio as he drove back to Greenwich Village. He was in one of those periods in his life when everything was as close to perfect as possible, and because life had taught him these intervals never lasted, he was simply enjoying it. Not only was he doing well, but so were the people he cared about. Grandma was thriving in the company of the Hatchet sisters. Marshall and Shari Ballard had reconciled and were working out their problems. Hatch, Chantal, and Sinclair adored Grandma, and they were also benefitting from having left Farmingdale. Chantal and Sinclair had adjusted to the world of suburbia with the resilience of the young. Anyone who met them would think they'd lived in Westchester all their lives.

He missed seeing Hatch, who was usually at work when he was over. In fact, he didn't think he'd seen her since the new year had come in, for she was working on New Year's Day when he drove up to see them.

Them. It was true. He didn't go to Tarrytown just to see Grandma, but all of them. The Hatchet sisters had become family. But it was almost amusing, Grandma worrying over Hatch's lack of a social life. The last time he saw Hatch she was so excited about starting classes. Her high school transcripts had been received, her financing arrangements made, and everything was in order. Her enthusiasm made her seem much younger—like a giddy teenager—but he knew how serious she was about getting a college degree. It was her priority, and he could understand why. Even with the accelerated program, she would be in her mid-thirties by the time she finished. He didn't see how she could manage a social life on top of everything else.

Skye opened the front door of his grandmother's house. "Anybody home?" he said, even though he had recognized Ruth Perkins's Ford parked out front. Grandma's longtime caretaker still came by to visit, this time not as an assistant, but as a friend.

"Skye! I didn't expect you today. When did you get back?" Hattie asked as she put her arms around him.

"I just got in a little while ago." He knew Grandma would be surprised to see him and was embarrassed by it, for he'd told her he wouldn't be arriving home until Sunday because of a personal plan that failed to materialize. He turned to his former employee. "Good to see you, Ruth. How've you been?"

"Fine, fine. Miss Hattie was just telling me about your latest assignment. Pretty nifty, getting sent down to the Florida Keys in February."

"Yeah, I'm all for that. I'll be working on local stories this week, but if that airline strike they're threatening happens I've got a feeling they'll be sending me down to Charlotte."

"Well, you're doing just fine, and the only one more proud of you than me is your grandmother here."

"Thanks, Ruth. So, Grandma, where are the girls?"

"Chantal and Sinclair went to the mall. They should be coming back any minute now. But Hatch is here. She's studying in her room."

"I guess I'll go and say hello." He heard between the lines of Grandma's comment; she was telling him that if he wanted to get Hatch out as he'd promised, he didn't have much time before her sisters returned. That was fine with him; he hadn't eaten since breakfast.

He knocked on Hatch's closed bedroom door, which was promptly opened. She didn't have to say she was surprised to see him; it showed in her expression.

"Well, this is a nice surprise," she said. "How was Florida?"

"Warm, sunny, all those things you think about associated with the sun belt. I haven't seen you in ages, Hatch. How've you been?"

"Busy."

He glanced at the open textbook she held. "Grandma said you were studying."

"Yes. Economics."

"So you like school, I take it."

"Who wouldn't like something that's going to change their life?"

"So how long have you been at it?" he asked.

"Most of the afternoon, I think. I'm off today. The store's in a postholiday slump. Miss Hattie's got company, and Chantal and Sinclair are out. It's the best time for me to study."

"Have you had dinner yet?"

"Actually, no. We had some leftover meatball minestrone Thursday. I had planned on serving the rest of it for dinner tonight. Miss Hattie loves it, and so do Chantal and Sinclair. There's plenty if you'd like to have some."

"I've got a better idea. I'm starved. Why don't you come with me to get something to eat? You could use a break after studying all afternoon."

"But Miss Ruth is still here. Did you want to bring her along?"

"No, I wasn't planning on asking Grandma or Ruth to join us. Grandma's fine with Ruth, even if Ruth leaves before we get back. Not that we'll be gone that long."

He saw a strange expression cross Hatch's face. It was gone in a second, before he could fully define it, but he decided part of it was confusion, as if she was unsure if traipsing off with him was proper behavior, especially since the person she was paid to look after stayed behind. Then again, maybe it was just a shadow.

"Well, if you're sure it's all right . . ."

"Sure it is. I know you're a great cook, but it's time you ate someone else's cooking for a change. Let's go. I'm so hungry I could eat one of those cardboard burgers they serve at the fast-food places."

"Skye, wait. I have to talk to you about something."

His empty stomach suddenly felt weighted down. He just knew something was wrong, but what could it be? "What is it?"

"My supervisor is going to be taking a maternity

leave in April and part of May. She's asked if I can change my schedule for six or seven weeks."

"Oh." A problem at Kmart. That was no big deal, unless she wanted to work days. "Change it to what?"

"She wants me to work from seven-thirty to noon every Tuesday, Wednesday, Thursday, and Saturday."

"Saturday isn't a problem, since the girls will be here with Grandma, but the other days they're in school. What'd you tell your boss when she asked you?"

"I said I'd have to check with my other job and let her know. I would never commit to a schedule change unless I talked to you about it first."

"Let me think on it, okay? I'll let you know by Monday. C'mon, let's go before I pass out."

"I'll be right there."

He sailed through the living room with Hatch following a few steps behind after getting her purse and turning off the light. "Hatch and I are going out for a quick bite," he said casually.

"I'll probably be gone by the time you get back," Ruth said, "but don't worry about your grandmother. I'll make sure she gets to bed all right."

"I'm not going to bed," Grandma said with almost childlike defiance. "It's not even six-thirty. I'm eighty-nine, not nine."

Ruth laughed. "All right, Miss Hattie. Don't get salty."

"We'll probably be back by eight," Skye said.

"The girls should be in within the next half hour or so," Hatch added, tucking the hairbrush she'd just used into her handbag.

Outside, Skye seated Hatch in the passenger side

158   *Bettye Griffin*

of the Cougar, and as he turned on the ignition he said to her, "What do you feel like eating?"

"Oh, I don't know. I'm pretty flexible. What would you like?"

"How about Mexican?" He sensed her hesitation, and suddenly it occurred to him that she probably never had Mexican food, other than perhaps the fast-food offerings of Taco Bell. "There's a good place on Central Avenue. You don't have a problem with heartburn, do you?"

She laughed. "Heavens, no. My stomach is lined with cast iron."

"Good."

Hatch shifted in her seat. "This car is nice, but it rides very low. I guess I'm just not used to sitting so far down."

"It felt funny at first, but I'm used to it now."

"Doesn't it make you nervous when a big truck or sport utility vehicle is behind you or next to you?"

He chuckled. "Sometimes I can't help thinking about what an SUV can do to me if we were to collide. I don't worry too much about trucks; they're not allowed on the parkways. If I'm on a thruway or a turnpike, I usually stay in the passing lane. But you've ridden in this car before, haven't you?"

"No, I haven't. I think Chantal and Sinclair have."

Skye tried to remember when he had spent time alone with Hatch, and then he realized he never had, at least not in the months since she had been living with Grandma. It was nothing to feel bad about; after all, he was her employer, not her friend; but he did agree that Grandma had a point. It certainly wouldn't hurt to spend an hour with her just to see how she was doing and make sure there were no problems. It wasn't as if he had anything else to do, even though it was a Saturday night.

That thought made him frown. Diana was supposed to meet his plane. The plan was for them to have a quiet evening at an intimate bistro within walking distance of his apartment. He always kept his cell phone charged up if Grandma or Hatch called.

When he heard his name paged at LaGuardia, he knew in advance what the message would be. A multicar pile-up with ruptured spleens or lacerated livers, or that other one, whatever it was they called it when a gallbladder had to be removed. He'd heard it all before, and he was sick of it. He was genuinely fond of Diana and thought they might have a future together, and while he realized that responsibility didn't always mesh with a strict nine-to-five, he was becoming convinced that he needed someone who was a little less busy. He didn't like feeling like he was a distant second to her work, and if he couldn't deal with it in someone he was dating, he certainly wouldn't be able to cope with it in a wife, and he wouldn't want to cope with it in the mother of his children.

He'd taken a cab to the Village, dropped off his bags, picked up his car and headed north to Tarrytown. He knew Grandma wasn't expecting to see him, but it was fairly harmless to make up an excuse for her about finishing his assignment a day early.

"Skye? You all right? You're awfully quiet."

He shook his head, as if to clear it. "Oh. Sorry. My thoughts ran away for a minute."

* * *

Hatch waited as Skye unlocked the front door to Miss Hattie's. Standing outside in the dark with him gave her an odd feeling, almost like they were on a date and he would be leaning in to kiss her good night at any moment. But of course, that wasn't the reality.

She had allowed him to order for her at the restaurant, and she thoroughly enjoyed her meal. They talked about mostly impersonal matters, anecdotes about his work, and he asked her about her classes and her job. He sounded like he was really interested in knowing, and that made her feel pretty doggone good.

He held the door open, and she walked inside. Chantal and Sinclair were home, sitting in the living room with Miss Hattie, watching television. They looked up expectantly, and Hatch saw their gazes go to hers and Skye's hands, and the disappointment in their eyes when they realized they were empty. "You didn't bring us anything to eat?" Chantal said, a shade accusingly.

"I gave both of you money before you went out so you could get something," Hatch replied.

"We ended up going to the show, so after we bought our tickets all we could get was popcorn and drinks," Sinclair said.

Hatch felt her temper flare. "Well, I don't know how you expected *me* to know that. Just have some minestrone and bread if you're hungry."

"I had some. It tasted even better the second time around. Hatch, you really are some cook," Miss Hattie said.

"Thank you."

Chantal was looking at Hatch and Skye through slightly narrowed eyes. "So where did you guys go?"

"We went out for some dinner," Skye said. "I felt Hatch needed a break. She works very hard, in case you haven't noticed," he added pointedly.

"How was your trip, Mr. Skye?" Sinclair asked.

"It was good, Sinclair, thanks. Excuse me." Skye walked toward the kitchen.

"What'd you have to eat, Hatch?" Chantal asked.

"Never mind what I had to eat. You girls embarrass me, the way you're behaving. Skye's been out of town all week, but you two are so busy asking if we brought anything back for you that you don't even say hello to him. I thought I taught you better." Their insensitivity appalled her. She knew teenagers tended to be self-centered, but she was never that way. She never had time. She'd been too busy helping Anna Maria with her sisters after her father's leg amputation, and raising them after Anna Maria was killed.

"Oh, come on, Hatch. We didn't mean anything bad by it," Chantal said.

Hatch simply glared at her sisters. If Miss Hattie hadn't been sitting there, she would have reminded them that she didn't want them viewing Skye as some type of sugar daddy who stood by, always ready to finance their every desire.

Sinclair stood. "Come on, Chantal. Let's go get some soup."

Hatch took a seat as Chantal and Sinclair left the room. "Kids," she muttered.

"It's an age-old refrain," Miss Hattie said. "I think it goes back to the time of the caveman. Try not to take it too much to heart, Hatch. You're really doing a fine job raising them. Remember, it's the most difficult job there is."

Hatch was too upset to answer. Her sisters' self-ishness had ruined her good mood.

"Where did you two have dinner?" Miss Hattie asked.

Hatch opened her mouth to reply, then broke off to listen to the voices and laughter coming from the kitchen, Skye's voice included. The stiff-ness in her jaw relaxed as she recounted their out-ing. "We went to a Mexican place in Hartsdale, I think. I don't remember the name of it, but Skye can tell you. The food was very good, though."

Miss Hattie nodded. "Skye loves spicy food. I find a little of it goes a long way, personally."

Skye came into the living room and placed a reassuring hand on her shoulder. "Well, Hatch, you'll be interested to know that Chantal and Sin-clair just apologized to me for not saying hello. We smoothed everything over."

Her jaw tightened again. "They really need to pay more attention to what's happening other than how it relates to what they want."

"Don't be too hard on them, Hatch. You know how kids are." He removed his hand and took a seat at the edge of the sofa.

The outburst rolled off her lips before she could stop it. "No, I *don't* know how kids are. I wasn't allowed to be one." She watched as Skye and Miss Hattie exchanged glances, and she suddenly knew she had to be alone. "Please excuse me," she said as she rushed out. Chantal and Sinclair looked at her in bewilderment as she dashed through the kitchen toward her room.

She thought she was going to cry, but once her bedroom door was closed behind her, she merely breathed deeply as she struggled to get her resent-ment under control. She had no life now, nor had she ever had one. She was thirty-two years old, and her entire life was about giving of herself. The only thing she was qualified to do was take care of people. It would be three more years before she could get a college degree. Who was she kidding? Who would want to hire a thirty-five-year-old woman with no professional work experience? Anyone else her age would have been working for years. She might as well quit right now.

The thought of giving up was all she needed to restore her confidence. She wasn't a quitter, never had been. She took a deep breath and raised her chin a notch. She would continue with her classes and graduate near, if not at, the top of her class. And she would succeed.

Fourteen

"A pool? We have our own pool? All riiiiight, Mr. Skye!" Sinclair grasped Skye's shoulder with one palm and his upper arm with the other, shaking them in excitement.

Hatch, too, was impressed by the kidney-bean-shaped hole in the ground, the water that filled it looking like blue crystals sparkling in the sun. They had all seen the house, of course, but Skye hadn't said anything about putting a pool in. It was such a luxury. She never imagined herself living in a house with its own pool. She remembered looking down over suburban Chicago as the plane bringing them to New York took off from Midway Airport, and seeing the swimming pools and trampolines so representative of the middle-class suburban life she hoped would be hers one day. This might not be her house, but from late June to early September it would be her home.

"I wanted to surprise you. I'm proud of you, Grandma, for keeping our little secret."

"Miss Hattie! You knew?" Chantal asked.

"I knew. We both thought it would be nice if you all were surprised."

"Did you have a pool at the house in Sag Harbor?" Hatch asked.

"No, because the owners never put one in. I

figured since I'll own this place for a while I might as well get comfortable. It's not finished yet, but I'm having the garage converted to a studio with bath." He laughed as the girls immediately ran to the separate building that formerly housed a one-car garage. Within seconds they heard delighted squeals coming from inside.

"Come on, Hatch, let's see what all the excitement is about," Miss Hattie said, taking Hatch's arm for support. In her other hand she held the three-pronged cane she used when walking short distances. They fell into step with Skye, who held the door open for them to enter.

"Oh, this is lovely," Hatch said, looking at the freshly painted room. A wood-toned countertop with a still-empty space where the sink would be, two built-in burners, microwave and under-counter refrigerator ran against most of the far wall, which it shared with a bathroom, easily identified by a tiled wall, unfinished step-in shower and a small frosted glass window. There were additional windows on both sides and next to the door, and except for a two-foot area the length of the kitchen, the room's floor was covered by maroon carpet. "Or at least it will be when the plumbing is complete and it has some furniture in it. I'll be sleeping on the sofa for the next couple of weeks until this is livable."

"Did our furniture come, Skye?" Miss Hattie asked.

"On Wednesday. Mrs. Ballard was nice enough to meet the delivery truck." They had selected furniture from a Westchester store with a branch on Long Island. "But I haven't seen it yet. I've driven out, of course, to check on the progress they were making with the pool and remodeling the garage, but I haven't been here since last weekend."

"Let's go see it," Sinclair said. She raced for the door, Chantal on her heels.

"I don't know why they're rushing. The house is locked, and they can't get in before I get there," Skye said. "C'mon, Grandma." He took Miss Hattie's arm, and Hatch closed the door behind them.

The furniture they'd chosen looked even better here than it had at the store. The little house fulfilled its promise of becoming a comfortable and cozy abode. Chantal and Sinclair had argued for the Art Deco style so popular at the moment, but in the end Miss Hattie's more conservative taste won out, and they selected a contemporary style sofa and matching love seat in a soothing smoky blue, with gently rolled arms, a buttoned back, and a shirred skirted hem. Hatch agreed with Miss Hattie; these pieces would never go out of style, and the solid color would be easy on the eyes, while those busy prints the girls adored so much would quickly become irksome.

"It looks very nice, Skye," Hattie said. "But it makes me light-headed to think about how much you've spent on construction and furnishings."

"This isn't just going to be a summer place, Grandma. This is our home away from home. I plan to get out here often between Labor Day and next Memorial Day, and I want it to be comfortable."

They looked at the bedrooms. Chantal and Sinclair's room was furnished with a full-size sleigh bed, with a trundle pulling out from underneath for Hatch. Everyone pronounced the house perfect, and then they all left for the supermarket to stock the cupboards and refrigerator.

It was the Saturday before Memorial Day, and Skye drove them out for their first weekend in the new house. Hatch was glad Skye had chosen to ride with them rather than bring his own car. In the past weeks she'd grown accustomed to sitting next to him in the front seat. He'd come to Tarrytown just about every Sunday and taken them on a different outing. They'd had brunch at the famed Sylvia's restaurant, seen New York from the eighty-sixth-floor observation platform of the Empire State Building, taken a private tour of the news studio where Skye introduced his segments, and roller-skated in Central Park. Spending an entire afternoon with him was a welcome change from having him drop in for brief visits, and she was grateful he had agreed to let her change her schedule to weekday mornings for a maximum of eight weeks. If not, Chantal and Sinclair would be telling her about everything she missed while she was at work on Sundays.

She was undeniably curious about why he suddenly seemed to have more time for them, and by the third week she could no longer contain it. "You know I'm always happy to see you, Skye, but I've got to ask. You only get two days off each week. How does Diana feel about you spending one of them with us?" she asked as they rode down the West Side Highway.

"It doesn't matter. We're not seeing each other anymore."

"Oh, I'm sorry to hear that," she said, forcing herself to sound sincere. "She seemed like a nice girl."

"She was, but her work didn't leave her a lot of free time, at least not while I was in town. Our schedules never seemed to mesh."

"But wasn't she a surgeon?"

"Yeah, but she wasn't the type who'd say, 'Okay, next Tuesday at eight A.M. we're going to take out your tonsils.' If that had been the case, there wouldn't have been a problem. But she works with emergency surgery, and the fact is that she simply had one too many emergencies."

"Oh, I see." Hatch didn't want to lie and say she was sorry to hear of the breakup, but she also knew that the time he was spending with them was only temporary. Soon he would have another girlfriend, one whose schedule wasn't so demanding, and he'd go back to dropping in for a few hours. But at least her schedule allowed her to join them, and spring was the nicest time to explore New York.

One place they didn't go to was the Village, where Skye lived. Hatch couldn't understand why. "Miss Hattie, have you ever been to Skye's apartment?"

"Once, right after he moved in. It's very nice, but I don't plan on going back. There are too many stairs there for me. There's a flight outside the building, then two more flights inside."

"He's on the fourth floor with no elevator?"

"Yes. That's not uncommon in New York. Marshall and his family live on the first two floors, there's another apartment on the third and then there's Skye's place. The closest thing they had to elevators in those old buildings are dumbwaiters."

Hatch was too disappointed to even ask what a dumbwaiter was, but at least she understood why Skye never brought them to his apartment. She was happy just to be in his company, and she found herself taking special pains with her hair, clothes, and makeup on days he took them out.

* * *

When they returned from the market, Miss Hattie said she was going to lie down, Chantal and Sinclair went for a walk to acquaint themselves with their surroundings, and Skye said he was going to look up some friends from Sag Harbor. Hatch watched unhappily as he got into the car and drove off. She hoped it wasn't a female he was going to see.

On Sunday Hatch drove Chantal to nearby Riverhead to fill out job applications. Chantal had just turned sixteen and was eager to get a summer job. Sinclair remained at home with Miss Hattie and Skye. While the day was pleasantly warm, the pool water wouldn't be at a comfortable temperature for another few weeks yet, but Sinclair went in anyway. When Hatch and Chantal returned they found her wrapped in a towel, shivering, a bluish tint to her lips. Hatch insisted she go change into dry clothes. "And I think you need to forget about going in anymore this weekend."

In the afternoon Marshall and Lucien Ballard stopped by to see Skye, and Lucien invited everyone to a barbecue his parents were hosting on the holiday. "For once they're not forecasting rain on Memorial Day," he commented wryly.

As the two men were leaving, Hatch noticed Skye speaking privately to Lucien. Lucien nodded and patted Skye on the back.

"Where's Shari?" she asked Marshall.

"She's at my aunt's helping with the food. They did most of it today. The boys are swimming, even though the water's freezing."

"I'd be happy to help out with the food preparation."

"That's sweet of you, Hatch, but between Shari, my mother, and my aunt they've got it covered. We'll see you tomorrow, huh?"

"Sure."

"All right. Who wants to get some dinner?" Skye asked after the Ballard cousins drove off.

Chantal and Sinclair immediately raised their hands, as Hatch knew they would.

"All right. We'll go when everyone's ready."

Hatch glanced at her watch. "It's only a little after five. Isn't it kind of early?"

"It'll have to be early. Lucien and I are going out later."

"Oh, I see." Her heart felt heavy even as she tried to tell herself there was no reason for it to be. He'd hung around the house all afternoon. She really couldn't expect him to spend the evening in, too. Besides, it was Sunday. And he was going out with Lucien, not some woman.

They were among the first to arrive at the Ballards Monday afternoon. It was good to see the two retired couples again; each represented the easy camaraderie of long-term partnership Hatch hoped to have with her future, still-unknown husband.

It was also nice to see Shari again. In spite of their hopes, they hadn't seen each other since the Christmas dance. Shari, talking with Lucien, embraced her warmly. "I'm so happy to see you, Hatch. The boys and I will be out for the summer when school lets out the end of next month. We'll have to get together and have lunch."

Once again Hatch felt touched by Shari's genuine warmth, and she realized it had been years since she'd had any real contact with anyone her own age. Most of the people at work were teenagers or college kids in their early twenties, or considerably older, in their fifties or beyond. In Farmingdale, she knew most of the girls from growing up with them in town, and those she didn't, gave in to the mediocrity of everyday life there, with no aspirations of improving their existence. It would be nice to have a girlfriend.

"I'd like that," she said.

Shari poked Lucien with her elbow. "Yeah, I've been waiting years for this fellow to get married and give me a sister-in-law, but I'm starting to lose hope."

Lucien shrugged. "What can I say?" He took another forkful of the potato salad he was eating.

The banter seemed good-natured and affectionate, but Hatch thought she saw a glimpse of sadness in Lucien's face. She wished Shari would change the subject.

"Great potato salad, Shari," Lucien said.

"You're not wasting any time digging in, are you?" she teased.

Lucien winked at Hatch. "Cut a brother some slack. I slept late this morning and didn't have any breakfast."

Shari nodded knowingly. "Yeah, I heard you and Skye painted the town last night."

"Not really. Some people Skye knew over in Sag Harbor had a few people in. We weren't out all that late. I was just tired, that's all."

Hatch didn't hear what they said after that. She remembered how handsome Skye looked last night in a pale yellow blazer worn over a simple black T-shirt and black cuffed slacks and T-strap sandals. She felt a sharp pang, a combination of longing and jealousy. Who was at the party? Had he met a woman there?

I'm being selfish. Miss Hattie deserves to see great-grandchildren, and that won't happen until Skye meets someone. But even though she knew she wasn't being fair, she couldn't give up on her dream. She simply wasn't ready to give up her place as the one who sat next to him in the front seat when they went out as a group.

She came to attention just as Shari excused herself to greet new arrivals.

"I hope you enjoy your first summer out here," Lucien said.

"I'm confused about something. Everyone talks about summertime in the Hamptons. But what's it like out here in the winter?"

He chuckled. "You either love it or you hate it. It's much different. It's not like Florida or California, where there's always activity going on at the beach. A lot of businesses close. Only two clubs stay open, one on Friday and the other on Saturday."

"How do you feel about that?"

"I've never been much for clubbing, so it doesn't matter to me. Things start to pick up during February and March, when people come out to look at rentals, and then it's quiet until now. Starting this weekend the roads are jammed. People staying out at Montauk or East Hampton have a long, slow ride in front of them on Montauk Highway."

"Why does the highway traffic move so slow?"

"Because it's not a highway, it's a one-lane road. And it's the *only* road until you can pick up the L.I.E."

She'd been in New York long enough to know

he meant the Long Island Expressway. "And you like living out here better than in the city?"

"I never lived in the city. Of course, I've been there, but this is where I was raised and educated. I went to Hofstra University. I do take vacations every year, but I've essentially lived my whole life right here in Westhampton Beach."

She nodded thoughtfully. Plenty of people in Farmingdale spent their lives there, but it never occurred to her that people in other places did the same thing.

"If you had a choice, where would you prefer to live—here or in the city?" Lucien asked.

"I like it out here. It reminds me of—" she paused, realizing she could no longer describe Farmingdale as her home. "It reminds me of where I used to live. I haven't spent much time in the city. In fact, I've never seen the apartment building your family owns, where Skye lives."

"Of course, I'd be living there, too, if I liked the city."

"You're certainly entitled to."

"Actually, it's all worked out very well. I built a little place between my parents' house and my uncle's. It's very comfortable. In the meantime, my parents and aunt and uncle get a good rental income from Skye and the other tenant. Hey, where are your sisters?"

"They're not here yet. There's a family across the street who have two daughters. They made friends yesterday and asked if they could go over there for a little while before coming here. I told them it was all right, since I doubt there will be anyone here their age."

"You're right. Some little kids maybe, but probably no teenagers. We're talking grandchildren of my parents and uncle's friends."

He had that sad look again. Hatch spoke in an upbeat tone. "Well, Chantal and Sinclair will be popping in as soon as they're hungry, I'm sure."

"It's nice that they've made friends."

"I don't know how much time Chantal is going to have to be social. She filled out applications all over Riverhead yesterday. Someone is sure to offer her a job."

"Is she old enough to work?"

"Yes, she just turned sixteen. I'd like to find something myself."

"Isn't your job taking care of Miss Hattie?"

"Yes, but technically all three of us are in Skye's employ. Officially it's only me, but between the three of us, Miss Hattie is never alone. And all three of us are getting room and board. I work Saturdays and Sundays in Tarrytown." She found herself hoping he wouldn't ask what she did. It wasn't like she cleaned toilets for a living, but sometimes she felt embarrassed nonetheless. He really didn't have to know, anyway. She'd already checked with the Kmart in Riverhead, and they weren't hiring. "They're going to give me a leave of absence for the summer. The extra money I make helps buy books and things for school."

"Oh. I wasn't aware you were going to school."

She named the college she attended. "I'm going to transfer to their Suffolk County campus for the summer semester."

"I think you're to be commended for taking on college at a later point in your life. It can't be easy, taking care of Miss Hattie and your sisters plus taking college classes. That's quite a load."

"I guess it is, but I don't really get discouraged.

I just keep thinking about how good it will feel to have that diploma in my hand, and that's enough to keep me going."

"Well, I don't know if you're interested, but my father and uncle do some landscaping. Actually, what they do is arrange to care for people's grounds for a certain price and then get someone else to do it for maybe half of what they're being paid."

"That's a sweet deal."

"We Ballards are very enterprising. I help out myself on weekends. I could always use a hand."

"I'm definitely interested, and I know all about yard work. Of course, we won't be out for the summer until the end of June, when Chantal and Sinclair are finished with school. I don't think we'll be out at all before then."

"No problem. We'll see about getting you set up when you get here."

Skye handed a plate of food to his grandmother, who looked quite the grand dame seated comfortably in a cushioned Adirondack chair, her wide-brimmed straw hat protecting her from the sun. He stood next to her and was talking to someone he knew when his gaze settled on Hatch, who was speaking with Lucien. He had been laughing with the person he was speaking with, but his smile faded like a haircut as he watched Hatch and Lucien talking like old friends.

Still keeping an eye on them, he leaned forward. "You okay, Grandma?"

"Oh, fine. This is delicious."

"Excuse me for just a minute."

"Go ahead. Don't worry about me."

Skye approached Hatch and Lucien on sturdy legs, but not understanding why he felt the need to join them so quickly. He knew plenty of people here, but for some reason he felt he had to be with Hatch and Lucien, and right away. It was all he could do to keep from running. Anyone would think he was an ant rushing to nibble on crumbs.

He stuck his hands in his pockets when he was a few steps away from where Hatch and Lucien stood. "Hey, there. What's going on?" he greeted.

Hatch's eyes were shining. "Oh, Skye, Lucien was just telling me he might have a job for me with his father and uncle's landscaping business. Isn't that wonderful?" Then she drew in her breath. "Oh. I guess I should have spoken to you first, to make sure it's all right. This would only be on the weekends. Chantal and Sinclair will stay with Miss Hattie while I'm at work . . . not that I've actually gotten the job yet," she added with an embarrassed smile in Lucien's direction.

"Of course it's all right. It didn't occur to me that you'd want a job, but I guess you can't exactly commute to Tarrytown every weekend from here, can you?"

"Thanks, Skye." She placed folded palms on her stomach. "You know, all this excitement is making me hungry. I think I'm going to go ahead and fix a plate and see for myself how good Shari's potato salad is. Excuse me."

"Nice girl, isn't she?" Lucien commented when Hatch was out of earshot.

"She's really very sweet. She hasn't had an easy life, but I have a feeling that giving up isn't something she would ever consider. She took care of her father, who was an amputee, up until he died last year, as well as raised her sisters."

"Well, she certainly has a way with your grand-mother."

Skye followed Lucien's gaze. Hatch stood by Grandma's chair. He watched the two of them ex-change a few words before Hatch moved on. He imagined Hatch asking if Grandma needed any-thing, not so much because she was conscious of being on duty, but simply because she cared.

"It's a joy having all three of them involved with Grandma. Chantal and Sinclair are like the grand-children she never had."

"I guess she sees it almost as if you had a sister."

Skye felt his shoulders go rigid. There was some-thing about Lucien's remark that rubbed him the wrong way, but he couldn't say anything about it . . . because he wasn't sure what it was.

Fifteen

"It's a good thing Skye is driving out separately. Otherwise, we'd have to tie someone on the roof of the car," Miss Hattie said as she cast a dubious eye on the numerous suitcases and boxes waiting to be put inside the car trunk.

It was the second to last Friday in June, and they were preparing to shift their home base from Tarrytown to Westhampton Beach until Labor Day. Miss Hattie's longtime neighbors Norma and Harry Williams would look in on the house regularly while they were away.

"So when is Mr. Skye coming?" Sinclair asked.

Hatch smiled giddily at the thought of Skye. He had spent every weekend in Westhampton Beach except one time when he had to fly out of town on Sunday for an assignment. They saw him on Fridays, when he would come by after work before heading for the island. Hatch had wondered why the rest of them didn't make the trip, as well, a question the typically bold Chantal saw fit to ask him.

He had shrugged rather sheepishly. "I just thought it would be more convenient for you to stay in town until school let out."

"C'mon, Mr. Skye. You just don't want us to

know what you're up to when we're not there,"
Sinclair teased.

Hatch had looked at him sharply. Was it her
imagination, or did he look uncomfortable, perhaps as though Sinclair had hit on the truth?

"Actually, all that traveling back and forth would
be too much for me," Miss Hattie had said. "We'll
be out there for the season in just two more weeks,
anyway."

"So, Mr. Skye, what's on your agenda for this
evening?" Chantal asked.

"A good night's sleep. But it's worth it to make
the drive late because the traffic's so much
lighter."

"As long as we're there in time for me to start
work," Chantal said. She had accepted a part-time
job at a water park in Riverhead and was quite
excited about earning a paycheck.

"Hopefully, I'll be working, too," Hatch had
said. It was the first time she was able to smile.
She turned her attentions back to the laundry she
was folding, and because of that she missed Skye's
frown.

They quickly settled into a comfortable daily
routine. Chantal worked afternoons on the cash
register at the water park. Sinclair was busy with
her friends from across the street, as well as the
kids who lived in the neighborhood year-round.
Hatch was taking morning classes for the summer,
and because she was at school when Chantal left
for work, it was Sinclair's responsibility to spend
those interval hours looking after Miss Hattie.
They had brought the sewing machine with them

from Tarrytown and spent many afternoons working at the kitchen table.

Skye came out on the weekends, but the time
went by all too quickly. Hatch eagerly anticipated
the long July Fourth weekend, in which he would
come out on Wednesday night and stay until Sunday. They were hosting a barbecue on the holiday
Thursday, or more accurately, *Skye* was hosting one.
He told Miss Hattie he had taken care of everything from New York, and that caterers were coming in to prepare the food.

She was washing the dinner dishes, trying to decide if she could afford to buy a new outfit for the
occasion, when Chantal joined her in the kitchen.
"Hatch, Jobari invited me to the movies Saturday.
Is it all right if I go?"

She nearly dropped the plate she was washing,
and it wasn't because Chantal seemed to have
adopted the New York lingo for what they had
always known as "the show." She quickly tightened
her grip on the plate. In hindsight she didn't know
why this had come as a surprise; all Chantal had
talked about since her first day at work was Jobari,
Jobari, Jobari. Besides, she was sixteen years old
and certainly should be allowed to go out on dates.
She'd gone out several times last winter, but those
were afternoon outings with a young man whose
family Miss Hattie had known for years, and whose
junior driver's license meant he had to be in before dark. Hatch knew Chantal was talking about
a more grown-up nighttime date. It had seemed
so far away until now.

"Hatch?"

"I suppose it's all right, as long as he doesn't
keep you out too late. Now, how old did you say
he was again?"

"Seventeen. He'll be eighteen in October, so he's about a year and a half older than me."

That was something else Hatch didn't want to think about, but at least by the time Jobari became legal they would be back in Tarrytown. "I see. Well, I see no reason why he can't have you in by midnight." The corners of her mouth turned up slightly as she waited for Chantal's response, which was sure to be an objection.

"Midnight! Oh, Hatch. That's so early!"

"Not really. Go to an eight o'clock show. It probably won't be any more than two hours. That way you'll still have a good hour and a half to get a quick bite before he brings you home. I'm not going to raise the roof if you come in ten or fifteen minutes late, but I'm not going to have you traipsing in at twelve-thirty or one A.M., either."

"But what if the movie we go see is three hours long?"

Hatch shrugged. "In that case I guess you'll have to skip the snack afterward."

"Oh, Hatch."

"I'm looking forward to meeting him. You've spoken about him quite a bit."

Chantal's mouth fell open in alarm. "You aren't going to tell him that, are you?"

"Of course not. I wouldn't embarrass you like that. Do you have something to wear?"

"I was going to ask you if you'd take me to buy something new."

"I will, if that's what you really want. You do have a closetful of clothes that he hasn't seen you in." All employees of the water park wore shirts with the park's logo while on duty. "You promised you'd put some of what you make away for college. Remember, you're the daughter of a poor man, and you have a poor older sister," she said with a smile. "I'm sure you'll get a scholarship with those good grades you're getting"—both Chantal and Sinclair had excelled academically after moving to Tarrytown, in spite of the district having a more advanced curriculum—"but it's not going to cover everything, just like my loan doesn't cover everything."

"I'm not going to make it a habit to go out and buy new clothes, I promise."

Hatch couldn't refuse. A girl's first real date was an important event in her life.

"I have a date," Chantal proudly announced over dinner the following evening.

"Oh! Is it Jobari?" Sinclair asked, her voice squeaky with excitement.

"Yes, Minnie Mouse."

"Well, this is a special occasion," Miss Hattie said. "It's wonderful being sixteen and going out on a date with a special young man."

"It would be even nicer to be thirty-two and go out with a slightly older special man," Hatch said wistfully.

"I'm surprised Lucien hasn't asked you out," Chantal said.

"Lucien and I are friends, nothing more."

"What's your young man's name, Chantal?" Miss Hattie asked.

"Jobari."

"*Who?*"

Chantal repeated the name, and Miss Hattie shook her head. "I don't know what's wrong with people nowadays, coming up with all these crazy names for their kids. What happened to the solid names they used to give?"

Hatch smiled; Miss Hattie's sentiment was so typical of someone her age. "If by 'solid' you mean something like Cornelia, they've gone the way of the dinosaur."

"Hmph. All I can say is they'd better hope nothing happens to Affirmative Action, or else those résumés are going to go right in the trash. If you ask me, the only people who should have those ridiculous names that scream out 'Look at me, I'm black,' are the ones who can sing, dance, or dribble a basketball."

They all laughed, then Sinclair asked, "Where is he taking you?" The moment Chantal told her she asked, "What are you wearing?"

But Chantal didn't mind sharing information. "I'm trying to get Hatch to take me shopping so I can buy myself something new," she said pointedly.

Hatch decided to humor her sister. "Okay. We'll go after dinner."

Hatch smoothed the new culotte she'd bought. She would wear it for the barbecue on the Fourth. Skye had insisted all the arrangements had been made, and that she didn't have to worry about anything. Still, she wanted to look nice and make a good impression on Skye's friends.

She had everything planned. Skye would arrive late tomorrow afternoon. She was going to make her legendary tacos, even if it would mean spending over an hour making tortillas, and almost that long to fry them in deep oil with tongs to give them the U-shape. But it was the homemade shells that made them taste so good. She knew he'd be impressed.

If the way to a man's heart really was through his stomach, she was definitely flowing in the right direction.

She was doing the deep-frying when she heard a car honking.

"That must be Skye," Miss Hattie said as she got to her feet. She had been sitting at the kitchen table, reading the newspaper.

Panicked, Hatch looked down at her faded T-shirt, which bore patches of flour and cornmeal, plus a few wet spots where she'd been splashed with batter. "Already? It's awfully early, don't you think?"

"I guess he left work early to try and beat the traffic." With that Miss Hattie was out the back door.

Hatch immediately sprung into action. There was nothing she could do about the raggedy way she looked, but at least she could straighten up the kitchen. She began tossing measuring cups, spoons, and frying pans into the sink along with the other baking utensils and turned on the water. She wanted him to think there wasn't anything to her efforts, not that she'd been cooking all afternoon. She covered the large frying pan she'd used to brown the ground beef and did a quick wipe-off of the stove, all while using tongs to hold the shell she was frying in a U-shape.

Skye's familiar voice rang out with what had become a standard greeting. "Something smells good in Hatch's kitchen."

"Hi there! I didn't think you'd be in so soon."

"Would you believe the scents from the kitchen beckoned me all the way from the city?"

"Yeah, right."

He sniffed. "What're you making? It smells spicy."

"Tacos. It's not really that spicy, at least not the meat. I bought two jars of sauce, one mild and one medium. At least they say it's medium, but I taste a whole lot of jalapeños. Your grandmother will have the mild, of course."

He moved next to her and inspected a shell. "Hey, you made these?"

"From scratch. Mine taste a whole lot better than Taco Bell's. That and the fact that I put more than a tablespoon of meat in mine," she added with a laugh.

"Any ready yet?"

"Not yet. These should really be in the oven."

"They look ready to me."

He sounded as though he were about ten, she thought. It was kind of cute. She had a visual flash of herself telling their son, Skye Jr., that he had to wait a few more minutes before he could eat. She blinked it away and responded to his statement. "I don't have any of the toppings prepared yet. I've got to finish frying the shells."

"All right. While you're cooking, I'm going to take a dip and cool off."

After the shells were complete and placed in the warm oven, a gleeful Hatch chopped lettuce, tomatoes, onions, and shredded cheese and divided them into bowls. She set each bowl on the table, along with a container of sour cream and jar of taco sauce. Everything looked perfect. She felt like Martha Stewart or B. Smith or somebody.

At that moment the doorbell rang. Miss Hattie was out back with Skye, and Sinclair was roller-skating up and down the street with her friends. Hatch flung a dishtowel over her shoulder and went to the door.

An attractive woman of about thirty-five stood there, and Hatch spotted one of those jazzy new Thunderbirds parked in the driveway next to Skye's Cougar. Her spine automatically stiffened, even as she prayed the woman wouldn't ask the question her common sense told her was coming. "Yes?"

"Hi. Does Skye Audsley live here?" the stranger asked, fulfilling Hatch's prophecy.

She forced her expression to be noncommittal. "Yes, he does."

"I'm Carla Kelly. He's expecting me."

"I see. He's in the pool."

"Can I go around the back?"

"The gate's locked from the inside. Come through the house. I'm Hatch; I take care of Skye's grandmother."

"Hello, Hatch. Nice to meet you."

As Hatch led Carla to the back door she bit down on her lower lip, and she could feel her forehead pucker. But this was no time to cry.

They had company for dinner.

Sixteen

The weekend Hatch had anticipated so highly passed in a blur. Skye's barbecue on the Fourth was a great success. Chantal had to work, but Jobari stopped in when he brought her home that day. He was a stocky young man of average height, with excellent manners and a seemingly sincere demeanor. Miss Hattie was only in attendance for an hour or so, then excused herself. A short time later Hatch decided to do the same. After all, it was Skye's party, not hers. He didn't need her to act as hostess; he had Carla.

Skye's latest romantic interest was very nice, complimenting Hatch's tacos when Skye invited her to join them for dinner when she arrived and showing the same friendliness that Diana Butler had demonstrated at the Christmas party. Hatch simply couldn't bear it. She said she was going to check on Miss Hattie and excused herself from talking with Carla and Shari.

She kept her word, checking on Miss Hattie the moment she got inside. She knocked on the closed bedroom door, entering when she was invited in. Miss Hattie was sitting in a side chair watching television. "I just wanted to make sure you were all right," Hatch explained.

"Oh, I'm fine. I just don't care too much for

some of that crowd, but I'll be back out in a few minutes. This is a silly movie. It's supposed to be a thriller, but I've seen this plot device a million times before. Someone who knows the identity of the bad guy arranges to meet the character who's in danger so they can talk in person instead of telling them what they know over the phone, and of course the bad guy will kill them before they can get to the meeting. It's ridiculous the way screenwriters overuse that gimmick."

Hatch smiled; Miss Hattie's assessment sounded like something Daddy would have said. "All right. I'll leave you alone, then."

Hatch stopped to talk to the caterer, who was busy shucking ears of fresh corn while her husband was overseeing the grill. It proved to be a beneficial conversation; the woman asked if Hatch would be interested in assisting them when they were especially busy, which during the summer season was often. Hatch felt so good about the prospect that she decided she could handle seeing Skye with Carla.

Outside, Hatch sat with Shari cross-kneed on the edge of the concrete pool deck, every so often cautioning Sinclair and Shari's sons, who were swimming, not to splash in their direction. Skye was sitting at a nearby table with Carla, Lucien, and Marshall, under the shade of a large umbrella.

"Carla's nice, isn't she?" Shari remarked.

"I thought so. She had dinner with us last night."

"She told me she and Skye met a couple of weeks ago when they were waiting for the shuttle to bring them to the parking lot at the airport. She had already been invited to spend the weekend with friends in Hampton Bays, and he asked her to stop by when she got here.''

Hatch's heart wrenched. No wonder Skye had driven out so early. He wanted to make sure he didn't miss Carla.

"She was telling me she's going to Memphis on business and then going down to Puerto Rico for vacation. Nice, huh?''

"What type of work does she do?" Hatch asked tonelessly.

"She's a chemical engineer for Union Carbide. I know they just met, but I think she'd be a nice match for Skye." Shari giggled. "Sometimes he cracks me up with that newscaster voice of his. I wonder if he talks that way when he's making love. You know, 'We'll have more right after this,' '' she said with exaggerated enunciation.

While Shari laughed at her joke, Hatch used the guise of adjusting the strap on her sandal to look over at Skye's and Carla's table. Carla was holding up the newspaper, and all four of them were laughing, probably about what constituted news out here. The local news consisted largely of inconsequential and embarrassing stories about arrests for reckless driving, disturbing the peace, even public urination. Carla's long nails were painted a neutral dusky rose, and they were so perfect Hatch knew they had recently been professionally manicured. Her chin-length bob was arrow straight, and her toes matched her fingernails. But, of course, with the position she held she could easily afford to patronize salons and spas for regular pampering. A chemical engineer, Shari had said. Hatch didn't even know what that was.

It was so utterly hopeless. How could she hope Skye would choose her over someone like Carla, someone who regularly flew to out-of-town meetings and probably supervised a staff? She needed to stop dreaming and get a grip. He was a professional man. His ideal partner would be a woman who felt comfortable in the business world and around the people here today, most of whom were professionals from the city or New Jersey—dentists, politicians, lawyers, and the like. She could never, ever be anything more to him than the woman who took care of his grandmother in her last years.

The party thinned out when darkness began to fall. She sought Lucien out and explained to him about the job offer from the caterers. "I hope you're not upset, but I think I'd enjoy that better than landscaping. I love to cook, and I might learn something."

"Of course I'm not upset. I'm happy for you. I was going to drive out and see the fireworks. Why don't you come with me?"

She didn't hesitate to accept. Jobari was taking Chantal, and Sinclair was going along with them.

Hatch drew in her breath when the finale, a likeness of the flag, lit up the sky over the Atlantic. "That was beautiful. I really enjoyed that."

"So did I. Why don't we do it again, say tomorrow night? No fireworks, of course, but maybe dinner."

His invitation caught her off guard, but this time she knew she couldn't accept. "I can't, Lucien. Chantal is going out with Jobari, and I need to be there when he picks her up and also when he brings her home."

"I understand."

"But why don't you come over and have dinner

with us?" She decided it was foolish to keep hoping
for something that would never happen. Skye was
not going to wake up one day and fall madly in
love with her. A perfectly nice man had just invited
her out. Turning him down would be silly.

"Did you enjoy the fireworks, Skye?" Hattie
asked the next morning.

"I did. It seems like they get fancier every year.
I thought you would have gone to see them with
Hatch and the girls."

"I didn't feel like being in such a big crowd.
Even if I did, I wouldn't have wanted to tag along.
It was bad enough that Chantal and her young
man brought Sinclair along."

"And Hatch, too."

"No. Hatch went with Lucien." She saw Skye's
expression harden. "Something wrong?" she
asked innocently. "Surely you can't have a problem with the two of them going out. I think I'm
a pretty good judge of people, and my feeling is
that Lucien is a very nice man."

"He is, but I don't see anything working between
them. Lucien likes living out here, and there's really
nothing out this far for Hatch careerwise."

"Oh, I don't know about that. I think architec-
ture is pretty healthy, with all the new homes and
businesses going up all over the island. And she
told me that Westhampton reminds her of her
hometown. But I'm just an old woman—what do
I know?"

She left the room, pretending not to notice that
he was still frowning.

* * *

Skye didn't know what to do with himself. Carla had a flight to Memphis Sunday afternoon, so she returned to the city on Saturday so she could prepare. He contemplated returning a day early himself, but quickly abandoned that idea as being silly. This was the tail end of a long holiday weekend. The millions of New Yorkers stuck in the steamy city would jump at the chance to spend it out of town.

He checked the time. Seven forty-five. Hatch and the girls were probably home. He'd walk over to the main house. Maybe they could get a movie on Pay-Per-View or something. Grandma might even watch it with them. All he knew was that he didn't feel like being alone.

He kept his cargo shorts on but changed into a fresh golf shirt. He was just a few steps away from the back door when he heard the rattling of dishes, suggesting after-dinner cleanup. Multiple voices laughed, giving him a warm feeling. His knuckle tapped on the screen door, stopping immediately when a male voice said, "Just a minute."

His hand froze midknock. He recognized Lucien's voice. What was *he* doing here on a Saturday night?

"Hey, man," Lucien said as his slight frame appeared at the screen door, which he promptly unlocked and pushed open. "I figured you'd be out for the evening."

Skye shrugged. "Carla had to go back to the city. I figured I'd stop by and see what the girls were up to."

"We just finished eating. I'm helping with the dishes."

Hatch entered the kitchen from the adjoining dining area, clasping two glasses between the fingers of her hands. "Hi, Skye!" she said in a surprised tone. "I didn't know you were home. Did you just get in?"

"I was out earlier this afternoon. I've been back at the guest house for a couple of hours."

"Well, why didn't you say something? You could have joined us for dinner."

"Is that Skye?" he heard his grandmother ask. For a woman who was about to turn ninety, she still had remarkable hearing.

"Yeah, Grandma, it's me. I'll be right in."

"Skye, you missed a great dinner," Lucien said. "Hatch made this pizza . . . thing."

Hatch shot him an amused look at his vague description of the meal she'd prepared.

"Let me just say that it was so good it left me speechless," Lucien concluded. He and Hatch burst into laughter.

Skye had the uncomfortable feeling that he was intruding. He quickly slipped into the dining room, where his grandmother sat sipping the last of her iced tea while Sinclair wiped down the table. "I hear dinner was pretty good," he said.

"Oh, it was wonderful," Grandma agreed. "There's some left. I'm sure Hatch will be glad to fix you a plate."

"I think I will try some. Hey, where's Chantal?"

"She's on a date," Sinclair answered.

"Oh, with the fellow who was by on the Fourth?"

"That's the one." Sinclair lowered her voice. "Hatch would be out, too, with Lucien, but she wants to see what time Jobari brings Chantal home. Like she couldn't trust me to tell her."

"Well, Sinclair, I don't think it's so much a matter of not trusting you as it is not putting off what's essentially her responsibility on anyone else. Your sister takes her responsibilities very seriously, as she should." *So that's why Lucien's here.*

"Speaking of dates, what are you doing hanging around home at eight o'clock on a Saturday night?" Grandma asked.

He explained about Carla.

"Oh. You two have an exclusive relationship already?"

"No, not really. We just met."

"I'm not one to interfere," Grandma said, "but I can't help thinking you'd be better off with someone who doesn't travel at all. With two people traveling all the time, they hardly ever get to see each other, and that always means trouble. Why do you think it's so difficult for actors and actresses to stay married?"

"Right now I'm not particularly concerned about it, Grandma."

"I'll be your date, Mr. Skye," Sinclair offered.

He smiled at the teen. "How about going into the village for some dessert?"

"You mean it?"

"Sure. I'm going to eat something first, though."

"Okay."

Grandma pushed back from the table. "You two have fun. I'm going to my room."

He helped her to her feet and held her arm as they walked into the kitchen.

"Miss Hattie, aren't you going to watch the HBO premiere with us? It's a comedy and is supposed to be real funny."

"No, thanks, dear. You and Lucien enjoy it. Turner Classics is showing *The Bad and the Beautiful*, one of my all-time favorites." She began humming a tune Hatch recognized as the film's theme.

"I'll see you later," she said, disappearing around the corner.

"Hatch, Skye's going to take me into the village for some dessert," Sinclair said.

"That's fine, but why are you in the refrigerator?"

"I'm going to fix Skye a plate."

He hadn't known she was doing that. "Sinclair, you don't have to do that. I can get my own."

Hatch put a hand on her hip. "My, my, what great service we give. Why is it that I have to remind you over and over again whenever I want you to do something for me?"

"Because you never take me out among all the beautiful people, Hatch."

It was a pizza casserole, Skye decided, a one-dish meal containing ground beef, Italian sausage, tomato sauce, mushrooms, sliced green pepper, and stringy mozzarella cheese surrounded by a garlic-and-cheese-flavored crust. It tasted fabulous.

He ate quickly, conscious of Hatch and Lucien sitting in the living room behind him, laughing at the movie on TV. She was sitting in the corner of the love seat and he was in the corner of the sofa closest to the love seat, but Skye suspected they might get closer once he wasn't hovering over them like a maiden aunt.

As anxious as he was to leave, before he left with Sinclair he looked in on Grandma.

She was sitting in a comfortable recliner, stitching a pillow. "I'm fine," she assured him. "But I'd like to spend more quality time with you, Skye. I'm getting on, you know."

"Getting on" was minimizing a life that had

spanned nine decades. "I know, Grandma. But you make it sound like we never see each other."

"All I'm saying is that you're always running here or there with this female or that one. I hope you'll cut back on your social life a bit and spend some time with your old grandmother next weekend, that's all."

He bent and kissed her cheek. "All right. Next weekend it'll be just you and me. Let me see what you're putting on that one." He adjusted the pillow in her hand and read aloud. " 'Can't see the forest for the trees.' "

"This one's for you, Schuyler," she said when she knew he had left.

Seventeen

"Are you all right, Grandma?" Skye asked for what must have been the fifth time in as many minutes.

"Schuyler, if I thought I was dying I would have suggested you call an ambulance."

In spite of her concern, Hatch laughed heartily; she couldn't help it. She supposed that if Miss Hattie was making jokes, she couldn't have been feeling too bad. At least, she hoped not. Abdominal pain could mean a whole lot of things.

"Skye, why don't you bring Miss Hattie inside and I'll park the car?" Hatch suggested as he followed the signs for the emergency room entrance of the hospital in Southampton.

"Good idea. Thanks, Hatch." He pulled alongside the curb and jumped out to open his grandmother's door. "Can you walk, Grandma?"

"Oh, I'm sure I can."

Hatch, who sat in the back next to Miss Hattie, stayed close, eager to help, but there was really nothing she could do. Miss Hattie had no problem shifting her body toward the door, and Skye's strong arms lifted her to her feet. Hatch quickly slid toward the other door so she could get out and take the wheel. When she looked at Skye, she saw the same worried expression on his face that she knew she must have on her own.

"Mr. Audsley?"

Hatch raised her head with a jerk as a white-smocked physician approached Skye.

"Yes," Skye said in an anxious tone.

"I'm Dr. Bartram. I'm evaluating your grandmother."

"What's wrong?"

"We don't find anything clinically wrong."

"Thank God," Hatch said in a whisper.

"She doesn't have an acute abdomen," the doctor continued, "and her lab values are normal for the most part. She does seem to be a little deficient in her potassium. We're giving her supplements, and I'd like to keep her just overnight as a precaution."

"She probably won't be too happy about that. She can be feisty when she wants to."

Dr. Bartram's forehead wrinkled. "Actually, she was quite amenable. I told her she'll be reevaluated in the morning and most likely will be discharged at that time."

Hatch frowned. She, too, had expected Miss Hattie to object to or even refuse an overnight stay. Was there some reason for her agreement? Did she suspect something might be wrong and that staying hospitalized would be in her best interest?

"Can we see her?" Skye asked.

"Certainly. Come with me."

Hatch followed the two of them, pleased that Skye had included her in the "we."

"She's really quite comfortable," Dr. Bartram

said as they walked. "She complained of being hungry, so I ordered her a dinner tray."

Skye was happy to see Grandma sitting upright, across her lap a tray holding a turkey sandwich. "Some dinner they give me," she complained. "Another couple of meals like this and I'll never get out of here alive. Hatch, you've really spoiled me."

"I'm sorry, Mrs. Jackson; it was the best the kitchen could do on such short notice," Dr. Bartram said. "Breakfast will be better, I promise."

"Well, I guess it's better than nothing. At least *I'm* getting something to eat." She looked at Hatch and Skye. "I know you two must be starving. Go on, get out of here. I'm fine."

"Don't rush us, Grandma. We just got here."

"We had some anxious moments while we were waiting," Hatch added.

"Well, now that you've seen me you know it's okay to leave. You both need to keep your strength up; you might need it to take care of me." She chuckled.

He watched as Hatch draped an arm on Grandma's opposite shoulder and leaned forward to give her a quick hug. "I'm going to call home and let Chantal and Sinclair know you're okay. It's been hours since we left, and since we can't use your cell phone in the hospital, they're probably worried sick. Excuse me."

"I think she'll be all right," Hatch said as she and Skye walked out of the hospital.

He knew she was trying to reassure him, but he

had to agree. Before they knew it, it would be to-morrow morning and time to bring her home. "I gave the staff the number to my cell phone, just in case they need to reach me."

"Oh, I'm sure they won't have to call."

"Well, I am kind of hungry. What say we pick up the girls and go get something to eat?"

"They're both getting ready to go out. Sinclair's going to go cosmic bowling with the Kirkland kids, and Chantal has a date with Jobari."

"Ah. So it's just you and me, huh?"

"Looks that way."

He seated her in the car and quickly got behind the wheel, steering the car east.

"Shouldn't we be going the other way?" she asked.

"I thought we'd try something different and go over to East Hampton, since we don't have to pick up the girls and we're halfway there already."

"Sure. I just hope we don't have to wait for a table."

"I don't think we'll have to. It's still pretty early for this crowd." He wasn't concerned about their casual dress; here in the Hamptons no one dressed for dinner, whether they were going to a restaurant or someone's house.

He drove to a restaurant that specialized in sea-food. Hatch tasted the crab cakes she'd ordered as an appetizer and proclaimed them perfection.

"Even better than yours?" he teased.

"I've never tried to make crab cakes, but I'm sure that if I did they'd be close." She smiled, then looked past him.

"What are you staring at?"

"I keep thinking that I've seen the woman be-hind you before, but I can't put my finger on where. It's not like I knew that many people in Illinois, but she looks so familiar, especially when she smiles."

Skye turned for a quick glance. "She should. She used to light up the world when she smiled, or something like that."

"What do you mean?"

"That's Mary Tyler Moore."

Her palm went to her heart. "It sure is. Oh, I feel so silly. Who would ever imagine that one day I would be having dinner in the same restaurant as Mary Tyler Moore?"

Skye shrugged. "Actors have to eat, too, you know. But I suppose it is quite a change from living in Farmingdale."

"Where there isn't even a restaurant."

He smiled, remembering their lunch that first day in Bourbonnais. "I've been meaning to tell you how glad I am that everything worked out for you with school and all, being able to switch campuses for the summer. It never occurred to me that summer in Westhampton meant you'd miss classes."

"You don't know how happy I am just to be going to school. My father was right; it wasn't too late, after all."

"You've still got plenty of time, Hatch."

"I just wish I could have my father here and still go to college," she said softly, her eyes focusing on the edge of the table. "I miss him, Skye. You have no idea."

"I think I do."

The faraway look in her eyes disappeared, and she turned a dangerously bright gaze to him. "Miss Hattie mentioned that you lost both your parents young. Were you and your father close?"

"I idolized him. Whenever I'd hear his key in the lock I'd go running to answer the door. I remember how I kept crying over and over that I wanted to see him after my mother brought me to New York and said that from now on we were going to be living with Grandma and Grandpa. I was heartbroken because Daddy had promised to take me fishing that weekend."

"Did you see him often after they broke up?"

"I never saw him again. He was dead a few weeks after we left."

"Oh, how awful!"

"I was too young to understand it all. My mother explained it to me years later, after she became ill. She said she wanted me to know the whole story, and she wanted me to hear it from her. My dad was having an affair with the wife of another man in their social circle, and my mother found out about it. All I remember about that time is that he started coming home later and later at night. Then Mom took me and left."

Hatch nodded. "I'm afraid that's not really an unusual occurrence, either today or back then."

"I suppose. I just wish the woman's husband had simply left her when he found out, but he went after them with a gun. He killed my father, and he did some major damage to his wife, although I understand she later recovered."

"Oh, Skye, I'm so sorry. I had no idea."

"No, you couldn't have known. I generally don't talk about it, and neither does Grandma, but with you it's—it's different somehow." It was true. He'd only shared the details of his father's demise with a handful of people in his entire life. Marshall didn't know, and neither had his former fiancée, but he felt like he could tell Hatch anything. He knew he could trust her with this intimate detail.

"And I won't say anything to anyone about it."

He blinked. It was almost as if she were reading his mind.

"How're you doing, Mrs. Jackson?" the nurse asked.

"Fair to middlin'. I was just about to doze off."

"They're showing an encore presentation of *A Day in the Life* tonight. It's one of those 'best of' compilations the network is using to fill in airtime during the summer."

"No one watches TV on a Saturday night anyway. But I'll watch it. I never get tired of seeing my grandson."

The nurse changed the television channel. Skye had filmed a special introduction to describe the segments being re-aired. "He sure is handsome. Nice, too. He gave me an autograph when I asked. If I was ten years younger I'd be all over him, Mrs. Jackson. Or is he married?"

"Not yet. But I think he might be getting closer to it."

Skye felt relaxed for the first time since Grandma started complaining about abdominal pain. "Okay, now that I've told you all about me, it's your turn, Hatch."

She chuckled. "Well, my life certainly won't win any awards for being the most exciting, that's for sure. You know about my mother running off and that I was raised by my stepmother."

"Who taught you how to be such a great cook,

God bless her." They laughed. "Yes, but surely there's something more, like a serious romance or two?" The question rolled off his tongue with an ease that surprised him.

She pretended—at least he hoped she was pretending—to be miffed. "Hey, no fair. We didn't discuss *your* love life."

He shrugged. "Thanks to Grandma, I know you know about my broken engagement, in which I was a prize fool."

"And since then there was Diana, and now Carla . . ."

He suddenly felt embarrassed. Did Hatch think he was some kind of Casanova? It was important to him that she didn't. "I just met Carla," he said. "There's no real involvement there."

"I'm getting the impression that you haven't been very lucky in love."

"I haven't."

"You're not alone."

"You have an unhappy ending, too?"

"It was years and years ago. My high school sweetheart and I worked hard for good grades and were awarded scholarships. Then my father had to have his leg amputated, and my stepmother was killed in that car crash. In the end he went on and I stayed behind. We broke up soon after."

Her voice had a rather matter-of-fact tone, as if she'd just stated the time. He got the impression that she had long since come to terms with her broken romance. "And since?" he prodded. Surely she'd been involved with someone since high school; even at her young age that was nearly half a lifetime ago.

Her lips formed a half smile. "Let's just say that most fellows were turned off by my having to work every Friday and Saturday night, but even if I was off those nights, living in Farmingdale was really another strike against me. It was a long drive from the Kankakee area, where most of the people I knew lived. But the bread man used to take me to breakfast a lot," she added.

They looked at each other and simultaneously burst out laughing. It felt good to laugh, especially considering the stress of the afternoon. What she said wasn't particularly funny; it was more the way she said it, as if she wanted to emphasize that even though her circumstances didn't allow her to date much, she could easily catch a man's eye. He was glad it had struck her as amusing also; he wouldn't want her to think he was laughing at her.

"That really sounded silly, didn't it?" she said when she caught her breath. "It just goes to show, that was the extent of excitement in my life before you came along and introduced my sisters and me to a whole new world. We'll always be grateful to you, Skye."

In the few seconds it took for her to say those seven words, the mood shifted from gaiety to seriousness.

"I'm very glad I ran into Chantal and Sinclair that afternoon. They made quite an impression on me. I never encountered young people so willing to take advantage of a stranger's predicament."

"I can't tell you how happy I am that I was able to get them out of Farmingdale."

"They tell me they were anxious to leave. That surprised me, especially for Chantal. At that age kids usually don't like leaving their friends."

"I think they enjoyed making the other kids envious by talking about the great life they were going to have in New York. I'm sure your name came up more than a few times, too. But they were secretly a little apprehensive. We all were."

"Now I don't know how Grandma managed without you. I don't think she does, either."

The house was dark when they drove up. They alighted from the car simultaneously, and Skye unlocked the tall wooden door of the backyard fence. "I'll have to call across the street and let Sinclair know I'm back," Hatch remarked as she stepped through the gate. Reflexively, she placed a hand on his upper arm. "Try not to worry, Skye. I'm sure Miss Hattie will be just fine. Just a few hours from now we can go pick her up. Why don't you stay with Sinclair and me for a while?"

"Thanks. I think I will. You know, Hatch, you've been a great help throughout this whole terrible day. I can honestly say that the only part of today that wasn't awful was the time spent with you."

"I enjoyed dinner, too. And wait 'til I tell the girls that Puffy was coming in as we were leaving."

"You mean P. Diddy. He changed his name, remember?"

"Yeah, but I still call him Puffy. People will always call you by your old name if you change it. Why do you think I've stuck with Cornelia?"

They smiled at each other, and when it came time for their smiles to fade, their eyes remained fixed. Hatch looked away, afraid that in the moonlight he would be able to see the yearning she'd kept secret for so long, that her heart would be exposed.

"Look at me, Hatch."

She raised her eyes, and something in his earnest gaze told her what was about to happen. She lifted her chin ever so slightly and her eyelids fluttered shut as his face came in close to hers.

The kiss was brief, only a few seconds, but it was enough to make her heart soar. "I guess that was inappropriate," Skye said. "I hope I didn't make you uncomfortable. It's just been kind of an emotional day."

She met his gaze and answered in a quiet voice. "The only way I would feel uncomfortable, Skye, would be if you were thinking I was Carla."

His reply was immediate and confident, but just as soft. "I kissed Cornelia Hatchet. I knew it was Cornelia Hatchet, and I didn't want it to be anyone else but Cornelia Hatchet."

She didn't know what to say to that, so she stood by silently as he unlocked the back door. "I'm going to call Sinclair," she said when they were in the kitchen.

Sinclair came home right away. She plopped on the living room couch, even though Hatch had told her a hundred times not to do that, and reached for the remote control. "Hey, that new Mel Gibson movie is showing on Pay-Per-View. Can I order it?"

"Yes, let's get it," Skye said.

Hatch looked at him curiously. Apparently he planned on staying a while. She feared he might change his mind and go home after what just happened outside. She liked having him around on a Saturday night, but part of her felt guilty. After all, if it wasn't for Miss Hattie becoming ill and being admitted for observation, he wouldn't be here . . . and he never would have kissed her.

Sinclair began yawning an hour into the movie, not because it was boring but because she said she

was tired. "That was good," she said the moment
the music swelled as the camera pulled away from
the last scene, "but I'm worn out. Good night."

Hatch glanced at her watch. "Chantal should
be coming in within the next half hour or so."

"Are you okay waiting up for her? I think I'm
going to turn in myself."

"Sure, I'm fine. Go ahead."

Skye, too, was yawning as he left. She locked the
door behind him, actually glad to have some time
alone to relive their kiss over and over. A part of
her even hoped he would kiss her good-night when
he left, even though sensibility told her the moment had passed.

She stretched out on the couch, her head resting on clasped palms, and dreamily stared at the
ceiling. Then she closed her eyes and raised her
chin, as though she were kissing Skye again. She
puckered her lips and made a soft smacking
sound.

Hatch decided that was enough fantasy and
opened her eyes, sat up, and reached for the remote control. The movie she settled on she had
seen before, but nonetheless became so engrossed
in it that when she looked at the clock it was twelve-
twenty A.M. and there was no sign of Chantal.

She immediately jumped up and went out the
front door, hoping to see the car Jobari drove, but
the driveway only held Skye's two Mercurys. The
street was dark. *I'll give her another ten minutes. After
that, she's seriously late.* Her mouth set in an un-
yielding straight line as she went inside to wait.

It was ten minutes to one when bright headlights
lit up the driveway. Hatch resisted the urge to run

outside and meet them, screaming, "You're late!" They knew exactly what time it was. Instead she waited to see if Jobari would escort Chantal inside, wanted to see if he would offer any type of explanation or even an apology, which she might consider. If they gave an excuse she felt was flimsy, she would simply forbid Chantal to date him the following weekend and make sure Jobari knew the reason why.

When the front door opened a full five minutes later, only Chantal came inside. Still, Hatch couldn't label Jobari as a coward for not coming with Chantal; for all she knew Chantal may well have insisted that it would be better if she spoke with her older sister alone.

Hatch folded her arms to demonstrate the sternness she was feeling, waiting for her sister to speak.

"Hi, Hatch. You didn't have to wait up," Chantal said, clearly taking the pretend-nothing's-wrong route.

"And if I hadn't, and I asked you tomorrow morning what time you got in. What would you have said?"

"I guess I am a little late."

"No, Chantal, you're a *lot* late. I gave you a curfew of midnight. It is now twelve-fifty-five A.M."

"I'm sorry. We got to talking, and the time just got away from us."

Hatch unfolded her arms and stood up. "You're going to have to learn not to let the time get away from you, Chantal. And just to make sure it doesn't, next weekend you can stay in the house."

"Hatch!"

Hatch held up a palm to silence her sister. "That's all I have to say, and that's my last word.

No dates with Jobari next week, unless you want to go out in the afternoon."

"You're not being fair, Hatch."

"I don't have to be fair. I'm your guardian, and what I say goes."

"And if we go out next Saturday afternoon? What are you going to do, insist I be in at six P.M.? And if I come in at seven, what are you going to do?"

"I can't believe you'd be silly enough to want to try me, but if you want to, go ahead."

"The point I'm trying to make, Hatch, is that Jobari and I can get into as much trouble during the day as we can at night."

She frowned. *Trouble?* "My preference would be that you don't get into trouble at all. You barely know this boy, Chantal. You've been out with him twice. You don't need to even be thinking about getting into any trouble with him."

"That's not what I meant, Hatch, but since you brought it up, can you honestly tell me that you and Trevor never slept together?"

Her eyes narrowed. "What happened between Trevor and me isn't any of your business."

"Yeah, well, maybe you're jealous that I have Jobari and you've turned into an old maid, pining away for Skye."

Her remark was so unexpected that Hatch was unable to conceal her shock. She drew in her breath audibly, and her mouth fell open. It was all Chantal needed to spur her on.

"Oh, you think I haven't noticed how you always style your hair and put on makeup every Friday when you know he's coming out? You even bought that new outfit for him. You just didn't expect him to invite that girl over. I know Lucien likes you, and I know why you haven't gone out with him. It's because you're holding out for Skye, but he's never gonna ask you out, Hatch. All the girls he dates have good jobs, like that doctor he brought to the church dance and the one he's seeing now."

"Enough! I want you to go to your room right now."

Chantal headed for the hall, her only response a sly smile, a silent way of saying she knew she had hit a nerve.

Hatch blinked furiously, trying to force the puddles in her eyes to dry up. In spite of her efforts a few droplets spilled out and ran down her face in cold, wet streams. She quickly shut off the television and the lights, then went into the sanctuary of Miss Hattie's room, where she lay across the bed atop the white eyelet quilt. She would sleep here tonight; she couldn't bear sleeping in the same room as Chantal.

As she closed her eyes, she thought how ironic it was that she had just a few brief minutes to savor kissing Skye before the heated exchange of words with Chantal. It wasn't the first time newfound happiness disintegrated. She would never forget how she and Trevor, in the bloom of becoming lovers, were relaxing in bed when his younger brother came home unexpectedly and reported to his parents what he'd seen. The Burtons informed her father and stepmother, who were livid and forbade her to see him.

Undaunted, she and Trevor made plans to attend college together, out of town, away from the interference of their families. The following week Daddy's doctors informed him that his leg had to come off. Was her happiness always going to be so short-lived?

Eighteen

Hattie picked up the phone when it rang at four minutes past three, knowing it was Skye. He was on assignment on the West Coast, but he called every day to check on her. She always heard from him daily, whether he was in New York or traveling, but since her brief hospital stay he made the call the same time each day.

She was pleased to learn that Skye and Hatch had gone to dinner in East Hampton after they left the hospital. They mentioned it when they picked her up the next morning, and she liked the affectionate smile Skye gave Hatch as she recounted the excitement of seeing two celebrities up close. Her plan was progressing nicely, but the tension between Hatch and Chantal was a distraction she hadn't planned on. The stilted atmosphere around the house suggested something deeper than Chantal's resentment at being punished for coming in late. Hattie had spoken to both Chantal and Hatch about it on separate occasions, trying to get them to make up, and not believing for a minute that they already had, although they both insisted that was the case.

She only half listened as Skye described the story he was working on. It was Thursday. He was flying back to New York tomorrow and would drive out straight from the airport. Was there anything else she could do to move things along?

The idea hit her like the shock of cold water on her face first thing in the morning. "Did Hatch tell you that the Kirklands invited both of you to a party they're having Saturday night?"

"No, she didn't mention it."

"I think she's apprehensive about going."

"Why's that? She's gotten to know Sheila Kirkland reasonably well ever since Sheila's daughters and Sinclair have been spending so much time together."

"I don't think it's that. I think she feels a little inadequate, because the Kirklands' friends are likely to be professional types. But I'm sure if you went with her it would boost her confidence."

"Sure, Grandma. You know I'll do whatever I can to keep Hatch happy. I know how much she means to you."

Oh, fine. "Can I tell her you're planning on going?"

"Sure, why not? I've got to go now. I'll see you tomorrow night, okay?"

Hattie pursed her lips thoughtfully as she hung up the phone. If Skye wanted to keep Hatch happy only because he was thinking of *her* feelings, then she still had loads of work to do. But she wasn't giving up. That night in the emergency room last Saturday had been uncomfortable, and she'd be doggoned if she'd done it for nothing.

"Oh, that's wonderful," Hatch said when Miss Hattie told her Skye would go with her. "I feel a lot better. Thank you."

"It's no problem, dear. You know that."

Hatch hesitated. "I have to ask you another favor, Miss Hattie."

"And what's that?"

"I need something to wear. Can you help me pick something out? Of course, I don't have a lot of money to spend."

"You won't need a lot. This is the Hamptons, where informality rules. Guests are likely to show up in Bermuda shorts."

Hatch was searching through the racks when Miss Hattie held up a yellow sleeveless dress. "You can never go wrong with a simple sheath," Miss Hattie said.

Hatch moved closer for a better look. The dress, made of an unknown textured material with a modest V neckline and slits on either side, had tiny flowers appliquéd about two inches from the hem. She didn't want Miss Hattie to think her ungrateful, but she didn't like it. "Oh, I don't know. It looks awfully plain, doesn't it?"

"Simplicity is what you want. Remember, it's always better to be underdressed than overdressed."

Hatch eyed the dress skeptically. Still, she had asked Miss Hattie to help her because she trusted her judgment. "Let's look a little more. I'm not crazy about pale yellow. I don't think it does much for my complexion."

"Here's one in fuchsia."

Hatch gasped. It actually was the same dress, but the vibrant shade was much more appealing. It was beautiful.

"I love it," she said.

* * *

Hatch found herself holding her breath whenever she heard a car outside on Saturday. Part of her expected to see Carla Kelly or some other woman drive up to see Skye. Just because he told Miss Hattie he would go to the party didn't mean he wasn't bringing a female companion along, and she couldn't think of a way to ask without feeling foolish.

As the afternoon wore on with no ringing of the doorbell, she began to feel comfortable with the idea of it being just the two of them. It wasn't likely that Carla would come out for another weekend with her friends. Of course, for all she knew Skye could have been seeing Carla or someone else in the city, but not last week while he was on assignment. Everything pointed to her being the only woman in Skye's life since that one quick kiss.

She hoped he'd thought about it.

Skye popped the remaining half of a turkey pinwheel sandwich into his mouth. The gathering at Tom and Sheila Kirkland's home was rather small, perhaps a dozen people. He looked across the room at Hatch, who looked delicious right down to her toenails, which were painted the same fuchsia shade as her dress. From the way she was laughing, he presumed she was finding plenty to talk about with the other women, most of whom were in their late thirties or forties and the mothers of adolescents and teenagers. But as guardian of two teens she could hold her own with any parent.

He hadn't spent any time alone with her at all last Sunday. Sinclair rode with them to pick up Grandma at the hospital, and they all spent a pleasant afternoon playing volleyball in the pool. After dinner he slept for two hours in preparation for the late-night drive back to the city.

He'd thought about Hatch during the lonely drive home, and many times during the week, as well. She had been so charming as she recognized Mary Tyler Moore at the East Hampton restaurant and later, P. Diddy. Somewhere along the course of the evening he'd forgotten all about his new friendship with Carla Kelly. He hadn't even called her since her return from Puerto Rico. Maybe Grandma had been right when she said only one person in a relationship should have to travel, or else it would fail. Or perhaps it was something else, something he couldn't identify. He just didn't have a good feeling about pursuing a relationship with her.

That brought him back to Hatch. He'd always given her credit for staying strong despite the tough breaks she'd gotten, but since he kissed her he realized his feelings ran deeper than mere admiration. He wanted to get to know her better as a woman, not simply as his grandmother's caretaker, someone he wrote a check to every two weeks.

He was happy to escort Hatch tonight, but two people attending a party together when both had been invited didn't really qualify as a date. He remembered her hesitation the first time he invited her to dinner, or, as he had casually put it, "to get something to eat." How would she react if he invited her out and made it clear it was official?

As Hatch looked at the other women present, she felt grateful to Miss Hattie for insisting that she not overdress. While no one wore Bermuda shorts, the mood was definitely casual. There wasn't a tie or a pair of stockings in sight. Most of the women wore summer dresses and sandals, like the inexpensive appliquéd mules she'd found at Kmart. Skye fit right in with the men in the group in his boxy blazer and cuffed slacks.

One of the women's husbands walked over to his wife's side. "Hey, what's with this breaking up into the men on one side and the women on the other?"

His wife slipped her arm through his. "We were just talking about female stuff. I was just about to join you."

That signaled the end of the girl talk, and Hatch watched as Skye approached her. "Having fun?" he asked.

"I really am. I'm so glad you came with me, Skye. I'm afraid that if you hadn't I would be home watching television or reading a book."

"I wouldn't have missed it. I've been thinking about you a lot, Hatch."

"You have?"

"Ever since last Saturday."

She nodded. "That was, as you said, a very emotional day."

"It was, but I can't forget kissing you."

"It really wasn't much of a kiss," she said, immediately regretting it.

"That's easy to rectify."

She breathed deeply, knowing she was on her own. This wasn't a quandary easily solved in the pages of an etiquette book. Her mind turned to the source of so much of her information about life, the movies. She'd seen one where Robert Taylor was a rich guy and Loretta Young was one of the household maids. She couldn't remember much else other than the head butler, the creepy Basil Rathbone, trying devious means to break them up, but true love had won out in the end. But she wasn't thinking about true love, she was thinking about how to handle her boss saying he wanted to kiss her. While she was human enough to feel that this development would shut Chantal up about Skye never looking at her twice, but what would Miss Hattie think?

"Hatch?"

She decided honesty was best. "I don't know what to say."

"I've been invited to a party next week at my producer's. Say you'll go with me."

Hatch paused, still at a loss for words. "You and I were both invited here tonight, Skye. But I don't know your producer."

"I'll introduce you," he replied dryly. "Seriously, Hatch, I think you'll enjoy it."

She shrugged, as much as her nerve-tightened shoulders would allow. "All right."

They said good night to the Kirklands and the other guests and crossed the narrow road. "Did you have a nice time?" he asked.

"Yes. I admit I was a little apprehensive, but people are just people, I guess, when they're at a social function."

"Sinclair and I were talking last week. She said that sometimes she feels lacking—she didn't use that particular word, but I know that's what she meant—around the Kirkland girls when they talk about their experiences. Apparently they've been all over the place—on cruise ships, the Caribbean,

Las Vegas and, of course, all the theme parks in Orlando."

"She's always been sensitive. I was worried about her spending so much time with them because I was afraid she might end up feeling inadequate. I mean, Tom is an ad exec and Sheila teaches at some exclusive private school. Naturally their girls have traveled. I can't blame her; I was hesitant to go over there tonight myself. But Sinclair never said a word to me about it."

"She asked me if I thought she would fit in when she goes to college."

"She did?" That was a surprise, and Hatch wasn't sure she liked her sister confiding in Skye.

He unlocked the gate to the backyard. The moon was a sliver, but the covered bulbs flanking the door to the guest house, as well as the back door of the main house, and pool lights provided minimum illumination. "Let's sit for a minute."

She sank into a patio chair, eager to continue their conversation. "So what did you tell her when she asked you that?"

"I told her there are always kids who are on skintight budgets and have to wait tables right alongside kids whose parents provide them with cars and generous allowances. She might fall in the first category, but as long as she remembers there's no shame in being poor and keeps sight of the fact that the whole reason for going to college is to avoid being poor the rest of her life, she'll be just fine."

She beamed. "I don't think I could have come up with a better answer. Thank you, Skye."

"Nothing to thank me for. I'm glad I could help. In my opinion, too many kids are held back by negative thoughts like 'I'll never fit in, I'll never make it,' and consequently they don't try. Sinclair's a smart girl. And she's ambitious. I think she'll do well."

"I think so, too. But Chantal has me worried."

"Last Sunday she filled me in on what happened between you two. I think she was hoping I would come to her defense, but she was disappointed when I agreed she had it coming."

"She didn't dare get smart with you!" So help her, if Chantal had given Skye any lip, she would *never* get to see Jobari.

"No, but it was clear she didn't like what I said. The whole thing kind of reminded me of my clashes with my grandparents when I was her age."

He looked as if he were enjoying the memory, but thinking about Chantal made Hatch suddenly feel tired. "I'm think I'm ready to call it a night," she said, standing.

"All right."

"You still have your keys out?"

"Yes. But wait a second." He stood, blocking her path.

She sighed. "What is it, Skye? I'm really beat."

He took her hand and led her away from the window, then swiftly pulled her into his arms. But this was no swift touching of lips; it was long, slow, and deep. One of his palms rested on the small of her back, the other on her shoulder. Their tongues mingled, and Hatch forgot her fatigue as it was replaced by a delicious feeling of weightlessness. It wasn't until the kiss ended that she had the presence of mind to hope her sisters hadn't witnessed them. She pulled a tissue out of her purse and dabbed his mouth with it.

"What's that for?"

"You've got lipstick on your mouth. I don't want anyone to see it."

"It's all right; I'm not going in, anyway. I just wanted to tell you good night."

"You certainly did."

Their eyes met as they exchanged heady smiles. He opened the screen door. "Here, let me get this for you." With one motion of his wrist he had the lock undone. "I'll see you in the morning."

She mumbled a good-night and disappeared inside. Their kiss felt so right, but she was flustered and anxious to get away from him before she said something foolish.

Chantal and Sinclair were watching television in the living room, a nearly empty bowl of popcorn set on the coffee table. "How was the party?" Sinclair asked.

"We had a nice time." Hatch noticed Chantal said nothing. *Let her sulk if she wants to.* No one was going to ruin the good time she had or the magic of what had just happened on the other side of the back door. Skye had held her like she was someone to be treasured. She'd never forget it, even if she got to be Miss Hattie's age.

Skye stripped down to his shorts and stretched out on his futon. He hadn't wanted to go in the house and witness more of the frostiness between Hatch and Chantal. Besides, it wasn't safe for him to be around Hatch. After having become so intimately acquainted with her mouth, the urge to familiarize himself with the rest of her body was overpowering.

Ever since they had dinner together in East Hampton, she looked different to him, and he made the startling discovery that Hatch possessed all the qualities he wanted in a woman. Some people would snicker at his interest in her and think he was only out for the physical, but let them. She might not hold a professional position, but she had the drive and ambition to succeed.

He wished he knew how to best handle the situation. If for any reason their changing relationship didn't work out, things would get awfully awkward around the house. Maybe he shouldn't risk it. A failed relationship was difficult enough without complicating matters by getting involved with someone so invaluable to him.

But even as he reasoned with himself he knew he couldn't stay away.

Nineteen

Hatch held a dress in each hand. "Miss Hattie, I can't decide which one to get. Both fit me nice."

"So get them both."

Hatch raised an eyebrow. She hadn't thought of that.

"The price is right, isn't it?"

"Absolutely. I'm so glad you told me about this place. I remember New To You in Tarrytown, but it never occurred to me there was a place like it in Riverhead." Hatch, knowing she couldn't afford a new dress for the producer's party, had confided in Miss Hattie. She didn't want to wear the same dress as she had last week; the evening was too important to her.

As much as she daydreamed about going on a date with Skye, she was worried about the appropriateness of attending the party with him. After all, he was responsible for the roof over her head, and Chantal and Sinclair's, as well. He signed her paychecks. The opportunity to get out of Farmingdale and go to college was something she thought would never happen, and now that it had she didn't want to do anything to jeopardize it. She felt like five feet, nine inches and a hundred and fifty pounds of confusion.

"These type of places are all over. You just have to look for them."

Hatch paid for the dresses, and she held the door for Miss Hattie to exit.

"Why, if it isn't Hattie Jackson! Fancy running into you here in Riverhead."

"Hello, Mavis."

Hatch stood a little apart from Miss Hattie as she greeted her friend, a fair-skinned woman in her late fifties whose ash-brown hair was obviously bottle-bred.

"What brings you to Riverhead? And a store where they sell used clothing? Don't tell me you're buying your things from them."

Hatch raised an eyebrow. What an odd thing to say.

"No, actually I got rid of a few things I know I'll never wear again," Miss Hattie replied calmly.

"Well, that's certainly a relief. I said to myself, 'I'm sure I saw Skye on television just the other week.' But I was concerned when he didn't rent the house this summer. You aren't staying in this town, are you?"

Even Hatch knew that Riverhead, being inland and lacking the posh restaurants and clubs that defined the Hamptons, was no place for summer people. That had to be an insult. She decided she didn't like this woman.

"He bought a place for us, in Westhampton." Miss Hattie turned slightly Hatch's way, then back again. "Mavis, this is my caretaker, Cornelia Hatchet. Hatch, this is Mrs. Clark."

Hatch nodded. "Very nice to meet you, Mrs. Clark." Her eyes narrowed when the woman's eyes swept over her dismissively, lingering on the bag she held.

"Nice to meet you," she said with that same air of duplicity, then returned her attention to Miss Hattie.

"I'm so sorry I can't stay and chat, Mavis, but I've got to get home right away to take care of something. But it was wonderful to see you again. Bye-bye." Miss Hattie linked her arm through Hatch's and fell into step, and the dumbfounded Mavis Clark said a lame good-bye.

"Miss Hattie, I get the distinct impression you wanted to get away from her," Hatch said. "Who was she?"

"She lives in Sag Harbor, on the same street as the house Skye rented the last couple of years. And you're right, I wanted to get away from her. She's a nosy witch, and I don't want to spend any more time talking to her than I have to."

Hatch remembered Skye saying that Miss Hattie hadn't been happy in Sag Harbor. "That really wasn't very nice, what she said about having seen Skye on television. It's like she was insinuating he's not doing very well and you have to buy clothes secondhand."

"It's just sour grapes. Her daughter likes Skye, or at least she did until it became clear he wasn't interested." She sighed. "It's really too bad. For every person who was worth getting to know out there, there was someone else who was only concerned with what your father and grandfather did for a living. I've always detested people who judge you based upon what your family was able to accomplish."

"I'm just happy you brought me to that store, because now I've got two nice dresses to wear. How did you know about that place, anyway?"

Miss Hattie laughed. "My dear, I used to be a

big patron of secondhand buying. I got most of my furniture secondhand years and years ago, and it still looks good. Just because Clarence and I were poor it didn't mean we couldn't have nice furniture."

Hatch's forehead wrinkled. "I don't understand. You and your husband were poor?"

"Of course. We got married in 1935, right in the middle of the Depression. Nobody had any money. We barely got by on what Clarence made as a redcap. Things didn't change until we got in the war. All of a sudden there were jobs everywhere. I remember people who actually were sorry to see it end, because they were making more money than they'd ever made before. Isn't that awful? People were dying all over the world, soldiers on battlefields and civilians of starvation, and all some folks could think about was how much money they were making.

"Anyway, after the war Clarence got on with the GM plant they used to have here, and a couple of years later we were able to buy our house."

Hatch was incredulous. "I never thought . . ."

Miss Hattie nodded. "I think I understand. You think that we always had people helping around the house and summer homes." She laughed. "Far from it. We never went hungry or anything like that, but I worked part-time in a laundry, starching shirts, and for many years we didn't even own a car. I made most of Barbara's clothes. What I couldn't make I bought from the Salvation Army. I got most of our housewares from there, too. When we bought an old '41 Ford, once a year we would drive up to Buffalo, where Clarence had relatives. That's how Barbara met Arthur, Skye's father. But the only reason I live so comfortably now is because Skye can afford to support me. Home care is very expensive, you know. If he worked as an accountant or something I'm afraid I'd be living in a nursing home right about now. And probably with a roommate."

Hatch stared at the corner, not really seeing it. Funny. She'd thought Skye's family always had money.

"That's why I don't really care for people like Mavis Clark," Miss Hattie said. "They're always talking about their fathers were professional men—dentists, attorneys, teachers, doctors. Well, my daddy was a ragman."

"A what?"

"A ragman. He went around in his wagon and asked people if they had any old rags, bottles, or newspapers. Today you would say he was in recycling. But people like Mavis make up their minds about what type of person you are by what your father and grandfather did. They're always very polite to me, of course. After all, I am old enough to be their mothers, and they were raised to respect their elders. But I get a funny feeling that they secretly feel I'm not as good as they are. That's why Mavis was coming up with all that foolishness about being worried that Skye might have suffered a financial blow that meant he couldn't afford to rent a house or buy new clothes. Hmph. I guess I told *her*."

"But she had no problem trying to get her daughter together with Skye," Hatch observed.

"I guess when it comes to the very successful types those snobs are willing to overlook a less than golden pedigree."

"What type of work did your son-in-law do?"

"He was on the Buffalo police force. That's a

respectable profession, but the respectability was only on the surface. But my Skye's a real catch. And when he does settle down he'll never run around. He knows firsthand what the consequences can be." She squeezed Hatch's arm. "Don't mind me. I was just thinking aloud. I don't mean to sound mysterious."

Hatch knew Miss Hattie's veiled comments referred to the circumstances surrounding Arthur Audsley's murder. She couldn't know Skye had shared that with her, and Hatch didn't want to let on that she knew. But she did agree with Miss Hattie on both counts. Those neighbors hung up on family background would view Skye very differently if they knew about the scandalous extramarital affair that had cost his father his life. And because of his father's fate, it was doubtful Skye would ever commit adultery.

All the talk about not fitting in brought her own concerns to the forefront. "Miss Hattie, Skye insisted I go with him to the party at his producer's house, but I'm real nervous about it. I did okay at the Kirklands', but who knows what type of people the producer knows? I'm just afraid I won't measure up, or that they might laugh at me behind my back."

"Well, you can't really help what goes on behind your back. Just remember, it's just a party. You're there to have a good time and meet people. Like you said, you did fine at the Kirklands' the other week, and you'll do it again. Never forget that you can never have too many contacts. You're very good at what you do, Hatch. Caring for old folks like me is an important function. It's too bad it doesn't pay a living wage." She patted Hatch's shoulder. "If I were you I'd make sure everybody there knows what you do. I hate to sound gloomy, but the fact is that your job security isn't very good. That's why you need to make contacts. Skye knows it, too. Why do you think he's so determined you go with him?"

Hatch didn't mind Miss Hattie thinking that Skye was only bringing her to the party to meet potential employers, but the mention of poor job security made her eyes grow damp. "Oh, Miss Hattie, you make it sound like you're planning on leaving us."

"No, dear; I'm not. I'm just talking about the inevitable."

Hattie placed the invitation back into the envelope and set it on her nightstand. This latest turn of events was just what she needed to hasten Skye's getting closer to Hatch.

When Hatch almost shyly told her that Skye invited her to a party at his producer's, she wanted to dance a jig. She'd been only too happy to help her find an affordable dress. Skye still hadn't mentioned it, probably because he didn't want her to think it was a big deal, but she could tell by the way he asked where Hatch was when he arrived this afternoon that he cared for her. His voice had been low and suspicious, his jaw set in stone. His expression convinced her that he was afraid she might be out with Lucien. He relaxed visibly when she informed him that Hatch and Shari Ballard had gone out for dinner and a movie.

Another sign of change was Skye's deviation from his usual routine of showering, changing, and going out for the evening. Tonight he treated Chantal and Sinclair to dinner in the village, along with the "beautiful people," as Sinclair nicknamed the wealthy summer Hamptonites. They'd asked Hattie to join them, but she declined. She took her evening meal early these days, and the last of the salmon cakes Hatch made the night before, along with a salad and some rice, made a satisfying meal.

Now she found herself almost too excited to sleep. Once more she glanced at the small white envelope on her nightstand. Her old friend Grace Moore didn't know it, but she might be responsible for getting Skye's entire future to fall into place.

"So what's Marshall doing tonight?" Hatch asked Shari over an appetizer of hot wings.

"I think he said he might go out for a little while with Lucien."

The mention of Lucien's name made Hatch's cheeks grow warm. She hadn't seen him since that Saturday night he was over for dinner. A few days later he'd called and asked her to dinner, but she'd declined. It hadn't been easy turning him down when he'd asked her for a date, but in spite of her efforts she couldn't stop longing for Skye, and feeling the way she did, she knew it simply wouldn't be fair to him.

"You don't have to feel guilty, Hatch."

"Huh?"

"I said you don't have to feel guilty about telling Lucien you weren't interested."

Hatch stopped chewing. "He told you?"

"He told Marshall. Marshall told me. But Lucien isn't for any woman who wants to get married and have kids. He's been nursing a broken heart for fifteen years."

"I had a feeling something was troubling him."

"Well, maybe I shouldn't say he's been walking around brokenhearted all this time. That makes him sound like he's some kind of a wimp, and he really isn't. It's just that nothing ever develops between him and anyone he's gone out with in all this time, and I think it's related to her."

"Well, what happened, if I'm not being nosy?"

Shari bit into a piece of celery. "I never really understood what happened exactly, but as far as I know he was on vacation in Las Vegas. He met some girl out there, and one night they apparently got too much spirit and impulsively decided to get married. At least, it was impulsive on her part. The next morning she insisted on getting an annulment. But I think he wanted to stay married to her."

"And they never saw each other again?"

"No. She lives out West, and when his vacation was over, he came home. He's been in Westhampton ever since."

"I don't like her," Hatch declared.

"I know what you mean. Lucien's such a sweetheart. I hate to think of him being hurt."

When Skye entered the house Saturday morning for breakfast, Grandma was sitting at the table having a corn muffin and coffee. He kissed her cheek, said good morning, and then announced, "I'm your caretaker today, Grandma. We're going to spend the day together."

"Good. I have some errands to do. But there's

something I need to talk to you about, so have a seat."

He did as she asked, taking a muffin from the cloth-covered basket in the center of the table. "What is it?"

"I've been invited to an anniversary celebration in Connecticut next Saturday."

"Oh? Anybody I know?"

"Grace Moore. Of course, it was her older sister Edna that I was good friends with, but she's been gone for years."

Skye nodded as he buttered his muffin. "Oh, yes. I remember Edna. Mrs. Tuthill, wasn't it? But I don't think I ever met her sister."

"I guess you wouldn't have. She lived in Connecticut from the time she married Fred, and that was sixty-five years ago."

"Sixty-five years! How old are these people?"

Grandma raised her chin defiantly. "For your information, young man, both Grace and Fred are younger than I am. She's eighty-four, and he's around eighty-six, eighty-seven. And you're obviously forgetting that Grandpa and I would have been married nearly seventy years if he was still alive."

"Sorry, Grandma. I didn't mean to insinuate you're a fossil or something."

"Anyway, Grace's daughter says she'll meet my ferry and arrange for all my transportation, and I'd really like to go." She raised her hand palm out when he started to speak. "I've got it all worked out. Chantal and Sinclair can come with me. They've never been to Connecticut. Not that there's all that much to see, of course, but at least there will be other people their age there."

"But where will you stay?"

"I'd like you to book us a hotel room. We can go late Friday and come back Sunday morning. The celebration is a luncheon on Saturday afternoon. You have to realize that people my age aren't much for late nights, but I'm afraid that traveling the same day as the party would be too much for me."

"I don't know, Grandma. I think Hatch should go along with you and the girls."

"Skye, please consider that Hatch hasn't had a day off since she started working for us. Besides, the caterers will need her for prep work. That's why she's not here now. She left right after she took the muffins out of the oven."

"I can go with you."

She snorted. "Oh, sure. I'll bet you'd like nothing better after a week of working than to bring me to Old Saybrook for the weekend so every woman there can offer to fix you up with one of their granddaughters."

He didn't deny how unappealing the idea was. "But I want you to go and have a good time, Grandma."

"I will. Chantal and Sinclair will take good care of me."

Skye couldn't help feeling uneasy. He didn't doubt Chantal's and Sinclair's abilities to handle an emergency at home, but being in a strange location could easily make them disoriented. They were only teenagers, and he didn't feel it was fair to saddle them with too much responsibility. It might be a hard truth, but it was the truth—the bulk of Grandma's care was Hatch's job.

"Skye? I'm waiting."

He tried to stall. "Have you discussed this with Hatch?"

"Yes. Right away she offered to take next weekend off from the caterers, sweet thing that she is, but I told her I don't feel it's necessary. Our transportation is being handled by Grace's daughter and grandson. All we have to do is get to the ferry and get on it."

"What did she say to that?"

"She said that if you gave the okay, she was going to sit the girls down for a serious talk about their responsibilities. But she said she was sure they could handle it."

He began to feel better. He knew Hatch would never go against her better judgment when it came to Grandma's care. The excursion was essentially an uncomplicated one. They would cross Long Island Sound late Friday afternoon and be brought directly to their hotel. Most of Saturday would be filled by the luncheon. Sunday morning right after breakfast they would catch the ferry back to Long Island's north shore, where he and Hatch would meet them. It shouldn't be bad at all.

"All right," he decided. "I just want to be with Hatch when she talks to the girls." He couldn't help thinking that Sinclair, at just fourteen years old, would be a more conscientious guide for Grandma than the good-hearted but more self-centered Chantal.

"Good. I'll call Grace's daughter and let her know we're coming. I already checked with her to make sure it's all right for me to bring two young people with me."

"I'm going to get some coffee," he said, pushing his chair back. It made him happy to see how tickled Grandma was at the prospect of seeing old friends. Who knew when, or even if, she would ever get to see them again if she didn't attend?

Twenty

"Now, I want you guys to have fun," Hatch said. "And remember, Skye always has his cell phone on."

"That's right," Skye agreed.

"Oh, we probably won't even need to call you," Miss Hattie said. "We'll have a fine time, won't we, girls?"

"Yes, you do need to call," Skye admonished. "I want to hear from you the minute you get to your hotel."

"Oh, Skye, you worry too much."

"I mean it, Grandma."

"We'll call," Chantal said. "And you two try not to be too lonesome all by yourselves all weekend," she added with a sweet smile.

Hatch glared at her sister. Leave it to Chantal to make a smart remark. She hadn't been too happy about spending a weekend away from Jobari, especially since last weekend she had to be in by seven P.M., but Hatch didn't regret putting so many miles between the young couple. If anything, she felt the distance would be good for them. She was afraid for Chantal; the teenager's feelings for her first serious boyfriend were much too intense.

* * *

During the drive back to the south shore, Hatch wondered if Skye was going out. She was afraid to ask; she didn't think she could hide her disappointment if he said yes, not while sitting this close to him. Better to just see what he did.

"I don't know about you, but I've got a sweet tooth. Let's stop and get some ice cream."

"I don't think I care for any, but of course if you want to stop . . ."

"Come on, Hatch. Help me put away a banana split, will you?"

So she did. And the ice cream, banana, syrup, and whipped cream were weighing heavily on her tummy when she and Skye got home. "I shouldn't have eaten that, Skye. It feels like somebody dropped a rock in the bottom of my stomach."

"We can take a walk around the block if you want."

"No, I think I just want to sit. You coming in?"

"Yes. Let's see if there's anything good on TV."

They watched James Cagney menace society for two hours in *White Heat* before meeting a fiery end shouting the famous cry of "Top of the world, Ma!"

Skye checked his watch. "They should be arriving at their hotel soon."

"You don't have to count the minutes, Skye. I'm sure they're fine."

"I'm not exactly counting the minutes. But you have to admit Chantal is awfully young for such a responsibility. I got the impression she didn't want to go in the first place."

"She wanted to spend time with Jobari this weekend. It's not enough that they see each other every day at work and that they talk on the phone for hours plus every night after dinner."

"Sounds like young love."

"More like fast love. I'm worried. What'll I do if she gets pregnant?"

"You want me to talk to her? I was a teenager myself, even if it was twenty years ago. I can give her the male point of view."

She considered his offer silently. The last thing she wanted was to stand by helplessly and watch Chantal go down the wrong path. A baby would mean the loss of her job. Babies might be cute and cuddly, but she also knew they could also cry at all hours of the night, and that they wouldn't mix well with anyone as old as Miss Hattie. But she couldn't trust Chantal not to say something impertinent to Skye, not after the cruel statements coming out of her mouth the night she was grounded. Best for her to handle it herself. "That's sweet of you, Skye, but I'm sure I can handle it. Do you mind if we talk about something else?"

"No, not at all."

"I've always wanted to ask you this. You've been all over the country. What's your favorite of all the places you've been?"

"That's a tough one." He grew silent as he thought for a few moments. "As far as cities go, probably San Francisco. But my favorite place is probably the water. For the last couple of years I've gotten together with two friends and chartered a boat. Not one of those fancy multimillion-dollar-yachts, just something comfortable, with three cabins, one for each of us. We've gone to various islands in the Caribbean. This year we're going to the Bahamas."

"That sounds wonderful."

"It'll be especially nice this year. Last year we

didn't go because one of the guys went on a safari instead."

A loud bolt of thunder made Hatch jump. "That was a big one," she said sheepishly.

"Looks like we're going to have a storm. I hope Grandma and the girls are in." He looked at his watch again, as she expected him to do, and the phone began to ring.

"That'll be them," she said. "Hello? Hi. Everybody all right? Good. I'm glad you made it. Skye's been worried." She waved off his wild gestures of objection. "How's your hotel? All right. Put Miss Hattie on so Skye can talk to her." She held out the receiver.

"I'm not worried," he said as he took it.

"You don't have to convince me," she said with a smile.

Skye talked to Miss Hattie for a few minutes. When he hung up he said, "I think it's going to be bad outside. Just before I hung up, I felt a little tingling in my ear from lightning. Do you have candles and matches?"

"Yes. I'll get them out."

"I'm going to go before the rain starts. I've got supplies in the guest house, too."

"Be careful," she said as lightning flashed, turning night into day for a few seconds.

"I will. I'll see you tomorrow. Lock up good." He ran out the screen door. Hatch watched him run across the yard to the guest house, inadvertently shuddering whenever she heard a boom of thunder. She closed and latched the door.

The house seemed so empty with everyone gone, especially with the bad weather outside. She lit candles in the living room and kitchen in case the lights went out, then turned on the television.

Nothing was on that she found even remotely interesting, and the constant thunder kept her from relaxing. She could hear the sound of a heavy downpour through the closed windows.

She stood by the front window. The lightning was more frequent now, and the rainfall so dense she couldn't see across the street. After one particularly clamorous thunderbolt that shook the house, and simultaneous lightning, the room went dark. Hatch whimpered in fear as she jumped back from the window. It sounded like lightning had struck something nearby.

She wished Skye had stayed with her instead of going back to the guest house. She couldn't even reach him; his phone was merely an extension of the one in the house. Besides, it was dangerous to use the phone with all the lightning. Her heart ached for the sound of his soothing voice. It felt creepy being alone. How ironic that she so seldom had time to herself, and now that she did, it looked like a flood was coming.

She decided it wouldn't rain for long; it rarely did when it came down this hard. But twenty minutes later, water still streamed from the sky, and the thunder and lightning hadn't let up. She sat uneasily on the sofa, her knees drawn up to her chest, trying not to quake with each boom.

She drew in her breath when she heard the screen door creak between thunderbolts, as if it were being opened. She picked up a heavy knick-knack from the end table and stealthily crept down through the dining area. Her heartbeat raced in panic. She wasn't hearing things; someone was at the back door, possibly trying to jimmy it open. Skye was right across the backyard, but she couldn't reach him by phone, and with the storm raging outside he wouldn't hear her scream. She had two choices. She could either try to clobber the intruder or call the police, but not from the kitchen phone, which was in plain sight. She'd go around and run to her bedroom, where she could close the door.

She gasped. The door was opening now. She had to hurry. Maybe she could block the bedroom door with a piece of furniture until the police could arrive. She turned and ran toward the hall, holding the sculpture with both hands.

"Hatch?"

Her feet stopped so quickly, she almost tripped over them. "Skye?"

"Where are you?"

She retraced her steps, entering the kitchen through the dining area, pausing to put down the sculpture. He stood just inside the back door, wearing a hooded red poncho dripping with water. Another thunderbolt boomed, and she ran to him as if she'd just been shot out of a cannon, whimpering like an injured animal. Instantly, his arm tightened around her waist.

"I didn't mean to frighten you," he said softly. "If we had another phone line I would have called to let you know I was coming."

"I'm so happy to see you," she said, her arms reaching around his slicker, not caring that the rainwater covering it was getting on her. "I know I sound like a little kid, but I was scared."

He pulled her closer. "Then I'm glad I came. I thought you might need me. Relax, Hatch; it's all right," he soothed. "I think it's time you let someone take care of you for a change."

She felt the softening in his tone; it was so strong she felt she could reach out and touch it. She loosened her grip on his waist, pulling back a little so she could look at him. "Do you really mean that?"

"I really mean it." He pulled her closer with the hand around his waist; his other hand cupped her jaw, simultaneously raising her chin. His mouth closed in on hers hungrily, powerfully. She raised her hands to his shoulders and returned his passion, knowing that a kiss this potent would not be enough to satisfy either of them. And when the thunder rumbled again, as explosively loud as it had been before, she barely heard it.

At last they stopped, if for no other reason than to give their lips a rest. The kitchen was quiet except for the pounding of the rain outside and the equally sonorous pounding of their hearts. "Your clothes are wet," Hatch said with a composure that surprised her.

"And so are yours now."

She hesitated only for a moment before voicing her thoughts aloud. "Maybe we should take them off."

The bedroom was dark, the furniture merely outlined. Hatch appreciated the opportunity for modesty. It had been many, many years since she had been intimate with a man, and she and Trevor were so young then, she couldn't even accurately describe him as a man. But Skye was a man, and she was a woman at the peak of her sexuality. The throbbing at her core reminded her of that every time she was close to him.

They undressed in the darkness, and then he came to her, gently easing her onto the bed. She was a willing player as he proceeded to kiss her senseless, his eager hands searching for pleasure points. Her skin tingled at his touch, and she moaned from the back of her throat. His mouth grazed her ear as he whispered intimacies, sounding very unlike the poised man who presented human-interest stories on television each week.

Then he shifted position, lying across her awkwardly as he reached for something on the floor. "I'm trying to find my pants," he muttered. "Ah. Got it." He pulled out his wallet, then opened it, still breathing heavily from his arousal. "Now, I don't want you thinking I came over here for the express purpose of hoping to make love to you," he said sheepishly as he held up the shiny foil pouch. "It's just that I always carry a few condoms in my wallet, since it goes everyplace I go, and some things you just can't plan on."

She smiled. How like him to make sure he wasn't giving the wrong impression. His consideration was just one of the reasons she loved him. "Skye?"

"Hmm?"

"Kiss me, you fool." She'd always wanted to say that.

The thunder and lightning provided background and lighting as they made love, winding down at the same time their passion peaked. Skye lay on his back, Hatch beside him on her side, his palm resting on her shoulder. He didn't remember the last time he felt so complete, and not just because he was sexually satisfied. He opened his mouth to ask if she felt as happy as he did, but she spoke first.

"Skye, I don't want anyone to know about us." That was the last thing he expected to hear. He removed his arm from her and sat up. "What do you mean?"

"I mean that I don't want anybody to know about us."

"You mean Grandma, Chantal, and Sinclair?"

"I mean *anyone.*"

"What's wrong, Hatch? Are you ashamed of us?"

She shook her head, and he recognized honesty in her eyes. "No, never. I just don't want people gossiping about us, making bets about how long it'll last. And I don't know what your grandmother would say about it. She might not like it, Skye. She might think I've overstepped my boundaries."

He could tell from the way her face suddenly puckered that it was the latter reason that bothered her the most. He took her hand. "Listen to me, Hatch. You can't stop people from talking, no matter what you do. I'm sure people are wondering why I've been turning down invitations. Sooner or later, somebody's going to put two and two together and get four. And as far as Grandma's concerned, I've got a feeling that she's been trying to get us together."

"Miss Hattie trying to get us together! That's the silliest thing I've ever heard you say." She snatched her hand away.

He suspected his grandmother would say something similar if he asked her if she had an ulterior motive in encouraging him to spend time with Hatch. "She knew we went to the party together."

"She thought you brought me so I could meet people who can afford home care for family members, if something should happen to her. She said that herself."

Skye was speechless. He couldn't make himself believe Grandma would object to his seeing Hatch.

She didn't have a snobbish bone in her body. She had said more than once that the people who thought so highly of him would drop him like the proverbial hot potato if they knew about his father's death. But Hatch was genuinely distressed. Their involvement was a sensitive subject for her, especially now that they had become lovers. But couldn't she see it was impossible to hide it? It probably showed every time he looked at her. He embraced her, rocking her gently. "All right, Hatch. I'm feeling pretty good right now, but if you don't want me to tell anyone, I won't. I promise."

He kissed her forehead. It was the right thing to say—the only thing he could say—at least for now.

Twenty-one

Skye flipped a page of the book he was looking at in Barnes & Noble. He was surprised when he noticed he was on page twenty-three. Had he really been standing here browsing all this time? No wonder this historical biography was on the bestseller list; it was fascinating.

He snapped the book shut. He'd better buy it so he could get back to the office before they sent out a search party for him. He had a meeting to attend at two, and he hadn't even had lunch yet. Jack Laughlin hated it when anyone was late, so he'd grab something from a pushcart vendor and munch on the way back to the office.

"In the mood for history today?" asked a female voice.

He glanced around, not sure if the speaker was addressing him or someone nearby. Carla Kelly stood smiling at him. She was the last person he wanted to see, but he couldn't let her guess he felt that way. "Hi there. What are you doing in the city?"

"I'm attending a one-day seminar. I just stopped here to pick up a paperback to go with my Papaya King hot dogs." She held up a paper bag. "I love these things, and we don't have them in Jersey. How've you been, Skye?"

It was a loaded question, one he had to think about carefully before answering so he wouldn't hurt her feelings. He really had meant to call her, had even lifted the receiver once or twice, only to put it down when he asked himself what he was going to say to her and realized he had no answer. "Oh, the same old same old," he said with a shrug, "except more unpleasant, now that it's the dog days of August." He lowered his voice to a level only she could hear. "I've been meaning to call you."

"Because you wanted to see me again, or because you wanted to let me know we wouldn't be seeing each other again?"

Her directness caught him off guard; he didn't know how to respond.

"Don't worry, Skye. I enjoyed myself very much that weekend in the Hamptons, but I had a feeling I might not be hearing from you."

"You did?" He was stunned. How could she have known something he hadn't known himself?

Carla nodded. "I couldn't help noticing how you kept following Hatch around with your eyes at the barbecue on the Fourth. She's the reason, isn't she?"

He raised his right arm to scratch the back of his head. "I don't know what to say, Carla. I feel a little embarrassed." He tried again. "This is all new for me. I don't even think she realizes." The way she was behaving he didn't know what to think. He decided it was best to enjoy the weekend and raise the issue when he got back out to the island on Friday.

Saturday they'd picnicked at Montauk Point and spent another night together, and they were careful not to give anything away when Grandma and the girls returned Sunday morning.

"Well, for heaven's sake, please tell her. You don't want to be like Niles on *Frasier,* admiring his father's health care worker from afar for years. I'm sure television comedy is a lousy example for real life, but he seems to have done all right." She patted his arm. "Good luck to you both."

"Thanks, Carla. You're a doll."

Sinclair sighed. "Hatch, do you know if we're leaving soon? I don't like it here."

"Why not? I know you were disappointed that Chantal had to work today, but there are a bunch of other kids here in your age group."

"They're all a bunch of show-offs. All they do is talk about all the stuff they've got and all the things they do."

Hatch put a reassuring arm around her sister. "It shouldn't be too much longer." Even as she said the words she feared she was being less than truthful. Skye had promised they wouldn't stay long at the Labor Day barbecue at the home of friends of his in Sag Harbor, but they hadn't even been here an hour yet. But she knew exactly how Sinclair felt. She had tried to join a conversation, but soon wished she hadn't. Never in her life had she seen a group of people so absorbed with other people's occupations. While the people at the Dune Road home of Skye's producer congratulated her and wished her well in her quest for a college education, the people here seemed almost shocked at her explanation that she was working as a caretaker companion while going to college. One man actually looked horrified when she named the college she attended. A woman with twinkling eyes and a mouth turned up at the outer corners asked in an innocent voice if Hatch was here with her employer. At that point Hatch merely excused herself, not even bothering to answer the question and stifling the urge to slap that smug smile off the woman's face. She didn't appreciate being the source of anyone's amusement.

"Why don't you go sit with Miss Hattie?" she suggested to Sinclair. "I'll go see if I can tell Skye we're ready to leave."

Skye was talking with two women, one about thirty-five, who met Hatch's approach with a cold stare, and a middle-aged older woman Hatch recognized as Mavis Clark.

"Well, hello there," Mrs. Clark said when Hatch joined them and stood next to Skye, but not too close. "Patch, isn't it?"

"It's actually Hatch. How are you, Mrs. Clark?"

"Oh, just enjoying this beautiful day, like everybody else. This is my daughter, Wendy. Wendy, this is Hatch. She takes care of Mrs. Jackson, Skye's grandmother."

Wendy's unwelcoming glare transformed into a smile as she said hello.

Hatch returned the greeting without smiling. *She doesn't consider me a threat now that she knows I work for Skye.*

"I'll bet you're enjoying summer in the Hamptons," Mrs. Clark said.

"It's very pleasant." She deliberately refrained from saying how the area reminded her of her hometown. A sixth sense told her the less she said to Mrs. Clark and her daughter about herself, the better. She watched uncomfortably as Mrs. Clark's sharp eyes took her in from head to toe, darted to Skye standing next to her and then back again. Was it just her imagination or did the woman seem particularly interested in her rayon print blouse and matching shorts?

"I'll bet you never expected to get out here at all, much less spend a summer. What part of the city are you from?" Mrs. Clark asked.

"I never lived in the city. I'm from a small town in Illinois." Mrs. Clark's raised eyebrows silently conveyed she hadn't expected this response, and Hatch enjoyed the older woman's confusion. Farmingdale was little more than a slum, but Mrs. Clark had no way of knowing that.

"And is that lovely young girl sitting with Miss Hattie your sister?"

"Yes, she is. She's fourteen." She felt herself relax a little bit. At least Mrs. Clark hadn't made the mistake Skye had that day last year, thinking Sinclair was her daughter.

"She should be with the other teenagers, making new friends. Everyone will be going back home this week. Perhaps she can join the Westchester chapter of Jack and Jill and form some lifelong bonds."

Hatch made a noncommital murmur. No way was she going to give this woman the satisfaction of asking what Jack and Jill was, but from the way Wendy discreetly lowered her head and covered her mouth with her hand, like she was trying not to laugh, Hatch knew there was a dig in there somewhere. It was probably some social club for kids from upper-income families, and of course Sinclair wouldn't qualify.

"I meant to tell you, Skye," Wendy said chattily. "I ran into someone you know, the other week on the jitney."

"Really? Who?"

"His name was Chuck something."

"Oh, that must be Chuck Mendehlsson." His next words were directed to Hatch. "You remember Chuck. You met him at the party the other week."

She nodded, noticing Wendy and her mother exchanging quizzical glances.

"Your grandmother is really getting around, Skye," Mrs. Clark said. "I'm so pleased she could join us here today, and she's going to parties, too? How nice for you, Hatch. The more places Miss Hattie goes, the more places you'll get to go so you can make sure she's all right."

"Grandma doesn't go out at night much anymore, unless the church is having a function," Skye said. "*I* brought Hatch to the party. Just the two of us."

Hatch drew in her breath. How could he spill their secret after he promised her not to?

Wendy gasped, and her mother wore an expression that looked like someone just informed her Mike Tyson was building a house next door to hers.

Skye rested a hand on Hatch's shoulder. "If you'll excuse us, I think we should check on Grandma."

"But why are you—isn't that *her* job?"

Skye didn't answer Wendy. Hatch suspected he was pretending he hadn't heard her, not that she cared. She had more important things to worry about. She started as soon as they were safely out of the Clark women's earshot. "Skye! How could you? You *promised* you wouldn't say anything about us to anyone!"

"I'm sorry, Hatch. I couldn't help it. She was

getting on my last nerve. I saw how Mavis was baiting you, trying to make you feel like you were hired
help or something."

But I am *hired help.* "I think we should get Miss
Hattie and Sinclair and get out of here. Too many
people have acted like I'm from another planet,
and I don't like it."

Miss Hattie, still seated with Sinclair, was talking
with an elderly gentleman who sat on her other
side and appeared to be having quite a good time.
"Looks like Grandma's just fine," Skye commented.

Sinclair rose when she saw them coming. "Can
we go now?"

"I don't want to interrupt Grandma. Let's give
her at least another five or ten minutes," Skye said.

Sinclair poked out her lower lip and made a
moaning sound. Hatch had little patience for
whiners, and she was about to tell her sister to cut
it out when she noticed Mavis and Wendy Clark
huddling conspiratorially with several other
women, Mavis glancing their way every so often.
She knew the word was spreading like a puddle
of spilled milk that she and Skye were seeing each
other socially. Her jaw felt like it had turned to
stone, and she realized she was clenching her
teeth. "Excuse me a moment," she said.

She headed for the back door of the house. Earlier she overheard someone asking for the location
of the "water closet," as well as the response they
received. She decided that was just an odd way of
asking for the bathroom. If not, she might embarrass herself and find that the third door on the
right in the hall was some other kind of room, but
she had to have a few moments of privacy to calm

herself down or else she'd get emotional right here.

Hatch looked at herself in the bathroom mirror and was surprised to see she looked normal; she expected the stress she felt to be visible on her face. She dabbed little pockets of sweat from her forehead and upper lip with a tissue, then silently counted to twenty. By then she felt better. If Miss Hattie was still talking, she'd simply go wait in the car. She'd had enough of these people.

Funny. She'd seen *Alice Adams* a dozen times or more, and she always felt like crying herself when Katharine Hepburn, portraying Alice, broke down and cried after being snubbed at a party by the wealthy folks in town, but Hatch never dreamed there would come a time when the same thing would happen to her.

The sound of hushed voices stopped her before she went around the corner leading to the back door.

"Someone should go stand guard."

"You're sure she came in the house?"

"Yes. She didn't ask for directions, just acted like she knew exactly where she was going. You'd think she lived here. Or at least that she'd been invited here."

"That's what happens when you get too close to your staff—they forget their place. Skye Audsley is the most eligible bachelor around. I can't believe he couldn't find a more appropriate date than someone who has to buy used clothing, for heaven's sake."

"I thought that outfit she's wearing looked familiar," someone said with a laugh.

"Well, I think it's awful. I'll bet she acts like she's the lady of his house."

"Suppose she's in one of the bedrooms? Oh, I hope nothing turns up missing."

Hatch held her breath and covered her mouth with her fingers. The hosts were talking about her, concerned that she was on the prowl inside their house. She let her breath out, and tears sprang to her eyes. All these people knew about her was her goals and her present occupation. The host family had smiled at her and welcomed her to their home, but that was when they thought she was one of them, growing up privileged in the suburbs. The moment they learned she was Miss Hattie's caretaker, their attitude changed to one of condescension. And now that they knew Skye was interested in her romantically they felt she wasn't good enough to use their bathroom. How dare they?

She blinked furiously, then allowed herself to come into view, looking straight ahead and holding her head up proudly as she walked past her hosts.

"Hatch, what's wrong? And don't tell me nothing."

"Nothing."

Skye let out an exasperated sigh. "I don't get it. I know Mavis Clark was her usual intolerable self, but that's just how she is. She was the main reason why Grandma wanted to spend the summers somewhere else. She's just trying to fix me up with her daughter. As soon as Grandma was finished talking, we left. End of story. I don't understand why you're so upset now." He paused a beat. "Why *are* you upset?"

"It's nothing."

He was beginning to lose patience. "Damn it, Hatch, will you talk to me?"

"All right." She cast an anxious glance toward the house, and he knew she didn't want Grandma to hear them. Chantal was out with Jobari, and Sinclair was bike riding with the Kirkland kids. He and Hatch were having drinks by the pool as the sun set on what for many was the last night of the summer season. "You and I will never work out, Skye."

"What are you talking about?"

"I overheard our hosts talking when I came out of the rest room. They said such cruel things. They thought I might be in the bedrooms stuffing my pockets with their belongings. They said I was too bold, just walking into their house without asking permission."

His eyes narrowed in anger, but she wasn't finished.

"They said I was acting like a guest, not someone who was there because I was working. They said the help tends to forget their place when they get cozy with their employers." She couldn't repeat what they said about her thrift shop clothing; it was too painful.

Skye cursed with a venom she found surprising. "I'd expect that type of behavior from Mavis and Wendy, but not from the others. I'm so sorry, Hatch. I wished you had told me."

"I didn't want trouble. I just wanted to leave. What's wrong with them, Skye? Have they lived within their own social circle so long that they don't realize there are decent people out there who maybe haven't had all the advantages they'd had? I'm working my butt off trying to get my degree. I've never stolen anything in my life, and

I've never tried to live off any man." The mournful theme music from the movie *Ruby Gentry* played in her head, and she remembered its signature line: Ruby Gentry was from the wrong side of the tracks, and the townspeople never let her forget it. The people at the barbecue had that same attitude. Someone in the film accused Ruby of "sashaying in from the swamp, thinkin' you're good as anybody." Well, she didn't come from the swamp, but a woman from a nowhere town in Illinois walking off with the most eligible bachelor around wasn't going to be stood for. Ruby didn't have a happy ending when she snagged the richest man in town, and Hatch suspected she wouldn't either if she stayed with Skye.

"I think you just answered your own question. But you mustn't let it come between us, Hatch. I think we've got something really special that's just beginning. We never have to see those people again. After the way they acted, I'm through with them."

"No, Skye, it just won't work. I'm sure now that everyone at the producer's house was thinking the same thing, wondering why you're going out with me when you can have doctors and lawyers and"—her voice dropped to a whisper—"chemical engineers." She spoke a little louder as she continued. "They were just too polite to say it. I don't have to accidentally overhear them discussing it. It's knowing they're thinking it that I can't bear. If you're with someone of your own caliber, you won't have this problem." *And I need to find myself a nice accountant or somebody.*

He couldn't believe it. In the last week he'd been happier than he'd been in months. He was looking forward to convincing her how futile it was to keep their liaison under wraps, and once she agreed, to spend more time with her now that she was returning to Tarrytown, even take her along on his upcoming vacation, and now she was telling him to forget it?

He fought to keep the desperation he felt out of his voice. "It's only a problem because you make it one, Hatch. You're letting other people's thoughts run your life, and consequently mine. I don't give a damn about 'caliber,' as you put it." He grabbed her hand and cupped it in both of his. "I never should have agreed to keep us a secret."

"You didn't keep us secret, remember?"

"I know. But I don't think this would have happened if we'd been more open. That way everyone would have known about us before the barbecue."

"A juicy piece of gossip like that would spread fast, I guess," she said dryly. She gently pried his fingers away and freed her hand. "Bottom line, Skye, is it won't work. You asked me what was wrong, and I've told you. I'm going to turn in. Good night."

He watched her disappear inside the house, but made no move to go after her. It was useless to try to do anything now; her hurt feelings were too raw. Best to hold off and try to reason with her next week.

Twenty-two

Hatch was pleased to hear Miss Hattie, Chantal, and Sinclair rave about the dinner she'd made. She'd tried a new chicken casserole, quite a simple one, actually, with cream of mushroom soup, onion dip mix, and rice. Miss Hattie commented that it tasted like a Sunday dinner, even though it was Thursday.

Cooking, along with her studies, had been Hatch's salvation since they'd been back in Tarrytown. Trying new recipes and the chopping, slicing, and careful measurements of the ingredients involved helped keep her thoughts away from Skye. She'd seen him since they'd been back, of course. He continued to visit each week, usually on Sunday, taking Miss Hattie, Chantal, and Sinclair out for an early dinner. By the time Hatch arrived home from work he was generally getting ready to leave, so their contact was minimal. She preferred it that way, and she had a feeling he did, too.

The one exception was her thirty-third birthday, when they waited for her to come home and took her to Ruth's Chris Steak House for a surprise birthday dinner. Sinclair had brought along gaily print cardboard hats, the kind children wore at birthday parties, and insisted they all wear one.

They went along with it, evoking curious glances from the other patrons of the restaurant.

The celebration caught her off guard, for her actual birthday was the following day. Looking at the caring, loving faces of her sisters, Miss Hattie, and especially Skye was suddenly too much, and as she tried to thank them, her voice broke and she couldn't go on. Skye was at her side in an instant, and she was only too happy to allow herself to savor his comforting embrace, to inhale his familiar scent, for once not caring what anybody thought. At that moment the wait staff brought out a chocolate cake with lit candles atop it. As they sang the birthday song, Hatch could only think about how good Skye's arms had felt around her. She never thought she'd embrace him again, and for the first time she wondered if she'd done the wrong thing by terminating their budding relationship.

She summoned enough breath to blow out the candles. Choosing a wish was easy. *If I was wrong, give me the chance to make it up to him.* "This is the nicest birthday I've had in a long time," she said when she could finally talk.

"Well, since it's not actually your birthday until tomorrow, we decided to wait and give you your gifts then," Miss Hattie said. "We wanted to save something so the actual day would be special."

"That's fine. I don't think I could take any more wonderful things happening to me today, not after this." She would remember this birthday for years to come. Funny how she kept her happiest moments alive in her memory bank, revisiting them like a favorite movie. The way Chantal, Sinclair, Skye, and Miss Hattie fussed over her made her feel special and loved. Skye and Miss Hattie were more than the people she worked for; they had become her family, and she loved them both. Miss Hattie was like the grandmother who had been Hatch's namesake that she barely remembered. And Skye . . . She loved him like a spouse.

She didn't get to talk to him alone that night; after bringing them home he left because it was late. When she woke up the morning of her actual birthday, she decided it didn't matter. She'd simply gotten caught up in the emotion of having such a pleasant surprise, to the point where she wasted her birthday wish. But nothing had changed. No way had she made a mistake.

She cleared her throat, determined to get him out of her thoughts any way she could. "Well, I'm glad everyone enjoyed it," she said, rising from the breakfast table. "I'm going to leave for school. I'll see you guys later."

"Before you go, Hatch, do you have a stamp?" Chantal asked.

"I just gave you a stamp yesterday. Anyone would think you had bills to pay."

"I wrote another letter to Jobari."

"Didn't you just mail a letter to him yesterday? And the day before?"

Chantal shrugged. "It's not like we can talk on the phone. At least not that often."

"Oh, young love," Miss Hattie said dreamily.

"All right," Hatch said. "Let me get my purse. I just hope all this letter-writing isn't going to interfere with your grades."

"It won't. But Jobari wants me to come out for a weekend."

"Oh, he does?"

"He said he's sure it'll be okay with his parents."

"I'm glad he's so sure. Listen, Chantal, I don't dislike Jobari, but don't you see something wrong with this picture? You're asking me for stamps just about every day, but I get the mail and I've only seen an occasional letter come in from him. And I don't see him getting on the Long Island Railroad to come see *you*."

"That's because he knows you won't let him stay here."

"Of course I'm not letting him stay here. We live here, Chantal, but it's not our home." Out of the corner of her eye she saw Miss Hattie shake her head in obvious disagreement, but her main focus was Chantal.

"You're just making an excuse, Hatch. If I'd gotten pregnant, you wouldn't be trying to keep us apart."

"What I was going to say was that if he wants to come for the day that's fine. But go ahead, Chantal. Get pregnant, marry him, and move to a place that's probably as dismal as Farmingdale except three months out of the year, when the wealthy people from the city pour money into the local economy. The water park closed Labor Day. Is Jobari even working now?"

"He got a job at a supermarket, doing stock."

"He stocks shelves at the supermarket. Chances are he'll still be doing that ten years from now, and beyond that. Maybe you can get a job checking people out. It's hard to support a family on low-wage jobs, Chantal. You'll be like I was in Farmingdale, standing on the outside envying those who live lives you can only dream about, and getting older every year while nothing happens to you." Desperate, she tried another tack. "You've been away from Farmingdale less than a year, Chantal. You're only sixteen years old. When I was sixteen, I had my whole life in front of me. I was going to do so much. But as you know, I just stayed in Farmingdale, driving to Bradley for work, and imagining what all the Kmart customers' lives were like." Wistfully, she added, "I'd give anything to have those years back."

Sinclair's gasp and the stricken look on Chantal's face made Hatch realize her statement sounded like she wished she had left them on their own. "I'm not saying I regret taking care of you and Sinclair and Daddy," she said quickly. "You're my family. I love you. What I'm saying is that you can't always control what happens to you. If you have a child at this point in your life you'll have to delay going to college, and you might not ever get there." She glanced at her watch. "I'm late. I have to go."

She thought about Chantal and Jobari as she drove to her class. She supposed she should be glad someone's love life was going so well, since hers was such a bust. Every time she saw Skye she was reminded of that one blissful weekend they spent together. When she shut her eyes she could practically feel his hands and mouth roaming her body, a squeeze here, a kiss there. It never failed to make her breath catch in her throat and her toes curl. The memory of those two days and nights would be with her for years, and possibly forever. It would only dissolve if she found herself able to love another man the way she loved Skye. For now, all there was for her to do was continue to earn her keep and to do the best she could at school, so when it came time for her to move on with her life, she could with preparation, satisfaction . . . and no regrets.

* * *

Hatch rushed for the phone as soon as she heard the ringing, for Miss Hattie began dozing on the sofa after lunch, and Hatch didn't want her disturbed. "Hello."

"Hatch, it's Skye. I'm glad you answered. I've been trying to reach you."

Her body tensed at the sound of his voice. "Miss Hattie's taking a nap."

"Good. I'm going to need your help planning her birthday party. Grandma's going to be turning ninety October twenty-ninth, you know."

"I know. How can I help?"

"I want you to help me plan it."

She frowned in confusion. "Help plan it? I'm not trying to be uncooperative, Skye, but I can't help thinking that you managed just fine by yourself with the barbecue on July Fourth."

He hesitated before replying. "Actually, I was hoping you could contact some restaurants for me. Get some menus and some prices."

"I can do that. Who did you want me to call?"

He named several places, adding, "They're all local hotels, which should be convenient for people coming from out of town. Tell the catering department you'd like a buffet featuring both chicken and beef dishes."

"All right, but you know her favorite place is the Italian restaurant right here in Tarrytown."

"I thought about that, but you know a lot of people don't like Italian food, other than spaghetti. You can't go wrong with chicken or beef."

She hadn't thought of that. *So much for my party-planning ability.* Just another example of how inappropriate she was for him romantically. "How many people and what date?"

He named the date. "Tell them roughly fifty to

seventy-five. I'm still working on the list. I need you to get on this right away, Hatch. I'm sorry to say that I'm a little late getting started."

"I'll start calling now. But I hope everyone has that date open. It seems to me that October is a popular month for weddings." The last word stuck in her throat.

"That's true, but most weddings will have a hundred or more guests. Our group can get by in a relatively small banquet room."

"Yes, of course." Her smile diminished. She was hopelessly out of her league. Dr. Diana would have known that. So would Carla. So would Wendy Clark. Anyone with the proper background and experience.

"If you can take care of that for me, I'll start checking into entertainment."

"Entertainment?"

"Yeah, music. We have to have music. I don't want to just sit and have dinner. Ninety's a real milestone, and everybody doesn't get to see it."

"Skye, does Miss Hattie know about this?"

"No. I think I'd rather just surprise her, tell her to get dressed up, that we're all going to dinner."

"You don't think it'll be too much for her? I mean, she is turning ninety."

"Oh, she'd figure it out the minute we head for a banquet room instead of a restaurant, so I'll have to tell her anyway. But she doesn't have to know about it until we're in the car and on our way. I don't see why Chantal and Sinclair should know about it before that. You know what blabbermouths kids their age can be."

"I won't say anything to them. But what about Mrs. Williams next door? She's no teenager, but

I've got a feeling she might have trouble keeping the secret."

"Good point. I'll call her and ask her to please not spill it. I guess I'd better include a few words of caution for the church people, too, with their loose lips. I'll make a decision about where the party will be and get out the invitations next week, before I leave for vacation."

"Vacation?"

"Yeah, the boat charter I told you about. Me and two friends. I'll be gone a week."

"Oh, yes, I remember."

"Oh, Hatch, take down my fax number, will you? Ask the hotels to come up with some sample menus and fax them to me."

"Sure."

Skye took in the view of the resorts lining Nassau's Paradise Island. Hatch would have loved this. The water was so much clearer and brighter in this part of the Atlantic than it was off Long Island. People on the beaches could see their feet through the green water, and sometimes be tickled by tiny fish swimming by.

He had wanted to bring her along. He knew he could rely on Norma Williams to look in on Grandma in the mornings, and of course Chantal and Sinclair were home from school before three. Hatch was certainly a good enough student to be able to make up the work she missed. She deserved a vacation, and she seemed so interested when he told her about it.

He had intended to ask her, but his plan extinguished when she pleaded with him to keep their involvement secret. He was determined to coax her out of that opinion, but nothing had been the same between them since the Labor Day fiasco. Instead of enjoying a relaxing trip with the woman he loved, spending some time away from the family members they both loved, he found himself alone for the first time since he and his friends had been chartering a boat.

"Don't sweat it, Skye," Zack Warner said, patting his back. "Everything will work out. True love always does."

"Yeah, maybe. How's Desirée doing, anyway?" He had briefly dated the former Desirée Mack, a travel consultant who fell in love with her boss, Zack's childhood friend Austin Hughes, "Ozzie" to his friends, to whom she was now married. "Having a baby, I'll bet."

"Not that I've heard. But Desirée's mother just married the fellow she's been dating, a retired judge, I hear. And a coworker of theirs is engaged to a woman he can barely talk to."

"What're you talking about?"

"I mean it. Ozzie's partner Phil was inspecting a hotel in Brazil with his wife, and they met this woman who cleaned rooms. They found out this woman came to work at the hotel after the family she baby-sat for on a live-in basis moved to another city. She had nowhere to live and was sleeping in one of the hotel rest-rooms. They offered her work taking care of their new baby and paid for her to fly to Colorado. That's how she met this other dude, Mickey, who works for Phil and Ozzie. They fell in love even though her English skills are limited, and Mickey doesn't speak Portuguese. I'm tellin' you, Skye, it's in the ozone."

"Wait a minute. How do they communicate if they can't talk to each other?"

"Apparently, they manage. Let's hope she really understood his proposal. I'd hate for it to turn out that she thinks he asked her to go to Vegas for the weekend instead of making a lifetime commitment. It's the craziest thing. This guy was a real Lothario, and Ozzie and Desirée are blown away at him being won over by a woman he's known for only a few months and who can barely speak English." He nudged Skye in the ribs. "I'm sure there'll be broken hearts all over New York when your lady gets you to, ah, retire."

"I don't know if that'll happen. It's complicated, Zack."

"Listen, Desirée worked for Oz, and technically, she still does. They opened a phone division which she runs, but it's owned by Austin and his partner, Phil. Mickey is marrying Phil's au pair. And since you mentioned complications, consider that Phil and his wife will have to find somebody else to change their baby's diapers. I see no reason why—what's her name?"

"Her real name's Cornelia, but she goes by Hatch."

"I see no reason why you shouldn't marry Hatch. At least you don't have any corporate hassles. Hell, you won't even have to find someone else to take care of your grandmother. And you won't have to pay Hatch anymore for taking care of family if she's your wife."

"Zack, you're twisted."

"Tell me I'm wrong."

Skye couldn't tell him that.

He thought about what Zack said as he tossed his fishing line into the water, a sun visor shielding his eyes from the late September sun. The activity on Paradise Island was a welcome change from the serenity of quiet Eleuthera, the Bahamian island where they spent the past two days. He certainly looked forward to the change of pace. Those quiet nights in Eleuthera, with its deserted beaches and romantic moonlight, were meant for love . . . and his love wasn't here. Zack and their other buddy, Ben Freeman, had their partners, but he was alone.

Ben and Joyce had been married about twelve years. They had two daughters, and Joyce was every bit as shapely now as she'd been the day they were married. If anything, the pregnancies made her more curvy. Skye liked being around the Freemans, and he wanted that feeling of comfort and contentment they so obviously had.

But Zack, like himself, usually brought a different companion every year. It had come as a huge surprise to learn his friend was settling down. Zack had made the most of his appeal to the ladies, but now it looked as though the E.R. physician so many women adored would be saying a final farewell to bachelorhood.

Skye glanced at Vivian St. James, who with Joyce Freeman was relaxing on a float in the ocean, her eyes closed and her ankles crossed. The sun caught the diamond of her glittering engagement ring, as well as the water surrounding her. With Zack's recent engagement, Lucien Ballard was the only single friend Skye had.

Skye knocked on his grandmother's front door to let them know he was coming in before he unlocked the door. "Anybody home?" he called, although the Marquis was parked outside.

Sinclair jumped up to give him a hug. "Hi, Mr. Skye! Did you have a nice vacation?"

"I sure did. Where's everybody?"

"Hatch is making breakfast, and Miss Hattie's helping. Chantal's not downstairs yet."

"Yes, I am. Hi, Mr. Skye," Chantal said sleepily as she came down the stairs, tying her bathrobe around her waist.

"Good morning, Chantal. You girls come in the kitchen with me. I want to see Grandma and Hatch before you open your souvenirs."

"Ooh, souvenirs!"

In the kitchen Skye hugged his grandmother and said a carefully controlled hello to Hatch, who looked delectable in a tie-dyed sleep shirt, its side slits allowing a generous peek at her firm brown thighs.

"How was your vacation?" Grandma asked.

"Nice, but it seemed like something was missing."

"I want to hear all about it," Hatch said.

He shrugged. "I caught some fish, did some swimming, parasailing, relaxed on the beach, gambled at the casino . . . that's about it. Breakfast almost ready?"

"That's what I like about you, Skye. You're so to the point. I'm still making pancakes. It'll be about another fifteen minutes. Hey, no fair," Hatch said when he reached for the oven door. "We have to wait for them all to be done so we can sit down together. Miss Hattie insists."

"All right. I picked up some gifts for you guys. You might as well open them now. Can you hold off cooking for a few minutes and come into the living room?"

"As soon as this batch is done."

* * *

His hands shook as he handed them their respective bags. In about three minutes it would all be over. He was taking a tremendous chance, and he knew it. But he couldn't stand Hatch acting like they should be ashamed of their involvement. He was in love, and he wanted to shout it from the rooftops.

Chantal and Sinclair squealed in delight when they removed their T-shirts and compact straw purses. Grandma dabbed her new perfume on the back of her wrists, saying her usual "Skye, you shouldn't have." But his eyes were glued to Hatch as she removed the tissue paper around her gift.

"Oh, isn't this pretty," she said, holding up the shell-covered box. "I can keep my jewels inside."

"It's too small for a jewelry box," Grandma said.

"I don't have much jewelry. Everything I have should fit in here very nicely." She opened the box and gasped. Her head sprang up like a jack-in-the-box to look at him, disbelief in her eyes.

"Yes, it means what you think it means," he said.

"What's going on?" Chantal asked.

Grandma, sitting next to Hatch, leaned over and looked inside the box. She drew in her breath and placed her palm on her heart.

"Miss Hattie, I don't know what to say," Hatch said.

"Will somebody tell me what's going on?" Chantal repeated impatiently.

Ignoring her, Hatch asked Grandma, "Are you all right?"

Chantal got up and took the box from Hatch's hand. "Oh, wow! This looks like an engagement ring. From you, Mr. Skye?"

"An engagement ring!" Sinclair was up in an instant.

Skye moved to stand in front of Hatch. "Grandma, I hope I haven't shocked you, but the fact is that in just the last few weeks I've fallen in love with Hatch, and I believe she's fallen in love with me. If she hasn't, I'm about to suffer the greatest humiliation of my life." He held out his hand before Hatch. "I just spent a miserable week on a vacation I generally enjoy, all because you weren't with me. I'm fed up with all this foolishness. I want to marry you, Hatch, and I don't give a damn what anybody says or what anybody thinks. I've been waiting for you for a long time, and I'm not letting you get away."

When she smiled at him with tears in her eyes, he knew she was his, even before she placed her hand in his.

"Well, it's about time."

Hatch turned to her, an astounded look on her face. "What did you say, Miss Hattie?"

"I said it's about time. I've known ever since last December that you two would be perfect for each other."

Chantal and Sinclair stood with their arms around each other, nervously wavering back and forth. "Hatch. You didn't give an answer," Chantal said.

"Yes, Hatch, you didn't give me an answer," Skye repeated.

She stood up and threw her arms around his neck. "Yes, yes," she said joyously.

Skye pressed his palms into her back and kissed her with all the hunger he'd kept stored inside for weeks. "Come on, girls," he heard Grandma say, "let's go finish making breakfast. Into the kitchen. Hurry it up, now."

"But I don't understand, Miss Hattie," Sinclair said as they left the room. "When did all this happen?"

"When we were in Connecticut, silly," Chantal answered. "I *told* them not to be lonely without us."

Skye and Hatch were sitting silently on the couch, her head against his chest and her hand in his, when Sinclair announced, "Breakfast is ready."

Hatch held out her left hand in front of her. Her ring was so beautiful. She'd have to take better care of her nails; it wouldn't do to have them broken off and uneven now that it was adorned with a ring she would wear the rest of her life. "I've been such a fool, Skye."

"It's all over with. We'll go forward from right now. Let's go eat."

And when they were all seated around the dining room table, Hatch said, "I guess I need to apologize to everybody for being so secretive. I pleaded with Skye not to tell anyone we were seeing each other. I was afraid people would laugh at us. And most of all, I was afraid Miss Hattie wouldn't like it. I was right about people snickering, at least some of the ones out on Long Island, but Skye tried to convince me you wouldn't object. I wouldn't believe him."

"Of course I don't object. You girls are my family, and now it's going to be official. I couldn't be happier."

"Grandma, I'm wondering about something, especially since you said you felt Hatch and I were perfect for each other," Skye said. "That afternoon we took you to the hospital, I expected you to refuse when the doctor recommended you stay overnight, but all you did was insist I take Hatch to get some dinner. Did you fake being ill?"

Miss Hattie waved him off. "Let's not talk about that now. We have a wedding to plan. Now, I figure we can announce the engagement at my birthday party."

Skye cast a stricken look at Hatch.

"I didn't tell her," she said.

He cast a suspicious eye on Chantal and Sinclair. "What party?" they asked simultaneously.

"Grandma, who told you what I was planning?"

"A couple of people at church."

Skye slapped the table with his palm. "And I put special instructions in with the invitations asking them not to say anything."

"You know how people gossip at church," Miss Hattie said nonchalantly. "Now, when we will have the wedding?"

Chantal and Sinclair both had opinions about that, but Hatch barely heard them. She gazed at Skye across the table. They really were a family now, and would be from this day forward, for the rest of their lives.

Epilogue

Hatch rubbed her damp palms together. Her hand went to her cap, making sure it was secure for about the fifth time in as many minutes, before smoothing down the sash across her front that distinguished her as an honors graduate. She couldn't help being nervous. It wasn't every day that she graduated from college.

The graduates would enter the chapel in pairs alphabetically, and she and Justin Barker would lead the group. As she stood in the doorway, all she could see was a blur of cameras held to the faces of the family members and friends, and especially the large camera hoisted in front of the platform capturing the entire ceremony on videotape. She stood on tiptoe, hoping to catch a glimpse of her family, but didn't see them.

It was time to begin. Flashbulbs lit up in her face as the guests snapped photographs. She looked straight ahead to protect her eyes. She could hardly believe it. At age thirty-five, she had earned a bachelor's degree. In two weeks she would begin work as a draftsperson.

She clapped enthusiastically at the end of the valedictorian's speech. She would have loved to have achieved that pinnacle, but it was enough for her to be among those at the top of the class.

When they called her name to get her diploma, she saw little Henry raised in the air, held securely by two feminine hands. That Chantal, she thought as she blew a quick kiss to the waving child. Chantal adored Henry. The rest of them usually intervened when she constantly let him have his way.

When the class filed out to the music of the recessional, Hatch fingered her diploma. Daddy and Anna Maria would be so proud of her. Their absence was the only blemish on the day.

Once in the large reception area, the graduates congratulated one another and looked for their loved ones. Their graduating class was small, less than fifty people, but there were easily six times that number of people filling the room. Eight of her most nearest and dearest were here . . . if she could find them.

Then she saw Skye frantically waving to catch her attention and she moved through the crowd as quickly as she could to meet him.

"You did it, Hatch! I'm so proud of you," he said as he wrapped her in a bear hug.

Her voice came out muffled against his chest. "I'm so happy, Skye."

She recognized Chantal's impatient voice. "Hey, Skye, can the rest of us say congratulations, too?"

"Of course." He kissed Hatch on the mouth before releasing her. "I'm just so proud of my wife I don't know what to do."

"I'm so proud you're proud," Hatch replied, smiling at him dreamily. He was even more handsome now with a sprinkling of gray at his temples. His hairline had dipped back in inverted crescents on the sides of his head, but seemed to have stabilized, just as his grandmother predicted.

"Oh, I'm going to be sick," Shari Ballard said

playfully. "You guys have been married for what, going on two years? You're not newlyweds anymore. It's about time for the mushiness to wear off."

Hatch embraced her friend. "Can I help it if we're still as much in love now as we were then?" She greeted them all one by one and accepted their congratulations: Marshall, Sinclair, Chantal, and Miss Hattie, who stood with her arm linked through Sinclair's. "Are you okay, Grandma?" she asked. Just as Chantal and Sinclair dropped the "Mr." preceding Skye's name when he and Hatch got engaged, Miss Hattie became "Grandma" to them at the same time.

"I'm fine. This graduation was my favorite kind; it was over in forty-five minutes. Those wooden benches are hard on my backside. At least when Chantal finished high school, the chairs were comfortable."

"I'm just glad you were here with us," Hatch soothed.

"I wouldn't have missed it. I'm planning on sitting right up front when Sinclair graduates, and for the college graduations, as well."

"Four more years," Chantal said mournfully. "That's a lifetime."

"Break it down into semesters, and it won't seem as long. You already finished your first one," Hatch said.

"Hey, Hatch, aren't you forgetting somebody?" Sinclair said.

Henry Audsley, seven months old, squealed at that moment, as if he knew his aunt was talking about him. "Hi, Poopah," Hatch cooed to her son, taking him from her sister's arms. "Mommy saw you waving when she got her diploma. I'm so glad you weren't bored, like your sister." She peered at the double stroller where Anna Maria, Henry's twin, lay sleeping.

"Let's see your diploma, Hatch," Sinclair said. She unrolled the rolled document Hatch handed her. " 'Bachelor of Science Degree awarded to Cornelia Audsley,' " she read. "You going to frame this?"

"I sure am. I already bought the frame."

Marshall Ballard, who had wandered off, rejoined them, biting into a piece of pink-frosted cake. "They're serving refreshments over there," he said through a full mouth.

"We've got food at the house. Peggy fixed a spread for us. If everyone's ready we can go," Skye said.

"Let's go," Chantal said. "I asked Aaron to come over, and I don't want to miss him."

Hatch met Skye's eyes. Chantal's romance with Jobari had run hot for a while, but the distance eventually burned it out. There'd been countless crushes since then, some of which were early casualties and none of them lasting beyond a few months. She was concentrating mostly on her studies at the state university in nearby Purchase. Sinclair, on the other hand, was now a high school junior and too busy with her studies and activities to have a boyfriend.

Twenty minutes later they pulled into their driveway. The house was all lit up for the upcoming Christmas holidays.

When they got married, they'd had no choice but to sell Grandma's residence of over a half century; they all had to live under the same roof, and that house wasn't big enough. After much searching, they found another house right in town, with an in-law suite and bath on the first floor for Grandma, a master suite and two more bedrooms upstairs, plus an attic waiting to be remodeled when it was time for Henry and Anna Maria to have their own rooms.

Hatch and Skye were married just shy of Skye's fortieth birthday, and they agreed to start a family right away. The twin delivery went undetected until just before their birth. It made for some frantic last-minute shopping, but the timing had been perfect. Hatch's labor pains started right after she took her midterm exams. She missed the first week of the new semester, but she eventually got caught up.

Peggy Walker met them at the door, carrying a bowl from the kitchen. In her late forties, Peggy had spent fifteen years working as an aide at a nursing home. She started working for them the week after the twins came home from the hospital, caring for them as well as Grandma while Hatch was at the morning classes she switched to after her marriage.

"How does it feel to have it all, Mrs. Audsley?" Peggy asked Hatch after offering congratulations.

"It feels pretty doggone good, Peggy. But wait until your son graduates, and he'll tell you himself." Peggy's nineteen-year-old son was a student at the same college Hatch just graduated from. "Oh, look at this!" Hatch exclaimed as she took in the food on the dining room table. Peggy had baked a ham garnished with brown glaze, pineapple, and maraschino cherries, and she also made potato salad, baked beans, and macaroni and cheese, with a marbled pound cake in the center of the table.

It was already going on nine o'clock, and since

it was a Tuesday night, their celebration broke up within an hour. Peggy, who had stayed late to prepare the food, left shortly after they returned. Grandma went to bed, the Ballards went back to the city, honor society member Sinclair said she wanted to do some studying, and Chantal bid a reluctant good-night to her latest boyfriend.

Hatch bathed Henry first, and Skye put him down while she bathed Anna Maria, who was now wide-awake. "I can manage from here. Why don't you go in, and I'll see you in a few minutes?" she told him.

"All right." Skye kissed his baby daughter. "Nighty-night, precious."

After Hatch put Anna Maria down in her crib, she sat in the semidarkness, the room lit only by a dim night-light, and gazed lovingly at her children as Henry slept and Anna Maria played with her toes. Peggy said earlier that she had it all, and Hatch had to agree. She had a loving husband, two healthy children, a beautiful home, and the career she'd always wanted waiting for her. Chantal and Sinclair were both doing fine, and so was Grandma at age ninety-two.

Daddy was right. Not only hadn't it been too late for her to leave Farmingdale, but she found a husband who understood not only her commitment to her sisters but also her fervent desire to have a career.

Maybe in the end she'd decide she'd rather stay at home with Henry and Anna Maria, but she could always do that if she changed her mind. There was a big difference between working most of the day and attending class in the morning, but for now she wanted to put her education to work, and of course pay back her student loans. Fortunately, her employer had agreed to a thirty-hour workweek rather than a forty. Since their office was less than a half hour from her home, at least she wouldn't have a long commute on top of working from eight-thirty to three.

Anna Maria eventually stopped squirming, and Hatch knew the infant's second wind was wearing off. She'd be asleep soon. She adjusted the volume on the baby monitor so she could hear them if they cried, then quietly went to her bedroom next door, where Skye waited.

Later, as she snuggled next to her sleeping husband, Hatch thought again about how hopeless her life seemed just three few short years ago. Now she had everything she had ever dreamed of. So many times she watched closing scenes of movies, where the camera showed the exterior of a happy house and pulled away before fading out, and here she was, with her own MGM ending, and she was the star.

Imagine that.

Dear Readers:

Ah, the end of another story. I hope Hatch's journey from hopelessness to achieving all her goals has left you feeling all warm and fuzzy inside.

My last several books have been spin-offs from supporting characters who become a little too real and started giving orders, demanding to be moved to center stage. My next book is more of the same, even though the character's initial introduction was quite brief. Ivy Smith, who hosted a fateful party attended by Vivian St. James in last year's PRELUDE TO A KISS, is getting her own story in CLOSER THAN CLOSE, to be released in early 2003.

Please note my new E-mail address. And remember, keep romance alive!

Bettye

bundie@directvinternet.com

or

P.O. Box 20354
Jacksonville, FL 32225
(Please enclose a SASE for a reply.)

ABOUT THE AUTHOR

Bettye Griffin is the author of four previous BET books: AT LONG LAST LOVE, A LOVE OF HER OWN, LOVE AFFAIR, and PRELUDE TO A KISS. When not writing, Bettye works as a freelance medical transcriptionist. Originally from Yonkers, New York, she now makes her home in Jacksonville, Florida, with her husband and is the stepmother of three children.

DO YOU KNOW AN ARABESQUE MAN?

1st Arabesque Man HAROLD JACKSON
Featured on the cover of "Endless Love"
by Carmen Green / Published Sept 2000

2nd Arabesque Man EDMAN REID
Featured on the cover of "Love Lessons"
by Leslie Esdaile / Published Sept 2001

3rd Arabesque Man PAUL HANEY
Featured on the cover of "Holding Out For A Hero"
by Deirdre Savoy / Published Sept 2002

WILL YOUR "ARABESQUE" MAN BE NEXT?

One Grand Prize Winner Will Win:
- 2 Day Trip to New York City
- Professional NYC Photo Shoot
- Picture on the Cover of an Arabesque Romance Novel
- Prize Pack & Profile on Arabesque Website and Newsletter
- $250.00

You Win Too!
- The Nominator of the Grand Prize Winner receives a Prize Pack & profile on Arabesque Website
- $250.00

To Enter: Simply complete the following items to enter your "Arabesque Man": (1) Compose an Original essay that describes in 75 words or less why you think your nominee should win. (2) Include two recent photographs of him (head shot and one full length shot). Write the following information for both you and your nominee on the back of each photo: name, address, telephone number and the nominee's age, height, weight, and clothing sizes. (3) Include signature and date of nominee granting permission to nominator to enter photographs in contest. (4) Include a proof of purchase from an Arabesque romance novel—write the book title, author, ISBN number, and purchase location and price on a 3-1/2 x 5" card. (5) Entrants should keep a copy of all submissions. Submissions will not be returned and will be destroyed after the judging.

ARABESQUE regrets that no return or acknowledgement of receipt can be made because of the anticipated volume of responses. Arabesque is not responsible for late, lost, incomplete, inaccurate or misdirected entries. The Grand Prize Trip includes round trip air transportation from a major airport nearest the winner's home, 2-day (1 night) hotel accommodations and ground transportation between the airport, hotel and Arabesque offices in New York. The Grand Prize Winner will be required to sign and return an affidavit of eligibility and publicity and liability release in order to receive the prize. The Grand Prize Winner will receive no additional compensation for the use of his image on an Arabesque novel, website, or for any other promotional purpose. The entries will be judged by a panel of BET Arabesque personnel whose decisions regarding the winner and all other matters pertaining to the Contest are final and binding. By entering this Contest, entrants agree to comply with all rules and regulations.

SEND ENTRIES TO: The Arabesque Man Cover Model Contest, BET Books, One BET Plaza, 1235 W Street, NE, Washington, DC 20018. Open to legal residents of the U.S., 21 years of age or older. Illegible entries will be disqualified. Limit __ entry per envelope. Odds of winning depend, in part, on the number of entries received. Void in Puerto Rico and where pro- ____ law.

ARABESQUE
A PRODUCT OF
BET BOOKS